THOSE WHO HUNT WOLVES

HARRISON TAYLOR

Interior design by Damonza
Cover design by Damonza

ISBN: 978-1-7372634-0-1 Paperback
ISBN 978-1-7372634-1-8 Ebook
ISBN: 978-1-7372634-2-5 Hardback

To my family.

Story Time

Remember the time 7721 gunned us down in that elevator? Don't look at me like that. It's a fair question. The brain has a funny way of forgetting things it doesn't want to remember. Since then, I always know when it's gonna rain. The slugs in my chest burn, and the day Leo stopped by, my chest was on FIRE. As always, I parked my Volvo in my one-car garage. Before you ask: Yes, it's leased. Don't know why more people don't do that. When I'm at home, there are two reasons I NEVER use the keyless entry to lock the door. Reason number two: I'll get to that. Anyway, I walked outside to get the mail. Gray clouds over me, thunder rumbling in the distance. The cool thing about living in a retirement community is that old people don't ask too many questions. At least the men don't. The ladies have tried to set me up with their granddaughters. No big deal. They're just sweet. I looked across the street and saw my neighbor, rolling along with his walker toward his mailbox. Nice guy. Don't know his name, though. I mentally refer to him as Walker.

"Looks like it's gonna rain," he said.

"Yeah, it sure does," I replied. Walker smiled. I could see from across the street he didn't have his dentures in.

"These April showers. So unpredictable."

I nodded and replied, "Stay dry." I waved at Walker before hopping up my black-and-white wooded steps. Always liked those steps. They looked like big piano keys. I unlocked the front door, and as soon I stepped into the house, I could see an image moving in the reflection of the mirror in the dining room.

"Come on, Shepard." I knew who it was. Can't mistake that thick raspy New York City accent for anybody else. "Not gonna make us run after you, are ya?"

"Nope," I replied. "Just locking the door so we won't be disturbed." I locked the door and walked out of the foyer and into the living room. "How'd you find me, Leo?"

"Easier than I thought," Leo said. He was sitting on the black leather couch in my living room.

Three of his minions appeared from the dining area. These guys were stocky. Tailored dark suits with silk ties. Threatening in stature but calm in demeanor.

"We followed you home last week," Leo said. "Shepard, I-I mean you didn't see us tailing you?" His voice sounded as if he was concerned.

I shook my head as I walked past my bathroom. This monster meathead comes walking out, just flushed the toilet, his shit wafting at my nose hairs. Nasty fucker couldn't even be bothered to wash his hands. Even at six feet I was only at chest level with this guy. I glanced over at the Glock holstered near his armpit. I tried to give them the impression that I was scared, but let's face it: That's like asking a crocodile not to fucking smile, right? I motioned over to the kitchen and started to unlock the door to the back porch.

"Now you ain't gonna try to make a run for it, is you?" Leo asked.

"Leo, I'm not a fucking moron," I said. "It smells like shit in here because your non-housetrained ox over there took a massive dump in my bathroom without turning on the fan. Just opening the doors."

"Hey big L," one of his guys said, "I gotta protest here. I mean no disrespect, but we made some serious moves with this guy."

"Don't you think I know that?" Leo asked.

Leo rubbed his face. With the bushy white beard and slicked-back white ponytail, he always reminded me of some skinny Italian Saint Nick.

"Man does his work, never rats on anyone, and look what he gets in return," Leo said shaking his head. "Shepard, I fought for ya."

"You don't say?" I asked as I opened both doors to the back porch.

"Bit of advice for the next life, kid?" Leo asked.

I turned around and smiled.

"All ears." I said.

"If Uncle Sam comes a-knockin', tell him to suck one."

"What?" I asked.

"Shepard," Leo said snickering. "Mayada knows. You're a spook. You and your band of merry men. That's the only way you would know about a score like this."

"What score is that, Leo?"

"The Blackout." Leo said.

I remember my smugness fading away.

"You looked?" I asked, sighing.

"Shepard," Leo said, widening his eyes and shaking his head. "This…changes everything. A weapon like this…"

"Who said anything about it being a weapon?" I asked.

"Fuck off, Shepard," Leo said grimacing. "Everything in Uncle Sam's hand is a weapon until proven otherwise."

I turned around to face them and took two steps backward onto the red brick. That porch was the reason why I bought the damn house. It was a gorgeous two-level patio with a built-in grill. By this time the sky was pitch-black. I could feel small rain droplets fall on the back of my neck. Leo pulled out his pistol. Of course, his drones mimicked him.

"It pains me to do this, kid," Leo said. "Really it does."

I looked at the old man and smiled. I put my hands in my pocket, my finger rubbing over the tiny keyless entry button for my Volvo. Like I was telling you, I never press my keyless entry button.

"You do what you gotta do, right?" I said pressing the red button.

Within seconds fire sprinklers throughout the entire house came on. Leo was startled as hell. The poor guido tried to cover his gelled, silver hair with his ancient, arthritic hands.

"What the fuck?!" Leo shouted. He held his hands up and surveyed his drenched clothes. His head ping-ponged for a while between looking at his men and gaping down at his clothing. "Do you see these shoes?"

"They looked nice," I said.

"Three-fifty, you asshole!" Leo shouted. He held up his pistol and pointed it at me. "This don't change nothin', kid." Leo wiped the hair gel trickling down his forehead with the back of his hand. "If anything, you just made my job a whole lot fucking easier!"

"Leo," I said, "Take a deep breath." I took two more steps back onto the brick patio.

Leo cocked back his pistol, as did his soldiers.

"I wouldn't do that if I were you," I said pulling out my lighter and a single cigarette from my pocket. I know. I'm trying to quit. But I digress. "Friction causes heat, which in your situation could have serious repercussions." I lit my cigarette. The few raindrops that were falling had turned into a soft drizzle. Leo squinted his eyes. I could tell the schmuck's wheels were turning.

"Kid," Leo asked, "You lost it at the end? What the fuck are you…"

"Leo, take a deep breath," I said again.

"What do you think this is?" Leo asked. "I can breathe just fine!"

"Yeah? Well, you might need your nose checked, cause that ain't water," I said. I took a couple of puffs off my loosey and took another step back. The connections finally came together in the old man's head. Leo looked up at the liquid coming out of the fire sprinklers. He took a couple of sniffs in the air, as if he was snorting cocaine.

"They say lighter fluid can give off euphoria if inhaled. Judging by the look on your face, though…" Leo did the math. The guns. The muscle. It's all irrelevant when your opponent brings fucking napalm to the fight. Leo dropped his gun to his side.

"Boss?" one of his guys asked.

"He fucked us," Leo said closing his eyes. "OK, kid, you're calling the shots now." I continued to puff at my Newport just before the light drizzle changed to an all-out rainstorm.

"No shot-calling here," I said using my hand to cover the flickering flame of my silver lighter. "Just for the record, I wish it wasn't you, Leo. I always liked you." Leo cracked a smile. He tapped the tip of the pistol on his thigh a few times before he shouted, pointing it at me. I flicked my silver lighter into the house. As soon as that lighter passed the porch door, the tiny flame ignited into a cloud of fire that took less than a second to engulf Leo and the others. I took a few steps back. Their screams echoed throughout the small suburban neighborhood. As I watched the blaze, stray bullets were flying by my face. This had to be a good two minutes, and wouldn't you know it: Leo was still firing his gun off at random. Eventually, he stopped.

∽

"Such a shame," Shepard said. "Always liked that house."

"So, you left?" Graham asked.

"Hot-wired Leo's Buick and drove off," Shepard said, pouring cream in his coffee and looking around the empty silver-and-neon-blue diner. It was quiet. Only the muzzled sound of the morning news could be heard, playing on a 24-inch flatscreen hanging in the back-right corner of the diner.

"So, what was reason number one?" Graham asked.

"What's that?"

"You said you had two reasons why you never pressed the key-less entry to your car, but you only gave one reason. What's the other one?"

"Oh," Shepard said, scratching the back of his neck, "I don't have another reason. That was just for dramatic effect." Shepard hailed one of the waitresses who was standing on the opposite side of a neon-blue-rimmed counter. The young woman smiled and power-walked over to them.

"Yes, sir?" She asked. Shepard looked up and smiled.

"What pies do you have over there, hon?" he asked.

"The key lime is real popular," she said with a valley-girl accent.

"Sounds good," Shepard said. The waitress was about to walk away when she took another look at Shepard's chiseled, tanned, middle-aged face. Black polo shirt with black slacks to match and a military buzz cut. Healed lacerations and burns covered Shepard's forearms like tattoo sleeves. She paused for a moment, noticing Shepard's pair of different-colored eyes: one green, the other blue.

"Sir," the waitress said looking around her feet, "I'm sorry but I think you dropped one of your contacts."

"I don't wear contacts, hon," Shepard said. The waitress raised her eyebrows and gave a gentle nod before walking away. Shepard placed his elbows on the table and clasped his hands.

"It's a residential home," Graham said. "Who puts water sprinklers in a residential area?"

"I don't know. Maybe the Blackout has influenced me."

"There you go with this influencing horseshit." Graham said, shaking his head.

"Have you ever looked at it, Graham?" Shepard asked, squinting.

"Don't give me that, Shepard," Graham said with a sigh. "Of course..."

"Not just in passing," Shepard said. "You ever just stared at it? That dark, beautiful, twisted void?"

"No, I haven't."

"Then you wouldn't understand."

"Shepard," Graham said, leaning forward, "I don't care if you looked into the void and saw the future. You act solely on emotion and improv. I wonder sometimes how you survived 7721 this long." The waitress brought over the key lime pie and placed it in front of Shepard. "Which is why I don't believe you pre-rigged your house with sprinklers and filled them with lighter fluid in the event of an ambush."

The waitress's eyes widened, her jaw slackened.

Shepard took a thin scoop of pie from his blue plate. He then used his fork to point at the TV screen. The newscast showed a small two-floor house smoldering in the rain with firemen pulling out bodies from the rubble. The bottom of the screen read FIRE IN RESIDENTIAL RETIREMENT COMMUNITY.

Graham squinted. The petrified waitress was startled when Shepard tapped her on the wrist.

"Can you get me a refill on my coffee?" She stared at Shepard's Cheshire-cat smile and gave a nervous nod.

"C-Coming right up," she said.

"So, how'd you get away?" Shepard asked.

"No one came after me," Graham scoffed.

"Seriously?"

"Well, they did send someone. If that's what you want to call it."

Shortly after Graham said these words, a woman in her mid-thirties hobbled into the diner clutching her back. Her T-shirt, fitted blue jeans, and sneakers all charcoal black, fair skin covered with soot and dirt.

"Look who's still alive," Shepard said.

"Barely," Graham said chuckling. The woman walked over to the men's booth and stood over the table silently, giving Shepard a vehement stare.

"Rosa!" Shepard said smiling. "You're still alive."

Rosa looked over at Graham, who wore a dark-gray T-shirt with tan slacks and black shoes as he chipped away at the key lime pie that Shepard had ordered. Running his manicured fingers through his short blonde hair, Graham acknowledged her presence by nodding. A smudge of whipped cream dangled from his groomed stubble.

"May I sit down, please?" Rosa asked, attempting to sound dignified. Graham scooted toward the window. With her eyes fixed on Shepard, Rosa sat down. The waitress returned and poured Shepard's coffee. She gasped at the debris falling from Rosa's long brown hair.

"Can I get you something?" The waitress asked with caution.

"May I have a glass of water, please?" Rosa asked. The waitress nodded with a furrowed brow and stepped away from the table.

"So?" Shepard asked. "What happened?" Blood from a fresh scratch over the right side of Rosa's forehead trickled down the contour of her cheek. She continued to stare at Shepard. The anticipating expression on his face angered her to no end.

"What do you think happened?" Rosa asked calmly.

"I don't know," Shepard said, excited. "It looks like you saw my note."

"Yeah, Shep," Rosa scoffed. "I saw your note, all right. Right before my fucking car exploded in front of me!"

The waitress came back to the table and placed a glass of water in front of Rosa, who regained her composure and took a sip.

"Thank you very much," Rosa said.

The waitress's dirty white sneakers squeaked against the tile floor as she power-walked away from the table.

"Rosa, I couldn't call you," Shepard said. "They probably had your phone tapped."

"So you spray-paint my car with some cryptic message?" Rosa asked.

"I wrote a warning," Shepard said.

"You wrote 'rabbit hole,' Shepard!" Rosa shouted.

Shepard stirred his coffee and said, "It was enough to save your life," finishing his sentence with a high inflection.

"It was enough for me stop and say, 'What the fuck,'" Rosa said.

"Which was enough to save your life," Shepard said.

"He's got a point, Rosa," Graham said.

"Stay out of this!" Rosa shouted. She looked at Shepard and asked, "So, what's the next move?"

"Raymond Mezzelli," Shepard said.

"Mayada's enforcer?" Graham asked. "I took care of that."

"What do you mean?" Shepard asked.

"It took some persuasion," Graham said. The waitress came back with a glass of water. "I have him in the trunk if you want to go ask him yourself."

"Seriously?" Shepard asked.

Graham nodded and said, "Let's go." He put eighty dollars on the table and placed his white coffee cup on top of it. Shepard popped up from his seat and the young waitress held her hands in the air. The glass pitcher of water she was carrying shattered on the white ceramic floor.

"Please don't kill me!" she shouted. Shepard, bewildered, stared at the waitress. He dug into the front pocket of his black slacks and pulled out a green ball of mixed bills.

"For the pitcher." He said, straightening out a ten-dollar bill and placing it on the table. "Mind the glass." He said as he walked out of the diner.

Rosa stared at her soot-covered reflection in the silver table. She slowly rose from her seat and trailed behind Graham and Shepard like a scared child.

"What are you doing?" Rosa asked Shepard.

"I'm sorry?" Shepard asked.

Rosa stopped and stared back into the diner where the waitress was cleaning up broken glass.

"You're just gonna leave her there?" Rosa asked as they walked over to Shepard's 1982 navy-blue Buick.

"Yo, dude, how many times I gotta tell you this?" Shepard asked, digging in his pockets and pulling out a set of car keys. "We don't kill innocent people."

Shepard placed the keys in the lock of the rusted trunk, which creaked as it was pried open. The inside was covered with blue carpet that smelled of oil. In the middle of this spacious trunk was a portly, graying man gagged and tied with duct tape. His knees were bent against the edge of the trunk and an oil-covered tire sat on his chest. He squirmed and moaned with a high-pitched voice as if someone was stabbing him to death. Rosa's body shuddered. She swiveled her head around the empty parking lot.

"Who the hell is that?" Rosa asked.

"Mezzeli," Graham said smiling.

"They sent this drunk piece of shit after you?" Shepard asked. Graham nodded. "Details?"

I was coming home yesterday evening. Nothing out of the ordinary. People letting other people into the building. Door without a doorman. I stepped into my complex and walked over to the gold-painted mailbox unit. As usual, nothing important. Just bills, which of course I throw in the trash. I stepped onto the elevator. That red-and-green velvet interior…bullshit. You know, paying that much for an apartment, you would think they could spring for a better lift that didn't make you feel like it was Christmas all year.

The elevator stopped on the seventh floor and I stepped out, staring down the off-white painted hallway. I can see my forest-green door at the end of the hall cracked open. The obvious thing to do here is to run, but why? Given the already MONOLITHIC fuck-up of a job this guy was doing, I figured I'd take my chances. I moved down the narrow hallway staying close to the wall. My shoulder touched every other door just in case I had to kick one of them down if bullets started flying.

When I got to the door of my unit, I nudged it open with my foot. It creaked until finally resting on the adjacent wall. I could already hear him panting. At first, I thought it was some young kid in over his head. But then the panting was alternating with this light squealing. I peeked my head in. Dummy is sitting in my lounge chair on the other side of the living room.

"You OK, chief?" I asked.

Then this jackass starts shooting. I stood outside in the hallway watching the bullets fly aimlessly down the empty corridor. Thankfully, it was late. I closed my eyes and listened to the gunshots being discharged. Oh, by the way, I took one out of your playbook and rented out a spot at a senior apartment complex. Those poor people wouldn't hear even the fucking building crashing on them. At first I thought I was mistaken, because no one could possibly be that fucking stupid. He fired his sixth and final shot.

"You gotta be kidding me," I said, walking into my dimly lit apartment. This wannabe assassin thought he could pull this off with a Smith & Wesson revolver. I didn't know whether to be grateful or insulted. I couldn't quite see his face. All I could see was this pathetic bastard, keeled over, holding his stomach and fumbling in his pocket, searching for more bullets to refill his outdated pea shooter.

"Hey, chubs," I said. "Let me get the light for you." I walked over to the lamp on the table next to the lounge chair that my killer was slumped over in. I turned on the lights. Wouldn't you know it? "Mezzeli," I said. This fat bastard was slouched over trying to pop bullets into his revolver. The beads of sweat trickled down his Captain Picard haircut onto my beige suede rug. He stared at me between hard blinks and gritting teeth.

"Mezzeli?" I asked again. This time worried. "You OK, pal?" The fat bastard tried to kill me with a bleeding ulcer. He fell out of my chair onto the floor, holding that big gut of his.

"H-Help me Graham," he said, squealing.

"What?" I asked.

"My stomach."

"And?"

"Get me a doctor," he said. I scoffed. "Please, Graham. For old time's sake." By this time, he was bent over in a fetal position. I locked the door.

"You know what you need?" I asked. "A drink."

I walked into my kitchen and opened the cupboard over the sink, thumbing through my small collection of spirits. "Let's see…" My finger stopped at the bottle of Bacardi 151. "Perfect." I looked under the sink and grabbed a funnel and tube. I walked over to him, who was doing his damnedest not to start crying in front of me. I knelt down next to him, dangling the bottle in his chunky, sweating face.

"Was it you or Ares who told me the story of the guy's nipples you cut off with a shaving razor to get information?" I asked. He didn't respond. "This is what's going to happen. This is going down your throat. Not a lot, cause I need you sober. But just enough to do the job. This here's gonna make you feel like you're burning alive from the inside out. Afterwards, you're going to tell me everything I need to know. Now you're probably thinking, *If you're gonna torture me anyway why should I tell you anything?* Keep this in mind: Shit can always get worse."

❧

"Oh, my God," Rosa uttered. "Who are you people? What the hell have I gotten myself into?"

"Badness, darling," Graham said. "A whole lot of badness."

"What does he know?" Shepard asked, looking down at Mezzeli's pain-riddled face. Fresh blood was seeping through the duct tape and dripping onto the trunk's carpet.

"Mayada's safe house," Graham said.

"Really?" Shepard asked. "Is Ares with him?"

"You know it," Graham said.

"Oh, my God," repeated Rosa, her head now in her hands. "So, what? You're just going to kill this guy?" Shepard grimaced.

"But you want our waitress in the diner to disappear?" Graham asked with sarcasm.

"Who do you think we are, Rosa?" Shepard asked. "Look at him. The guy's bleeding. We're going to take him to a hospital. He's not going scot-free, though." Shepard leaned closer to look Mezzeli in the eyes. "He's a message." Shepard whispered in his ear. Mezzeli's head trembled. His eyes widened. "Got it, pigeon?" Just before Shepard closed the trunk, he stared down at Mezzeli. "Tell Mayada and the god of war that Shepard Black says hello."

The Message

"It just don't make any sense," Ares said as he disassembled his cigarillo. He poured the tobacco out onto white notebook paper and pulled out the tan filter.

"Just let it go," Mayada said, irritated. His voice was raspy and deep. They were sitting in a jet-black Hummer with two black Lincoln Navigators sandwiching it. The convoy was traveling down Lincoln Avenue headed toward Sinai Memorial Hospital.

"Mezzeli's been in this game long enough," Mayada said as he straightened his black silk tie. "He's the family's enforcer. Stop drinking if you can't do the fucking job. It's that simple!" He wiped white specks off the shoulders of his matching black silk dress shirt. "This fucking dandruff. Hey kid, what you using for shampoo?" he asked, patting the top of his thin, receding silver hair.

"With all due respect, Mr. Mayada…"

"Ares, please. It's Uncle Raphe. You're my dead brother's bastard child, for God's sake. We're family."

"Uncle Raphe, we're dealing with a dangerous bunch here."

Mayada cocked his head to the side, causing his neck fat to roll.

"What do you think I was doing before you came knocking on my door?" he asked, scanning Ares from head to toe. "I deal with dangerous people all day, Ares. It's the highlight of what I do."

The convoy pulled onto the curb in front of Sinai Memorial Hospital.

"Mr. Mayada," the driver said, "we're here."

"Yeah," mumbled Mayada. He looked at Ares. "I agree this whole situation is fucked up."

"Thank you," Ares said. "Should have sent me to take care of things."

"That's not what I mean. We shouldn't be doing this in the first place. Shep and Graham are like fucking family."

Ares rolled his eyes.

"Here we go again with the sentimental bullshit," Ares said as he stuffed the tobacco back into the cigarillo.

"Shut your mouth," Mayada said, pointing his chubby index finger. He opened the car door. "Do yourself a favor, will ya? Your face is bleeding again all over my car. Have some respect for your appearance, huh? Fix that shit."

Mayada pried himself out of the black SUV. Once out, the old man brushed the dandruff from his black suit and caught his breath. He patted down the few patches of hair and gel that covered the crown of his head.

Ares finished twisting the end of his cigarillo and, using the rearview, studied the swollen bruises under his eyes. He lifted his chin to look at the fresh scar running along the right side of his jawbone. The bridge of his nose was still red from being set in place. Ares pulled out a white handkerchief and cleaned the blood dripping from his nose. He put his reflective shades over his dark-blue raccoon eyes and stepped out of the Hummer. His clothing matched his uncle's: tailored black suit, silk shirt, and tie.

"Mr. Ares, sir," the driver said, holding a lighter in front of him. Ares placed the cigarillo in his mouth and took a deep breath while igniting his vice. He surveyed the chaos that was New York rush hour. All walks of life power-walking with their faces in their cellphones brushing past his broad shoulders. Ares finished his cigarillo in eight puffs before crushing the roach under his black loafers and going through the automatic doors.

⁂

Ares strutted into the ICU, his head turning from side to side. He took a stick of gum from his pocket and popped it in his mouth. He glanced at the board, scanning for Mezzili's name and room number.

"Room 8435," Ares said.

Ares continued to walk down a taupe-colored hallway. The fluorescent overhead lights illuminated the ICU floor. His boyish face scrunched at the smell of feces and urine as he passed one of the rooms. "Fuck me, that's gross," he mumbled to himself covering his swollen nose. He could see Mezzeli's name written outside the second-to-last room on the right. The room was pulsating with the sound of IV machines and heart monitors. Ares stepped into the room. The potbellied gangster was oozing blood from his mouth. Mayada stood over Mezzeili, holding his hand.

"Shit. Can he talk?" Ares asked. Mayada shook his head.

"Poor guy," Mayada said. "They pumped four pints of alcohol and hot sauce from his stomach."

"What?" Ares asked.

"Maybe we should talk to Shep," Mayada said. "Tell him if he runs now…"

"Uncle Raphe, is this what I'm hearing now?" Ares asked, pointing to his ear. "They fucking maim your partner and your only regret is that we should have appeased that cocksucker?"

"Ares…"

"Why are you tying my hands, Uncle Raphe? Why won't you let me…"

"We are meeting him tonight." Ares placed his hands on his head before clasping them together in front of him.

"What the fuck do you mean, 'meet'?" Mayada remained silent. "You can't be serious. I mean, you're acting like you let this guy suck your..." Mayada spun around. The old man threw a right hook, which landed square on Ares's chin, dropping him to the floor.

"Get up," Mayada said. Blood trickled from Ares's reopened wound. He slowly lifted himself from the floor and stood under Mayada's glare, looking down at the tile like a scolded child.

"You see?" Mayada said, handing Ares a tissue. "You're not a god. It's a nickname. That's all. Just a nickname. Try not to get caught up in names. 'Cause when you do that, you get caught up in your own ego. And when you get caught up in your own ego, you ostracize family. Which makes it real hard for family to see *you* as family. Which means that family," Mayada said pointing at his chest, "wouldn't hesitate to put you down like the stray fucking dog you are if you step out of line again."

Ares quickly nodded.

"Good," Mayada said. "You made a name for yourself. That's good. I don't mind a little bravado. But you best to remember who's in charge. Now, when we see Shep tonight, no surprises. We're just gonna talk. And by talk, I mean you keep your fucking mouth shut. Got it? Are we square?"

"As a boxing ring," Ares said.

I hate coffee, Shepard thought to himself. *I hate coffee shops even more.* He looked up from his dark-blue mug half-filled with cold coffee and stared at the wooden sculpted sign that read THE BLUE BEAN. The sign was suspended by two bicycle chains connected to the rafters. Just under it were three industrial-size coffee makers and two espresso machines, all of them hissing and vibrating on a wooden bar. Behind the tall machines were the bobbing dark-blue hats of baristas calling out orders. Each time he heard a name called, he'd glance at the pickup counter to see if it was her. Shepard sat in a high wooden stool at a wooden table. He looked at his watch and sighed. *Maybe she called in sick today.* He thought to himself. *Probably for the best. We got bigger fish to…*

The single door to the coffee shop swung open. Shepard perked up in his seat. He could feel his stomach drop when she rushed in. The woman straightened her dark-blue T-shirt and put on her dark-blue apron. Her long, frizzled black hair was tied in a ponytail by a dark-blue ribbon to match her apron. She turned her head in Shepard's direction for a split second. She had intensely focused light-brown eyes and high cheek bones. She turned her head to look at the barista standing behind the register as she made her way behind the bar. Every muscle in Shepard's body relaxed. He chuckled and smiled, watching her feverishly clock in and pin her name tag onto her apron. She picked up the remote to the satellite radio and pressed a button. The music changed from light jazz to Joe Jackson's "Breaking Us in Two." He looked at the tag resting on her apron: TRISH spelled in dark-blue capital letters. Shepard took a sip of his cold, black coffee. He snarled and rubbed his tongue on the roof of his mouth to get out the bitter taste. He got up from his stool and walked toward the register. Trish had her head down, bobbing to a subtle cowbell in the song. She lifted her head up and smiled. Shepard could feel his eyes mist at the sight of Trish's bright smile and imperfectly perfect left dimple.

"Can I help you?" she asked.

"Uh…" Shepard said, looking at the chalkboard menu behind him. "One for the road, please."

"Sure," Trish said giving him a blank stare. Shepard stared back at her with a goofy smile. He squinted his eyes.

"Oh," he gaped pointing at her. "You need to know what my order was don't you?"

Trish laughed and said, "Kinda. Yeah."

"Small cup of coffee. Black."

"OK," she said, punching the order into the register. Shepard looked down at the buzz coming from his side pocket. He pulled the phone out and looked at the screen.

"Here you go," Trish said, sliding a blue paper cup in a blue paper sleeve across the counter.

"Thank you," Shepard said with a bright smile.

"You're welcome. Come back and..." Trish gasped. Her eyes started to flutter as she buckled under her own weight. She extended her arms against the counter, bracing herself from falling.

"Oh shit," Shepard said grabbing her by the arms. "Are you OK?" Trish grabbed her chest and took a deep, labored breath.

"I'm fine," she said looking at Shepard's hands gripping her armpits.

"I-I'm sorry," Shepard said slowly, letting go.

"D-don't apologize."

"Maybe you should see a doctor about those lungs."

"What?" Trish said squinting her eyes. "How do you know I have artificial lungs?" *Shit.* Shepard thought to himself.

"Well I..." Shepard said, his eyes wide and voice high-pitched. "You were holding your chest. I guess."

"Oh," Trish said sighing. "I-I'm not supposed to tell anyone that. You a doctor or something?"

"No..." Shepard said. His shoulders relaxed as he stared into Trish's light brown eyes. "Secret is safe with me, though." Trish smiled and took another deep breath.

"I appreciate that," Trish said. Shepard looked down at his cellphone buzzing again. "You might want to take that," she said, walking away. Shepard nodded as he grabbed his small cup of coffee and walked out of the coffee shop. Shepard took ten paces toward his black Lincoln before tossing his coffee cup and putting his cellphone by his ear. "I see you got my message."

"How did you know it was me?" Mayada asked.

"You're the only person I know in the 212."

"That's sad." Mayada said chuckling. "Shepard, I think it's time we had a sit-down." Shepard laughed.

"OK," Shepard said with a wide grin, his eyes wide, his blue eye sparkling. "Make sure the meet-up is public. Preferably with law enforcement close by."

"I understand. Need a little extra protection."

"It is protection, Mayada. I'm less likely to kill you with cops watching." Shepard hung up the phone and got into his Lincoln. He turned the ignition and placed the cellphone to his ear again. "It's me."

"Where are you?" Graham asked.

"That's not important."

"You're at that coffee shop, aren't you?" Shepard was silent. "We're in the middle of Mobcon fucking five and you're out here chasing skirts?"

"The meeting's on. Going by myself," Shepard said, turning the Lincoln out of the coffee shop parking lot onto the highway.

◦§◦

"Uncle Raphe?" Ares asked.

Mayada sighed. His brown eyes floated between an empty glass and a bottle of gin. Mayada and Ares were sitting at a round table facing a faded red door.

Old peanut shells crunched under Ares's dress shoes. In his periphery he could see two off-duty police officers plopped on tan leather barstools. One was slumped over nursing half a mug of beer, while the other was watching the news on a 27-inch flatscreen mounted in the corner of the wall. Waitresses standing at the bar counted tips while periodically glancing at Ares from across the room. It couldn't be helped. With his light-brown hair, green eyes, and boyish face, he stood out amongst his company.

"Hate fucking cops," Ares said curling his lip.

"What?" Mayada asked.

"It's been over two hours," Ares said. "I don't think he's coming. I mean we just tried to kill this guy, right?"

"He will," Mayada said. "A guy like Shepard Black don't intimidate easily."

Moments later, Shepard walked in. He was wearing a light-blue dress shirt shrouded by a dark-gray trench coat. Beads of rain slid down his lapels. The downpour tapped against the roof of the bar. He took two steps inside and looked around. Mayada signaled Shepard by raising his hand. He grabbed the bottle of gin and poured it in the glass. Shepard strolled toward the table. He looked at Mayada and then the glass of gin in front of him. He picked up the glass and poured it on the ground.

"I know this might sound funny, but don't you trust me?" Mayada asked.

"That wasn't out of paranoia," Shepard said, sitting down. "But out of respect." He poured himself another glass of gin, taking the shot down in one gulp. "Mezzeli was a good guy."

"That he was," Mayada said. "A real soldier."

"You did break one of your cardinal rules," Shepard said.

"Yeah?" Mayada asked. "What's that?"

"You always said contract killing was a young man's game," Shepard said.

"I gotta agree with the prick," Ares said. "You shoulda sent me."

"I said 'a young man,' not some pup with the temperament of Scrappy-Doo," Shepard said as he took off his trench coat.

"Eat a fat one, Black," Ares said. Shepard placed his trench coat over the back of his dark-brown wooden stool. He picked up the bottle of gin and refreshed Mayada's glass.

"Leo was a good guy, too," Mayada said, picking up the glass. "Salud." He took a sip. "Lost a couple of real upstanding guys to you

21

and your counterpart this week." Shepard nodded. "The way you took out my guys…" Mayada looked up at the ceiling. "It's as if…"

"We saw you coming?" Shepard asked. "Yeah, we kinda did."

"Is this funny to you?" Mayada asked, grimacing. "If you weren't such a good friend, I'd have put a bullet in your head as soon as you walked through that door."

"Have another drink, Raphe," Shepard said.

He poured himself and Mayada each another shot of gin.

"None of this is even fazing you, is it?" Mayada asked.

"Oh, it's fazing me," Shepard said, staring at Mayada. His bright-green eye sparkled in the reflection of the overhead light while his blue eye was dim. "You tried to kill me and my crew after we did our job. So yeah, I'm pretty fucking fazed right now."

"I see anger," Mayada said, scanning Shepard's scowl. "But not an ounce of fear."

"When you walk through the fire, you'll never be afraid of the sun," Shepard said. He looked over at Ares who was mouthing, "FUCK YOU."

"Shepard, you know my hand was forced on this one, right?" Mayada asked.

"I know," Shepard said.

"As cliché as this may sound, it was nothing personal. Just…"

"So where's Barbara?" Shepard asked. Mayada sighed.

"You mean the ghost bitch you've been pining to gut for the last three years?" Ares asked.

"Glad we're all on the same page," Shepard said.

"Look Shepard, it was a brilliant heist," Mayada said. "To be honest, I'm still in shock how you guys knocked off the damn spooks in another country. It was the right thought but the wrong people. I told you this when you came to me with this con, and you wouldn't listen. This is the fucking federal government we're dealing with. They don't pay people to keep secrets, they bury people to keep secrets."

Shepard smiled.

"The deal was that you get me information on Barbara's whereabouts, and I give you the Blackout," Shepard said.

"Blackout?" Mayada asked. "Fuck the Blackout. If I don't clip you and your people, they're gonna wipe out the organization. This harebrained scheme put the whole family in jeopardy. So, what? You think I want you dead because I just don't want to pay you? This hit on you is about minimizing collateral fucking damage."

Shepard swallowed another shot and slammed the glass on the hardwood table.

"Leo told me you peeked," Shepard said. Mayada's eyes darted away. "You know what it is. And now that you know what's in your possession, I doubt the spooks are going to walk away."

"Let me give you some advice," Mayada said. "Run. If you run, I may be able to buy you some time so you can sort this all out. As a friend…"

"You keep saying that," Shepard said holding up his index finger. "Me and you, we are not friends. We're animals. Any group of mammals can run as a pack when sharing a common interest. But they won't hesitate to rip out one another's throat if survival called for it. Look, I've been very calm this evening and your little self-proclaimed god of war has tried my patience, so let me be clear." Shepard looked down at his silver-plated watch. "Today is Saturday, six o'clock. I'm gonna need that Blackout back. You have forty-eight hours."

"Let me walk you out," Ares said, popping up from his seat. He followed behind Shepard as if he were his shadow. "I'm gonna hunt you down, rip out your boyfriend's tongue and use it to eat out that hot piece-of-ass translator." Shepard stopped. He turned around and laughed. "What the fuck is so funny?"

"I meant what I said about Mezelli and Leo," Shepard said. "They were good guys. And when I kill your uncle, I am gonna feel truly, *truly* bad. These men I respect. But you? It won't be murder. Just another abortion."

Ares's eyes widened. He placed his hands in his pockets and smiled.

"See you in forty-eight." Ares said.

Token

"Senator John Upstead was laid to rest in his hometown of Montgomery, Alabama," the news reporter said. Senator McCray leaned forward in his seat, his elbows resting on his knees. He watched the coverage of Senator Upstead's passing on the flatscreen of the C lounge, a communal area in the east wing of the congressional building on 7ᵗʰ Street Northeast. Reclining on a black leather sofa, McCray watched Senator Upstead's funeral trying his best not to slam his fists through the circular glass coffee table in front of him. His eyes teared up each time they showed a picture of the senator.

"Georgia's most loved and hated senator's funeral procession crossed the entire state. Per his will, the procession did not pass through Selma, part of the senator's final protest against the civil rights movement. The senator held strong to his beliefs and took a firm stance against current socially accepted movements such as affirmative action and equal pay for women." McCray's attention was interrupted by the rumbling sound of the doorknob twisting. He turned around and saw three house members walk in.

"Walter," one of the congressmen said.

"Joe," McCray said, glancing at the young congressmen over his shoulder. Joe towered over the other two House members. Two of the congressmen sat down at one of the square mahogany high tables while Joe walked to the fridge and took out three Heinekens.

"Making sure he's dead?" Joe asked, chuckling. His black mustache contrasted his light complexion. McCray didn't respond. "You mind if we turn it to the game?" Joe asked as he sat with his friends at the table.

"I'm watching this," McCray said. He fixed his black-rimmed glasses and focused back on the TV. The news had changed to a panel of four reporters separated by a vertical split screen. McCray undid the first button of his light-blue oxford shirt and loosened his red tie.

"I'm not saying he was a bad man," one of the pundits said. "He was a wonderful father and loving husband according to his family. But the level of narrow-mindedness, the hatred for people who were remotely different than him. You know, this man owned a country club in Georgia, and do you know that to this day African Americans are still not allowed to be members?"

"Is it bad to say I'm glad he's dead?" one of the congressmen asked. The three of them laughed.

"We'll give you a pass this time," Joe said, chuckling. "Son of bitch probably pledged Kappa Kappa Kappa in college. Pillow sheets with eye holes was part of their uniforms."

McCray scoffed and looked over his shoulder, giving Joe an uncomfortable stare. Joe stopped laughing.

"There a problem, Senator?" Joe asked.

McCray didn't say a word. He turned his head back around and continued watching TV.

"A toast," Joe said as he held up his Heineken, "to one of the most influential, nefarious, evil sons-a-bitches ever to be sworn in." The other two congressman held up their bottles.

"Hear, hear," one of them said. Joe took a sip of his beer.

"Seventy-three," Joe said. "Bastard died from some blood clot in his lungs. Hope it was slow." McCray threw the remote across the room, cracking it on the dry wood wall. The impact startled the three congressmen.

"Shut up," McCray said pointing his finger at Joe.

With a crinkled nose and a single raised eyebrow, Joe asked, "What?"

"I said shut the fuck up!" McCray shouted. "You didn't know him."

"I didn't know him?"

"No, you didn't," McCray said. "You're basing your opinions on this cum and vomit they call journalism!"

"I don't need to watch the news, Walt!" Joe shouted. "I had front-row seats to that racist bastard every term! And why the hell would a member of the Black Caucus stand up for that guy?"

"Walt?" McCray asked as he approached Joe. "It's Senator McCray."

"So, it's 'senator' now?" Joe asked.

"Hell, yeah, it's 'senator,' Joe!" McCray said, pointing at Joe's chest. "I don't give two shits about what you think you know about that man. You didn't know him." McCray grumbled to himself as he turned around and headed for the door.

"They warned me about you, you know," Joe said. McCray stopped. "They said you were a sellout. I figured since I respected you, I'd give you the benefit of the doubt. Guess they were right. You just anotha house nigga. Ain't you too dark for that?"

"Respect?" McCray asked, cracking a smile. "You don't need to respect me." His smile faded. "You need to fear me." He walked toward Joe with his hands in his pocket, staring at the hardwood floor. "House nigga, huh? Funny thing about the house nigga is that he knew all of massa's secrets. Where all the skeletons are hidden. Where all the bodies are buried. I take it Mrs. Harold doesn't know about that young little blonde surfer girl you got in Malibu." Joe's eye's widened.

"I do," McCray said chuckling. Joe leaned in, grabbing McCray's wiry arm with his huge oven-mitt hand.

"Keep your voice down," Joe said.

McCray looked behind Joe to see the two other congressmen staring down at their beers, desperately trying to give the illusion that they weren't listening.

"That wasn't a threat. That was just a warning shot. A graze, if you will," McCray said, making a gesture as if he were combing the side of his short Afro.

"You would leak that?" Joe asked. "You would really screw over another member of the Black Cauca-"

"Save the I-have-a-dream speech for your constituents," McCray said, holding up his hand. "You aren't Fredrick Douglass and this isn't the Underground Railroad. This is politics. Grow up." McCray looked at the TV displaying old satirical cartoons of Senator Upstead. "And you didn't know him." He looked at his watch and stormed out, slamming the door.

The driver held the door open for McCray as he stepped into the black limo and scooted to the middle of the back seat. The driver then walked around to the driver's side and hopped in.

"Congressional library, right, sir?" The driver asked, staring at McCray in the rearview mirror. McCray nodded. The driver turned on his signal and forced his way into the oncoming traffic. "I'll have you there in less than five minutes, sir. General Ashcroft and Commander Bradshaw are already there."

"Have they finished 'debugging' the room yet?" McCray asked while making air quotes with his fingers.

"Sorry, sir. I can't confirm that."

McCray shook his head.

Minutes later, the limo pulled up in front of the library.

"Sir, we're here."

Walter nodded to the limo driver. Before he could grab the handle, the door opened. He looked up and saw a security guard in a black suit wearing an earpiece.

"Senator McCray," the guard said. "An honor, sir. We'll be your security from here on out."

McCray closed his eyes and pursed his lips. "Security?" He asked.

"If you'll follow me, sir. General Ashcroft will make everything clear shortly."

McCray stepped out of the limo. As he walked toward the library steps, he noticed two more guards behind him dressed in dark suits. The front guards held the door open as the senator walked into the library. The echoing of their dress shoes clacking in tandem against the gray marble floor was the only sound being made at this late hour. They stepped into the elevator, and one of the guards pushed the B button. Walter glanced at the four armed men surrounding him and exhaled sharply.

"Sir?" A guard asked. "Are you OK?"

"Well," McCray said, rubbing his sweaty palms, "I'm going into the basement of a vacant library with four... I'm guessing ex-Marines? Who work for a general no one even knows exists?"

The elevator doors opened.

"Sir," the agent said, extending his arm, "I assure you that General Ashcroft will explain to you in full detail what is about to happen."

McCray sighed and stepped out of the elevator while the four agents stood still.

"You're not coming?" McCray asked.

"No, sir," the agent said. "We need to guard the perimeter and make sure you won't be disturbed. Is there anything else that

I can do for you, Senator?" McCray furrowed his eyebrows and shook his head. "Then we'll see you in exactly thirty minutes, sir."

McCray watched the elevator doors close before he started down the hallway of the library's basement. It was a wide hallway with a pair of double doors at the end marked CONFERENCE ROOM. McCray pushed open the doors to find Ashcroft seated across from the entrance, under a portrait of Alexander Hamilton. He sat in a leather chair with his right elbow on an arm rest, rubbing his forehead. The ambient light shined on his black military attire. No medals or ribbons. Not even his name was on his uniform. Just a single black star the size of a quarter stitched on his lapel. Bradshaw was standing over Ashcroft wearing a standard-issue military blue uniform, his wrinkled hand patting against the patch of hair plugs planted at the top of his scalp. The two were speaking indiscriminately and were unaware of the presence of McCray, who stood at the entrance letting the double doors slam shut.

"Senator," Ashcroft said without looking up. His raspy voice hanged on each syllable. McCray slowly walked toward the leather chair across from Ashcroft and Bradshaw. He pulled it back and sat down.

"First off, let me offer my deepest condolences," Ashcroft said. He leaned back in his seat. His graying auburn hair and stubble complemented the intensity of his piercing blue eyes. "I know you and Senator Upstead were very close."

"The room's clean I hope?" McCray asked.

"It's been debugged, yes, sir," Bradshaw said.

"Wasn't bugged in the first place," McCray mumbled to himself. "Who would bug for random numbers on a government budget list?"

"Upstead thought the same," Ashcroft said smiling. "But 7721…"

"Let's cut the bullshit," McCray said. "What's with the guards?"

"I'm sorry?" Ashcroft asked.

"The guards," McCray said. "The men-in-black motherfuckers that escorted me down here. Thought they were gonna chop me up."

Ashcroft roared with laughter.

"He didn't tell you?" Ashcroft said.

"Tell me?" McCray squinted his eyes. "Tell me what?"

"You have no idea what you are about inherit, do you?" Ashcroft asked. He leaned back in his seat and folded his arms. "Alan." Bradshaw pulled out a folder from his briefcase. He placed it on the table and slid it to McCray.

"What's this?" McCray asked.

"Senator Upstead's true estate," Bradshaw said. "Or more specifically his political estate."

"I don't understand," McCray said.

"Let me explain, Senator," Bradshaw said. "In this series of bank accounts and hedge funds lies close to one hundred billion dollars. Ninety percent of that money will be used to fund 7721, seven percent to run your campaigns and the other three percent to go to your personal estate."

As Bradshaw continued, McCray sunk back in his seat. He looked down at his lap, rubbing his left eye with the back of his hand. Each time he'd try to speak, he couldn't get the words out. All he could do was scratch the bottom of his salt-and-pepper goatee.

"It's a lot to take in," Ashcroft said. "7721 is yours now, Senator. You will never have to worry about another reelection because you will win every election. Now before you get on your constitutional high horse, understand politics is no longer your job. Hope you didn't have plans to be the next black president."

McCray scoffed.

"Who the fuck wants that job?" McCray asked.

Ashcroft gave a sly grin. Bradshaw grabbed his briefcase and stood up from his seat. He glanced at Ashcroft, whose eyes were trained on the door.

"Well then, sir," Ashcroft said, scooting back his seat. "If there's nothing further…"

"Wait," McCray whispered. "Sit down."

Ashcroft and Bradshaw did as they were told. McCray placed his hands on the table. The news of being responsible for one hundred billion dollars was still settling in his mind. He patted at the table to the rhythm of his pounding heart while taking deep breaths.

McCray then gathered his thoughts and said, "I was looking through the numbers from last year and noticed there was a five-hundred-million-dollar surplus. Care to explain?"

Bradshaw and Ashcroft looked at each other. McCray snapped his fingers at the two officers as if they were toddlers.

"Hey, fellas," McCray said. "I asked a question."

Bradshaw cleared his throat and said, "It's just…"

"Are you about to ask me why I'm asking about more money in the bank account?" McCray asked.

Bradshaw sighed and said, "Well, I…"

"Of course you were," McCray said. "A surplus of this magnitude must mean one of two things. Either you found a more efficient way to run 7721—and if so, great. Or you're cutting fucking corners on an operation that can *not* afford to do things half-assed—and if so, we have a problem."

Ashcroft straightened his black tie.

"We do have a bit of a problem, Senator," Ashcroft said as he leaned forward in his seat. "The five-hundred-billion-dollar surplus comes from outsourcing maintenance of the Blackout."

McCray's eyes widened. "Outsourcing it where?"

"Iceland," Bradshaw said.

"It was cheaper for us to have a software expert from Iceland step in and take care of the basic programming behind the

Blackout. One month out of the year the technician would be able to access the main terminal and do his job from the American embassy in Iceland."

"Are you two out your minds?" McCray asked, rubbing his forehead. "You put the Blackout online just to save a few dollars?"

"Senator," Ashcroft said, holding up his hand, "I assure you, we placed it on a secure line."

"That's not the point!" McCray shouted. "You got to use some common…"

"The American embassy in Iceland was hit," Ashcroft said.

"It was what?" McCray asked.

"They got access to the terminal. We lost the Blackout," Ashcroft said. McCray fell back in his seat and wiped his face with his hands.

"Shit."

It's a Small World

"Jonah, did you get the beer?" Carol asked as she tossed a garden salad in a brown wooden bowl. Jonah did not respond. The jazz music playing in the background was drowning out her meek voice. She put down the wooden fork and leaned over the kitchen island. Jonah was crouched on the other side, pouring ice into a large blue-and-white cooler. "Honey?"

"Yeah?" Jonah asked, standing up.

"The beer?"

"Brent's bringing it."

"Brent?" Carol asked in a whining voice. "He always brings that cheap stuff."

"No. he doesn't."

"He buys that Miller Lite shit," Carol said, laughing.

"Who doesn't like Miller Lite?" Jonah asked with a mischievous smile.

"Just because you don't drink doesn't mean the rest us have to suffer."

Jonah walked around the kitchen island. He gently pulled back Carol's hair and kissed her cheek.

"Maybe because I love you and your precious liver," Jonah said.

"Mm-hmmm," Carol said sarcastically. Jonah glanced over the dark-brown roots of her auburn dyed hair.

"Why don't you just let it grow out?" Jonah asked.

"What?"

"Your hair." He pushed the ice-filled cooler to the sliding glass doors leading to a flat cement patio. "It's a pretty brown. Why all the chemicals?"

"I like red."

"But your hair is too dark to dye it red."

"Oh, so you're a beautician now? The big-time physicist here is giving me beauty tips." The conversation was interrupted by a knock on the door. Jonah could see Brent's spiked blonde hair through the shutter blinds. "Any other tips for me, Vidal?"

"Fuck you," Jonah said, smiling. Carol slapped Jonah on the butt as she passed by him.

"With pleasure," she said as she placed a salad bowl on the square glass dinner table.

Jonah walked to the door and opened it. The humid summer air had melted Brent's hair gel. His spiked hair curled and gel dripped down the sides of his face.

"Wednesday, man," Brent said as he and Jonah fist bumped. "We present our thesis and *boom*! It's over!" He walked inside and waved at Carol.

"Brent," Carol said pointing her kitchen knife, "you take him outside to smoke and I will peel the skin off your fingers."

Brent gave a nervous smile. He waited for Carol's expression to lighten but it never did.

"Whoa," Brent mumbled.

They picked up the cooler and hauled it outside onto the patio.

"She is chilly!" Brent said, wiping the sweat and hair gel from his forehead. They walked around the apartment complex to Brent's car.

"She can get that way," Jonah said as he picked up one of the two cases of light beer. Brent grabbed the other, and they headed back to the patio.

"Strange," Brent said. "Older women tend to like me."

"Bullshit."

"For real, though, how old is she again?"

"Thirty-four."

"How your parents feel about that?"

Jonah lifted one side of the cooler trying to shake loose the ice cubes that had frozen together.

"I don't know," Jonah said as he opened the cooler, "I'm twenty-eight. It's not like she's robbing the cradle."

"Well, I got to hand it to you," Brent said, ripping open the case, "she is fine as hell. How did a nerd like you pick up a fly girl like that?" The high-pitched inflection in Brent's voice made him sound like a chipmunk. Jonah laughed.

"Stop."

"What?"

"The slang shit. Please stop. I can't take you seriously."

"OK, asshole," Brent said while jamming the Miller Lites into the packed ice. "Seriously, though, how'd you two meet?"

"At the gym. I was squatting when I saw her from the corner of my eye laughing at me."

"How much were you squatting?"

"One fifteen," Jonah mumbled.

"What?" Brent asked holding his hand up to his ear.

"One hundred and fifteen pounds. OK?"

Brent laughed.

"You fucking sissy!"

"Shut up."

"OK. OK," Brent said catching his breath., "Shouldn't be surprised. Your legs have the circumference of a twig." Jonah looked down at his thin, pale legs partially covered by his baggy tan shorts. He looked in the reflection of the sliding glass door to see a dirty blonde–haired stick figure with the face of a fifteen-year-old. "Why are you so sensitive? Sorry. Tell me what you did when she saw you squatting the weight equivalent of a twelve-year-old girl."

Jonah rolled his eyes.

"She walks over to me chuckling while I'm getting off the rack. And I flipped. Told her to go fuck herself. She gave me this look as if she was going to tear my head off."

"What did she say?"

"That normally she would rip off a guy's fucking head for talking to her like that, but in my case, it was charming."

They each grabbed the handles of the cooler and pushed it up against the sliding door.

"Shit," Brent said.

"I was pissed, but those eyes, man. Those big, light-brown eyes. Like a Margaret Keene painting. It was like staring into the eyes of…" Jonah paused. "I can't explain it. Anyway, I asked her out on the spot."

"You asked her out," Brent said, more of a statement than a question.

"Yeah, and five months later I asked her to marry me."

Brent looked through the sliding glass door at Carol. She was wearing a long blue backless sundress. Multiple scars adorned her tanned, toned physique.

"Are those gunshot wounds?" Brent asked squinting his eyes.

"What?" Jonah asked.

"Your wife," Brent asked, tapping on the window. "Did she get shot?"

"Hunting accident, she said. Doesn't like to talk about it."

"Oh," Brent said, continuing to stare. Her long, slender neck was leaned to one side as she chopped vegetables into fine pieces. Brent then looked at Jonah, who was struggling to push the cooler out of the path of the sliding door.

"Well, just try not to piss her off," Brent said.

"No shit."

"Girl like that, you'll be definitely wearing the panties in the family."

"She's already raped me twice." Jonah's face was expressionless.

"How was it?"

"Awesome."

Jonah popped open the cooler and tossed Brent a beer. They leaned back against the sliding glass window watching children in the backyard across from them play basketball as the sun set.

"So, man of the hour," Brent said. "You decided on your employment?"

"I don't know. There's a thousand physicists out there ten times smarter than me."

"Most of them from India," Brent said. They chuckled.

"Seriously, though, I'm just a bench rat who got lucky."

"No. I'm not gonna let you do that. It was a huge discovery you made. It takes more than some fucking benchwarmer to find what you did. I say you sign with the D.O.D."

"And let those assholes turn my shit into a weapon?" Jonah asked. "Fuck that."

"Then what?"

"I think I'm going nonprofit."

"Really? You'd give up all those offers?"

"Why'd we become physicists, man?" Jonah asked. "To join the rat race? Make some fucking bomb that ends up killing millions? There's got to be more out there than just...*that*." Jonah looked down at his beer, wiping the top with his gray T-shirt. "Everyone gets that one big discovery in their career."

"Not everyone," Brent said, pulling out a pack of cigarettes. He handed one to Jonah.

"Do you know there're kids in Africa using windmills to power their homes? I'm mean, they're walking miles to go to school. All the shit we take for granted and bitched and complained about as kids. Always wanted to go to Kenya. Start a science-and-math school. Build a well or two while I'm out there."

Brent lit his cigarette and smiled.

"You'd be good out there. Just bring a lot of sunscreen."

"Ha."

"Like a shitload. You're as white as the color."

"Boy, quit that smoking!" a subtle, Southern voice said. Brent and Jonah looked up. A stalky silver-haired gentleman wearing a blue polo shirt and kakis came from around the corner.

"Dad!" Jonah said. He walked up to his father and gave him a hug. "I thought you said you couldn't make it."

"If you thought that I would let a couple of millennial tourists keep me away from my boy's graduation, think again."

"Mr. Hayward," Brent said, shaking his hand.

Jonah dove his hand into the cooler and grabbed a beer.

"Where's Mom?" Jonah asked, tossing a beer to his father.

"She went on in," Mr. Hayward said. "Figured she could meet the new Mrs. Hayward and give her the third degree before I swoop in and smooth things over."

Jonah turned his head and peeked in at his mother and Carol talking, their backs facing the window. Jonah shook his head and gave a labored sigh when his mother grabbed Carol's waist.

"Aww man, Mom," Jonah said scrunching his face. "Enough with the birthing hips."

"You know your mother," Mr. Hayward said, laughing. He squinted his eyes trying to look inside the condo. "Can't see a damn thing these days without my contacts." He leaned his back against the white stucco condo wall. "Good thing the tourists don't know that."

"Got to go to the restroom," Brent said.

"Hey, kid," Mr. Hayward said, gesturing for his son to pass him the lit cigarette. Jonah handed it to his father. The old man closed his eyes and inhaled, relishing the nicotine. He held his breath for several seconds before letting the smoke out through his nose, where it rolled over his silver mustache into the evening summer air. "Shit, I miss that."

"You don't sneak a smoke or two at work?"

"I retire from the military, and the whole world done gone smoke-free, sugar-free, gluten-free."

"How's that by the way?"

"What's that, son?"

"Retirement."

Mr. Hayward took another puff.

"Well, your mother has some peace of mind, that's for damn sure. Don't have to worry about some Marine knocking on her door holding a folded flag."

"She's not the only one relieved about that."

"I know, I know. And it's nice to be home every night for dinner." Hayward took one last puff and flicked the cigarette butt onto the concrete patio. "Still, I sure do miss it."

"Miss what? You're still flying helicopters."

"It's not the same," Mr. Hayward said with a smile. "Flying black ops is like heroin and hovering these rich pricks over the Grand Canyon is methadone. It'll never truly replace the high." They sat quietly for a moment when Mr. Hayward finally asked, "Son, are you sure that she's the one?"

"Yeah, Dad. I'm sure."

"Your mother almost had a heart attack when she found out she was almost six years your senior. Let alone that you eloped."

"Dad…"

"Listen, you don't owe me an explanation. You are your own man. I trust your judgment."

He placed his hand on Jonah's shoulder.

"Thanks, Dad."

"So, are you going to introduce me to this lovely lady or not?"

Jonah laughed. He opened the sliding doors and the two men walked into the condo. As Mr. Hayward wrapped his wired reading glasses around his ears, he could hear his wife and Carol in the kitchen talking.

That voice, Mr. Hayward thought to himself. Carol's back was still facing Jonah and his father. *It can't be.*

"She's…" Mr. Hayward whispered.

Carol whipped around laughing.

"Honey, your mother is hilari-" Carol looked at Hayward and flinched. She tightened her grip on the knife while dropping down her shoulders and giving her guests a warm smile.

"Dead," Mr. Hayward whispered.

Jonah walked over to his wife and placed his arm around her shoulders.

"Dad, this is my lady," Jonah said.

Mr. Hayward could feel his heart beating out of his chest. His eyes glanced at the knife that Carol was clutching. Mr. Hayward scanned the room, trying to find something he could defend himself and his family with. Carol placed the knife on the counter and looked at Mr. Hayward with a blank stare.

Carol cocked her neck to the side and asked, "Are you OK, Mr. Hayward?"

"Honey?" Mrs. Hayward asked. "You look like you just saw a ghost."

"I…I'm fine," Hayward said.

Jonah's eyes darted between his father and Carol.

"Um, do you two know each other?" Jonah asked with a single raised eyebrow.

"Not at all," Carol said staring at Mr. Hayward.

"Complete strangers," Mr. Hayward said.

"O…K…," Jonah said. "Dad, I'm gonna grab Mom a beer. You want one?"

"No, thanks," Mr. Hayward said, smiling at Carol. "I think I'd like to get to know my daughter-in-law a little better."

Jonah nodded and walked out of the kitchen.

"Well," Mrs. Hayward said. "Let me set the table."

Carol smiled at Mrs. Hayward. She turned the stove to low and waved her hand for Mr. Hayward to follow her. He slipped a steak knife in his pocket and followed her into the empty one-car garage and closed the door behind him.

"The knife isn't necessary, Joe," Carol said.

"You sure about that, *Carol?*" Joe asked.

She walked down four wooden steps to the empty garage floor.

"If I wanted you dead, that wouldn't help. You should know that by now, right?" Joe pulled the knife from his pocket. "Why don't you put that down before I shove it up your ass, flyboy." He sighed and placed the knife on the wooden bannister, wiping his sweaty palms on his pants.

"What are you doing here?" Joe asked. "You're supposed to be…"

"Yeah, thanks for selling me out."

"Fuck you," he said, pointing his finger at her. "You sold the entire unit out. You and those other two bastards."

"It was an order."

"Bullshit. Shepard was trying do something good. It wouldn't have hurt nobody. And *you…*" Joe could hear his voice raising. He slammed his fist against the wooden banister. Joe looked at Carol's blank expression. "You may not care or know how to care, but he deserved better."

"Fuck Shepard," Carol said through clenched teeth, her left forearm shaking with tension.

"What was it with you and him?" Joe asked, shaking his head.

"Does it matter?" Carol said as she clapped her hands together. "He's dead. Let's not bring up the past. You want to know why I'm here? After I recuperated from what happened, my intentions were to hunt each and every one of you down. I figured you'd be the easiest, so I started with you by starting with your family."

"You evil bitch! They have nothing to do..."

"So, I started with your son. He was easy enough to find. The plan was to kidnap him. Torture him," she said with a chuckle. "Chop off a piece of him one day at a time until you take his place. The day I was about to abduct him, I made the mistake of meeting him. Well done, Joe."

Hayward scoffed.

"He asked me out on a date, and I said yes. Hayward, I have never been happier since." Joe folded his arms. He licked his teeth as he stared down at the ground, shaking his head. "I-I love him, Hayward."

"Are you even capable of love?" Joe asked, laughing. "You're a fucking psychopath."

"Hayward, listen, I..."

"Enough," Mr. Hayward said, waving both hands, "I don't care if you parade in front of my son with this Donna Reed persona you've made for yourself..." He paused, noticing Carol's eyes welling with tears. "Well, this is a new trick. I know what you are, darling. You and those other Wolves. You're incapable of love. And any man who stands by and lets their child fall in the clutches of a Wolf ain't a man."

"Hayward, if you would just..."

"I can't kill you. If I could, I would have slit your throat with that steak knife before you walked down those steps. But what

I can do is call Ashcroft." As Carol squinted her eyes, tears fell down the side of her face. "That's right. I'm giving you a head start, darlin'. The dogs are coming for you. I suggest you leave tonight." He hopped back up the steps and walked back into the kitchen.

"Hayward. Hayward, please." Carol stood at the bottom of the steps, wiping tears from her eyes. She shook her head and hopped up the wooden steps. When she stepped into the kitchen, Mrs. Hayward had already set the table.

"Carol," she said as she poured water into the glasses. "This dinner smells amazing. What are you baking?"

"Chicken," Carol said.

Jonah walked into the kitchen holding a bottle of wine.

"Special occasion Ri…" He noticed Carol's fading smile. "What's wrong?"

"Nothing," Carol said, slowly and passionately kissing him on the lips. She took a deep breath, grabbed his head and gently pressed her forehead against his. "Have a seat," she whispered in his ear. Everyone except Carol sat down at the table. Jonah popped open the bottle of wine. He poured a glass each for Carol and himself before passing the bottle.

"I just want to say that this is as close to a family as I've ever had," Carol said, standing behind Jonah. She placed her hands on his shoulders.

"That's sweet, honey," Mrs. Hayward said. Carol closed her eyes and took a deep breath.

"The Buddhists have a belief in letting go," Carol said.

"Here she goes with the philosophy," Brent said. Mr. Hayward's eyes widened. As everyone at the dining table laughed, he leaned forward in his seat.

"Let me finish!" Carol said, smiling. "Letting go is something I've had to do my whole life. Being an orphan an all, letting go is a part of life. What I'm realizing is…"

"Barbara..." Mr. Hayward said grabbing his butter knife. Everyone at the table turned to him with confused expressions.

"Life is all about letting go," Carol said with tears rolling down her cheeks.

"Barbara, don't..."

"Even death itself—it's just a transition. A way for you to let go of life."

"Barbara, please..."

"So, this evening, as much as it pains me to do this, for the first time actually, I'm going to ask you to remember as you're forced to let go..."

"Dammit, Barbara..."

Jonah could feel her tears tapping at the back of his neck. He twisted his head to look up at his sobbing wife. Jonah scrunched his face before staring back at his father sitting across from him.

"Dad, who's Barb—," Jonah said before he felt a sharp pain in the back of his neck. His hands dropped to his side. The last image Jonah saw was his father hopping on top of the table. The screams coming from his family became more distant until finally echoing in the background of his subconscious.

Life Is but a Dream

"No, baby," he said with a thick Italian accent. "You always assume that I'm not where I say I am. You're the mother of my children. Why would I lie to you?" He was driving a burnt-red catering van, speeding through traffic and running red lights. On the sides of the vehicle read TONY'S LITTLE ITALIA. The young man would periodically look over his shoulder and sigh with relief that none of the food had spilled. As he was preparing to run another red light, he mashed on his breaks. The van screeched along the paved street, stopping just a few feet in front of a green SUV. Black smoke rose from the open hood.

"Shit. I do *not* have time for this shit!" he shouted.

He turned off the ignition. A young lady appeared from behind the SUV. Her hands were tucked away in her gray peacoat that came down to mid-thigh. Her black six-inch stilettos stomped against the pavement. The van's fluorescent headlights made her pink glitter lipstick shimmer. She pulled her long brown hair behind her ears and flashed a demure smile at the deliveryman.

"Hello," he said with a pleasant tone, stepping out of the van. "You need help?"

"I'm so sorry. My car just died on me," she said. The deliveryman kept his cellphone close to his ear, whispering in Italian.

"Cars don't die," he chuckled. He was missing one of his incisors. The young woman gave a polite smile and nodded. "Don't worry. We get fixed."

She placed both her hands over her chest just a few inches above her cleavage. She sighed with relief.

"Thank you so much."

"I go take a look." He stuck his head under the hood with his cellphone close to his ear. *Perché ti ho sposato?!*

"Excuse me?" she said.

"Oh, no," he said, hitting his head on the hood and pointing to his phone. "Talking to friend. I think you need tow truck."

"Aww, no. Really?"

"Don't worry. I stay until help arrives."

"Thank you so much. That's so sweet of you."

"No problem, no problem." His eyes wandered to her legs, which were scantly covered by her pink lace dress. "Kinda late to be out here all alone," he said.

"Or pretty early, depending on your point of view."

The deliveryman laughed. He patted at his uneven mullet, flipped his cellphone shut and edged closer to her.

"You coming from a party?" he asked.

"More like I'm going to one."

"Ooh, sounds fun," he said, inching even closer to her. "This party that you go to in the middle of the night, what's the occasion?"

"I don't know," she said, rolling her eyes. "But I can tell ya, I am *not* looking forward to it."

"Well," he said, touching her shoulder with his short, hairy hand, "maybe it's a party I'd be willing to join."

"It's not that kind of party," she said as she stepped away from him.

"Hey, take it…"

"Didn't you say you were going to call me a tow truck?"

The deliveryman curled the right side of his upper lip.

"You fucking American women," he hissed and marched toward his van. "Just a big tease you are."

"So that's how it is?" she asked, trailing behind him.

"Look, lady, I'm already late with a delivery."

"So why did you marry your wife?" she asked.

He stopped and turned around.

"How did you know that I…"

"I know a lot, Andre. I know you're on your way to Mayada's to drop off a late-night snack." He stepped back until he hit his head against the side of the van. "I know you're a womanizer who'd cut off his arm for a BJ."

The cold metal of Graham's silencer pressed against the side of Andre's forehead.

"Oh, my God!" Andre said, sobbing.

"What I didn't know before tonight is that you're married. You told me that."

"Wh-when did I…"

"When you were speaking to her."

Drops of sweat dangled from Andre's lashes and coated his eyes like a saline moisturizer. His red eyes darted back and forth between the blurry images of the young woman and Graham.

"Hey, Andre!" she said snapping her fingers. "Can I call you Andre?" He nodded feverishly. "Wonderful. You didn't ask me my name. Would you like to know?"

"Um…s-sure," Andre said.

"It's Rosa," she said.

"Say hi to Rosa," Graham said, poking the gun at Andre's temple.

"Hi…hi," Andre said.

"Now, Andre, listen carefully," Rosa said. "I need you to sing 'Row Your Boat' in Italian. Can you do that?"

"What?" Andre asked.

"'Row your boat,'" she said, deepening her voice. "Sing it."

Andre looked up at the night sky. He took a deep breath, clenched his fist and sang:

> *"Rema, rema, rema la tua barca,*
>
> *Dolcemente lungo il ruscello.*
>
> *Allegramente, allegramente, allegramente, allegramente,*
>
> *La vita non è che un sogno."*

"Keep going," Rosa said, closing her eyes. She placed her hand on his chest as he continued to sing. The words echoed in her mind. "Countryside. Northern Italy…Northwest?" The echoing faded and was replaced by a choir of children singing on a lush, green patch of grass. They stood in front of a stone castle with a cool wind blowing their wolfskin coats. Rosa took a deep breath. "Morgex wine?" The children in her vision started to sing in rounds. "I hear French." Dancing in the wind was a black-and-red flag. Rosa smiled. "The Aosta valley. That's where you're from, right?" She opened her eyes.

Sweat dripped from the eyelashes of the wide-eyed delivery-man. He asked, "How did you…" Rosa pressed her finger against his lips.

"Shhhhh…." she said, shaking her head.

❧

"It's not the dead baby they murdering for this stem-cell thing?"

"Naw," Ares said, shaking his head. He was surrounded by Mayada's bodyguards. They were standing by a large gray concrete pillar, one of five holding up the second floor of Mayada's mansion. The pillars made a square, in the middle of which was a small garden clearing. The bodyguards each had on tailored pinstriped slacks with satin ties and white cotton dress shirts. Their sleeves were rolled up, showing off arms with ink-pen prison tattoos. Semiautomatic pistols were holstered under their armpits.

"It's like this," Ares said. "If the price is right, you can get a whore to do whatever you want, right?" The crowd laughed and cheered. "Naw, naw, I'm serious," Ares said, catching himself chuckling. "You can get a trick to fuck, suck, piss, whateva's your pleasure as long as you come correct with the dough, right?" The crowd nodded. "Let me ask you this. And let me preface this by saying first, no disrespect. I fucking love you guys. But when's the last time your wives sucked you off?"

The crowd erupted into multiple protests: "Whoa, Ares!" "You go too far, boyo!"

"Let me fucking finish, all right? I'm making a point," Ares said, holding up his hands. "Now, you don't have to answer this, but I would bet that the last time any of you got some head was back before you got married. People mature. Wives mature. She's proper and good, you know, she's the fucking mother of your children, right? Think of a mature nerve like that. It ain't growin' and it ain't changin' for shit."

One of Mayada's men was leaning on an adjacent pillar, glaring at Ares. He was stocky, wearing a white oxford shirt with a black tie and an obvious chip on his shoulder. His sleeves were rolled up to his elbows. His arms were folded and his eyes did not waver, hoping that Ares would notice his stare. One of the capos, a tall thin man with dark-brown hair and thick black glasses, gave a nervous chuckle before backing out from the crowd and walking over to the mobster seething in the corner.

"What's your problem?" he asked.

"What the fuck you think?" the mobster asked. "He's my

fucking problem. He got all these fucking wise guys around here on his fucking jock."

"You gotta stop this shit, man."

"Or what?"

"Or what?" the thin capo repeated. "You deaf or somethin'? Or what…"

He nudged the thin capo out of the way and walked over to the crowd.

"Tony!" the capo whispered.

"So, your old ladies are the nervous system of your house, right?" Ares asked. The crowd laughed and nodded. "That's good. The backbone of your homes and you should be proud of that. It means you chose well. But like anything mature and proper, they only gonna do so much before they tell you to go fuck yourself— or in this case, suck your own cock."

"Get to your fucking point," Tony said.

The crowd of gangsters glanced at Tony before focusing back on Ares.

"My point is a stem cell isn't a whore, they're better than that. They're that fresh piece of ass that just got off the bus from nowhere. Young and dumb. You know the type: perfect, flexible Midwestern body, comin' to the city to be a dancer. You ain't gotta pay 'em, you ain't gotta buy 'em cars or jewelry. You can just take 'em out once in while, show 'em a good time, and they'll do whatever you want 'em to do. That's a fucking stem cell. It can change into any cell with a little bit of tender love and care, including nerves."

The flash of insight ignited across their faces.

"So, what you're saying," one of the wise guys said, scratching his eye, "Is that when I get home, if my wife don't give me some head, I tell her she's a broken nerve that needs to be replaced by some hot-tit stripper?"

The crowd erupted.

"Hey," Ares said, "it's your funeral!"

"That's funny," Tony said. "Where'd you learn all that shit anyway?"

"The news," Ares said. "That's all I did in Rikers—read and watch the news."

"News and books, huh?" Tony asked. "You never had to put any work in?"

Ares's smile faded. He placed his hands in the pockets of his black slacks, and the crowd parted for him as he slowly approached Tony.

"What do you think?" Ares asked softly.

"What do I think? Nothin'," Tony said, staring timidly at the ground. He looked up, squared his broad, muscular shoulders, and locked eyes with Ares. "You seem to enjoy talking about fellatio. Just wonder whose balls were you suckin' on in the pen?"

Ares scoffed. He patted himself down until he felt a pack of cigarettes in his back pocket. Tony took another step toward Ares. His height and imposing arms gave Tony the advantage. The two were standing within a few inches of each other. He looked down at the back of Ares's bowed head. Tony flexed his broad shoulders and cracked his knuckles.

"You got everybody here afraid of you. But not me."

With his head still down, Ares placed the cigarette in his mouth. He patted himself again, looking for a lighter.

"That's what I think. You phony little shit."

Ares pulled a lighter from his pocket and lit his cigarette.

"Fuck you and the cunt whore who bore…"

Ares flung his head back like a whip, forcing the back of his head into Tony's jawbone, breaking his jaw and shattering teeth. Tony's head flew back, his body stumbling backward. Ares took a quick puff off his cigarette and pulled out a .45-caliber pistol, shooting both of Tony's kneecaps. Tony crashed to the concrete floor. He curled up in a ball and clutched his bleeding knees. Ares took one last puff on his cigarette before flicking it away. He straddled Tony and picked him up by the collar of his shirt. He raised the butt of his handgun and slammed it into Tony's broken face. Tony tried to yell but could only let out small whimpers in between each strike. Ares continued to hit Tony until all he could see was mangled blood and flesh, the remnants of Tony's face. Out of breath, Ares took the black handkerchief from Tony's shirt and threw him onto the concrete.

"You his boss?" Ares asked, pointing at the thin capo.

"Yeah, Ares," he said with a cracking voice.

"A mouth on him, huh?" Ares said, wiping the handle of his gun with Tony's handkerchief.

"Y-yes sir," the thin capo said. "My apologies for his manners."

"I know he was your friend, and I respect you. So, I'm gonna do you a favor. I'm gonna allow you to toss this bastard in front of a hospital." The capo nodded. He and a few other men grabbed Tony and started dragging him toward the entrance. "Wait." They turned around. "You might have thought that by 'toss' I meant to place him carefully in front of some random emergency room. What I meant was as you are driving no slower than sixty miles an hour that you open the door and *toss* his ass within proximity of said hospital. Understand?"

"Yeah, Mr. Ares," the capo said.

"And hurry up," Ares said, wiping his blood-splattered face with the back of his bare forearm. "We got company coming." Ares holstered his .45 and went inside. He stepped into a tan oak living room, glancing at the head of a stuffed elk on a mantle propped over the fireplace. Armed gangsters nodded in respect as Ares passed them. He walked up a broad spiral stairway covered by red-and-gold oriental carpeting. Mayada's study was about five steps from the stairwell. Once he reached the top, he could hear voices in the study. Ares stood next to the cracked double doors.

"You don't get it," Mayada said. "I'm not giving you a damn thing until you help me take care of these guys."

"Mr. Mayada, we are not here to assist you in controlling the help. You told us you had the Blackout." The voice was deep, yet soft.

"Let's not be coy here, agent…whatever your name is. Black suit and tie, G.I. Joe–build; I know what you are, and I know whatever it is those guys lifted from that embassy was shit you spooks had hidden for a reason. Reasons that I don't even want to know about."

"You can call me…"

"Ah bup, bup, bup," Mayada said holding his hands up. "Now, I ain't no rat. OK? Fuck the cops. But I am a patriot. Figured this was some shit that was a matter of national security."

"In other words, you knew you couldn't sell it."

"You gonna blame me for being a red-blooded capitalist?" Mayda sighed. "Fuck, if I didn't know any better, I'd think you two were hatched from the same pod. You fucking stand just like him."

"Stand like who?"

"Shepard Black."

There was silence in the room. Ares peeked through the narrow hinges of the double doors. He could see a middle-aged man with short dark-brown hair and olive skin stood. Mayada was seated behind his broad oak desk. Carved elephant heads, each with thick ivory tusks, propped up the solid slab of oak that made the desktop. Mayada sat in a large tan leather chair twice his size.

"That…it's not possible," the man in black said.

"What do you mean 'not possible'?"

"You must be mistaken."

"He's not," Ares said, walking into the study. The man in black scanned Ares from head to toe before turning back to Mayada.

"Be that as it may, a dispute between a couple of common thugs is just that. Common," the man in black said.

"What?" Ares asked. Mayada motioned for Ares to keep quiet.

"Whoever this guy is that you're obviously afraid of, it seems to me that you're heavily guarded, and he should not pose a problem. I, however, am a different story all together. Now, if I do not have the Blackout within the next five minutes, it will not be your death but your torment," the man in black said.

"Uncle, who the fuck is this guy?" Ares asked.

"The boogeyman," the man in black replied. "Please stop interrupting me."

"Uncle Mayada, fuck this guy," Ares said, edging closer to the man in black. "We need to make moves."

"Son, you are truly trying my patience," the man in black said.

"Ares, enough," Mayada said.

"Fuck your patience," Ares said. "How about you try this bullet in your fucking mouth?"

The man in black chuckled.

"Huge error, young man," the man in black said. "Declarations are for foolish romantics and spineless politicians."

"What?" said Ares, furrowing his brow.

"Whenever you wish to shoot a man, just shoot him, don't say it. Now I'm on the defensive, and I can guarantee my draw will be quicker."

Ares's eyes widened. He looked down at the ground for a split second before reaching for his holster. The man in black stuffed his left hand in his pocket. When his hand emerged, a metal object projected, hammering into the bridge of Ares's already-broken nose. Ares was blinded by his own blood and tears. Caught off-balance by the projectile, he unholstered his .45 and waved it in the air. Through his tear-filled vision, Ares could see a blurred image approaching him. The man in black grabbed Ares's wrist and started twisting. His grip felt like a vise, cracking the bones in Ares's forearm. Ares then felt a sudden sharp pain in his right side as the man in black rammed the palm of his hand into his floating ribs. Ares dropped his pistol. He then spun behind Ares, still holding onto his broken wrist. The man in black bent down and brought Ares's wrist to the ground. The force lifted Ares off of his feet, propelling him into the air crashing through the double doors. The man in black stood up and straightened his tie, staring at Ares's slumped body in the hallway. Mayada jolted himself up from his seat. The man in black picked up his metal case.

"Cigarettes," he said to Mayada, waving the metal case in the air. "I swear this is going to be the end of me before any bullet." He slid the case back in his pants pocket. "Where is the Blackout, Mr. Mayada?"

"Is he still breathin'?" Mayada asked.

"For now. That can change, though."

"You kill me now, and you'll never see it again. Spooks or no spooks, I have something you want."

The man in black sighed. He placed his hand in his jacket pocket and pulled out a single syringe.

"You don't listen very well, do you, Mr. Mayada? I didn't say anything about death. Just torment."

⤎

"It's about time!" the wise guy said. He and a group of armed men dressed in dark tailored suits were standing guard outside Mayada's brick mansion. "Andre, where the fuck have you been?!" His bulbous gut bounced as he walked down the long set of brick steps toward Andre's delivery van parked in the circular driveway. "Andre, you hear me?"

Rosa stepped out of the van wearing Andre's stained black slacks and a red T-shirt that read TONY'S LITTLE ITALIA. She had on a black baseball cap with her hair in a ponytail.

"Who the fuck are you and where's Andre?" the wise guy asked.

Rosa whipped her head in his direction and said in Italian, "Some mouth on you." She looked down at his stomach. "Some belly on you, too. Stop being a filthy pig and help me with your food."

The wise guy shook his head and opened the van's sliding door. There were six large metal tubs of pasta resting on a set of warmers.

"Don't you have help, Miss?" he replied back in Italian.

Rosa slammed the door.

"Those animals Tony and Andre sent me out here by myself to go gambling!"

The wise guy waved for help. Soon a group of men walked out of the house and headed toward the van. They lifted the large metal warmers back to the house.

"You from Aosta?" The wise guy asked. Rosa nodded. "That's nice. My grandmother's from there."

"Yes, I came here to live with Uncle Tony for a better life," she said with sarcasm. "I only traded delivering milk for delivering grains and tomato sauce."

The wise guy chuckled and said, "You shouldn't think of it that way. You can go to school…"

"Yes, yes," she said, walking away. "I am aware of this so-called American dream. Enjoy your meal."

"Hold on," he said grabbing her arm. "Stick around." Rosa looked at her watch.

"I-I have more deliveries to make."

"To hell with the other deliveries," he said. "Come on, break bread with us."

Rosa grimaced while taking a deep trembling breath.

"O-ok, just for a minute," she said.

"Dada girl," the wise guy said in English, patting down his gray sideburns with his thumb.

He wrapped his arm around her elbow and the two walked

up the lit brick-and-cobblestone path toward the mansion. They stepped inside the foyer. The other guards had just finished placing the metal warmers on a long plastic foldout table in the middle of the dining room. Rosa couldn't stop her body from shaking. Noticing this, the wise guy rubbed her arm.

"Relax, darling," he said. "You're among friends."

Rosa gave a nervous chuckle.

"Hey, Joey," the wise guy said. "Get the other guys together. Tell them dinner's here."

"Ain't we on like Defcon 5 or somethin'?" Joey asked.

"Two guys," the wise guy replied. "It's overkill. We'll keep a couple guys watching the front entrance. Everyone else get in here." He looked at Rosa. "You don't mind standing up eating, do you?"

"Oh, no," she said covering her mouth, "I didn't bring the… the plates and the cutlery."

"It's fine," he said.

"No, it's not," she said walking away, "Let me go get it."

"Will you relax?" he said, grabbing her arm. "Why are you Italian women so wound up? I'm sure we have all that shit in the kitchen. Why don't you go over there and get the food warmed up."

"Warm up the food?"

"Yeah," he said, squinting his eyes. "You do know how to do that right?"

"Yes. I can."

She walked over to the metal pan, took a deep breath, and turned the knobs of each propane burner propped under the metal pans. She stepped back and watched as the small blue flames ignited under the stainless metal tubs. As she stepped away from the buffet, she could feel the wise guy's hand on the small of her back.

"So," she said in Italian, "why so many people here at this time of night?"

"Nothing to worry your pretty little head about," he said, touching her chin with his index finger. "Just a little security work."

"So, you guys are security guards?"

"You could say that."

"I see." Rosa grabbed her stomach.

"You OK?"

"I-I'm fine," she stammered.

The room was now spinning. The wise guy scrunched his plump cheeks at the dazed expression on Rosa's face. He looked over at the platoon of gangsters congregating around the buffet. He turned his head back to Rosa, who was now flat on her back, her mouth and nose covered by a white gas mask.

"What the fuck?" the wise guy murmured to himself. He walked over to the crowd surrounding the food and shouted, "Wait!"

"Hey, Harvey wants us to wait for him," one of Mayada's men shouted. "What the hell for? You want a pan to yourself?"

The crowd laughed.

"I said stop!" Harvey shouted. He slapped a plastic plate from one of the capos standing next to him. Marinara sauce splattered all over his dark pinstriped suit.

"What the fuck ya do that for?" the capo asked.

"There is something wrong here?" Harvey said.

"What?" said the capo.

"I don't know," Harvey said holding his head, "This girl was standing right here talking to me and the next thing I know..." Harvey started to stagger.

"Harv?" said the capo.

Harvey looked around, confused.

"It's fine," he said. "We should be fucking fine if we don't eat..." His eyes rolled into the back of his head as his body crashed onto the wooden floor.

❦

Outside Mayada's mansion, two men stood guard with their backs against the brick wall. One of the guards looked at his wristwatch and gave a frustrated sigh. Moments later, they heard a loud thud. The two guards glanced at each other but didn't budge. They then heard multiple thuds, picking up in tempo and resonating throughout the mansion. Plates and glasses shattered, while metal cutlery banged. One of the guards walked over to a window seal to look inside. Mayada's men laid lifeless, splattered with pasta and shattered china across the checkered wooden floor. He looked over and saw Rosa wearing her gas mask, squirming under a capo who had fallen on top of her.

"What the fuck?" the guard said.

"Hey…" A voice whispered from the bushes.

The guard looked up and saw a shadow pointing a sawed-off shotgun. Buckshot ripped through the guard's chest and lifted him off of his feet. His limp body came to rest at the foot of the other guard, who looked down at his partner, then in the direction of the shadow standing in the bushes. As he lifted his Glock to open fire, his head was jolted. Brain and skull painted Mayada's oak door. His body slumped against the door before sliding to the ground. Graham stood over both corpses with a silenced nine-millimeter in his hand. He looked over at Shepard emerging from the bushes wearing a black gas mask. Graham quickly put his on mask, and the two walked into the foyer. They surveyed the area until they noticed Rosa trying to bench press the portly capo off her chest. Graham gave a dull whistle to get Shepard's attention. He pointed at Rosa, and the two stepped over the bodies toward her. Shepard kicked the capo off of Rosa's petite frame. She rolled onto her stomach, coughing and gasping for air. Shepard and Graham each grabbed an arm and picked her up.

"Is this everyone?" Shepard asked. Rosa didn't respond. "Rosa."

"Dammit, Shepard! Give me a minute!" Rosa said. She ripped her arms from the two and bent over, placing her hands on her knees. "This is everyone. Except for Mayada."

"Ares?" Graham said.

"He's definitely not here," Rosa said.

"Get back to the hideout and stay put," Shepard said.

Rosa nodded and staggered toward the entrance. They walked across the foyer to a wide spiral wooden stairwell upholstered with a red-and-gold oriental rug.

"Can't believe they just left two people on guard," Graham said. "First the geriatric hitmen, then the guy with the ulcer…"

"It's a dying breed, the mob business, I guess," Shepard said.

They reached the top of the stairs and walked down a dimly lit hallway leading to Mayada's study. The oriental rug trailed past the door to the study, which was broken in half and dangling from its hinges. Ares was on the opposite side of the hall slumped over with his body propped against the wall.

"Is he still breathing?" Graham asked.

They saw a slow rise from Ares's chest.

"Shit," Shepard said, taking off his mask.

"What are you doing?"

"He's still breathing, right? We don't need these up here." Shepard looked at the shattered door and glanced back at Ares. "He's here."

Graham took off his mask and took a deep breath.

"Shit."

As Shepard emerged from the hallway, the man in black's pupils grew. Shepard looked over at Mayada, who was sitting at his desk. His body was tense, his teeth and fists clenched, rooted in agony. The man in black stood silently across from Shepard. His initial expression of shock was replaced by confusion.

"Shepard?" the man in black asked.

"Been a while, Santiago," Shepard said.

"How is this possible?" Santiago asked, staring at Shepard. "I..."

"Killed us?" Shepard asked. "Almost."

"No...I emptied my clip in that elevator. We dragged your bodies..." Santiago shook his head. "Well, I guess the next plausible question is..." Hearing the footsteps coming from behind Shepard, Santiago placed his left hand behind his back, drawing a double-edged hunting knife. He wound his arm like a pitcher at a mound and released the knife from his hand just as Graham was emerging from behind Shepard. The force of the knife pierced Graham's right wrist, pinning him against the wall. Shepard didn't move.

"Guess that answers my next question," Santiago said. He placed his hands back in his pocket. "How goes it, Graham?"

"I've seen better days," Graham said, grunting. "See you still go for your knife before your gun."

"Old habits," Santiago said. "You know how it is." Santiago unholstered his nine-millimeter and held it at his side. "You never intended to sell the Blackout." Santiago tapped his gun in the air in Shepard's direction. "No, you went into hiding, licked your wounds, and when the time was right, shot us a signal."

"More or less," Shepard said.

"What's this about?" Santiago asked, opening his arms. "Revenge? That never seemed to be your style, Shepard."

"You're right," Shepard said.

"But it is Barbara's," Graham said, glancing at the light switch a few feet next to him.

"Barbara?" Santiago asked.

"She *has* paid you guys a visit, hasn't she?" Shepard asked. There was a blank expression on Santiago's face.

"We'll take that as a no," Graham said. He flipped down the switch. In that split second, shots rang through the study. With each blast, Graham could see snapshots of Shepard navigating his way through the room toward Santiago. After the final blast, there was a painful grunt followed by silence. Graham flipped up the switch. Santiago stood in the middle of the room with his gun pointed at the broken door. He glanced over at Graham, who was hunched over and cradling his wounded wrist, his knife nowhere in sight. He looked down to find Shepard crouched under his left arm. The same knife that he had used to pin Graham against the wall was now deep in his chest. Santiago coughed before collapsing to the floor. He looked up at Shepard now holding him, trying to get his last words out but each time interrupted by blood gushing from his mouth. Shepard clutched Santiago's dying body close and started whispering in his ear. Graham walked over to find Santiago cracking a smile before drifting away. While carefully laying Santiago on the floor, Shepard closed his tear-filled eyes and said, "*Ave Maria, gratia plena, Dominus tecum. Benedicta tu in mulieribus, et benedictus fructus ventris tui, Iesus. Sancta Maria, Mater Dei, ora pro nobis peccatoribus, nunc, et in hora mortis nostrae.* Amen."

"Shepard?" Graham said.

Shepard got up and walked over to Mayada, still seated behind his desk, tense and silent. His eyes were red and drool oozed from his mouth. Shepard grabbed Mayada by his shirt and dragged him from behind the desk. He flung the old man onto a zebra-print sectional sofa and sat down on an adjacent dark-gray wool ottoman.

"Mayada," Shepard said. The old man remained silent. "Mayada!" Mayada, trembling, looked at Shepard.

"It hurts, doesn't it?" said Shepard.

"W-what did he d-do to me?" Mayada murmured.

"It's called the lake of fire," Shepard said. "It acts on a relay center in your brain that interprets pain. It's designed to intensify. Soon the pain will be so strong that you'll lose your mind."

"T-turn it off!" Mayada shouted. "I'll tell you whatever you want!"

"Doesn't work that way," Shepard said. "I can't reverse it. There is only one way to end this." Mayada looked at Santiago's body.

"You have t-to promise me y-you won't go after my family," Mayada said.

"You have my word," Shepard said.

Mayada's tense trembling fingers pointed in the direction of the bookshelf.

"It's in alphabetical order," Mayada said. "You like H-Hemingway? A fan of *Old Man and the Sea* myself."

Graham walked over to the bookshelf, scanning with his fingers the spines beginning with the letter *O*. He pulled a book and flipped through the pages. On page seventy was a black thumb drive. Graham pulled the thumb drive from the page and held it in the air. Shepard walked over to Santiago and picked up his gun.

"So, this is how I go out," Mayada said with a chuckle. Shepard cocked the pistol. "Well…" A shot from the doorway cut Mayada's words short. His head fell back on the couch with blood trickling from his temple onto the floor.

"Shut the fuck up!" Ares said, hobbling into the study, his right arm dangling at his side. Shepard kept his gun pointed on him. "A year and a half, been dealing with this guy." He looked at Shepard and Graham. "This is the most racist, misogynistic, homophobic…" The thick Jersey accent melted away as Ares continued on his tirade. Shepard sighed, lowering his weapon.

"Glad to see you're still breathing, Ares," Shepard said.

"Stop calling me that!"

"Why do you get so annoyed by that nickname?" Graham asked.

"Because my name is Jonah."

"You sure it isn't Ares?"

"Look at me, Shepard," Jonah said, pointing at his boyish face. "If I was gonna ride up the ranks of this bunch, I needed to give the appearance that I was war incarnate."

Graham rolled his eyes.

"Well, you certainly proved that," Shepard said.

"Save me the piety, preacher. We all have blood on our hands," Jonah said. He walked over to Santiago's body and knelt down. "This is a one of those Wolves, huh?"

"Uh-huh," Shepard said.

"How'd you do it?" Jonah asked.

"We told you not to engage him, Jonah," Shepard said. "You're lucky to be…"

"Have you found her?" Jonah asked, his voice flat and stern.

"They haven't seen her," Shepard said.

"Bullshit," Jonah said. "You expect me to believe he didn't tell you anything?"

"Believe it or not, it's the truth kid," Graham said.

"Liars," Jonah said. "You two still don't trust me."

"More or less," Shepard said.

"You think as soon as I find out where she is, I'm gone. Don't you?" Jonah said, walking toward Shepard.

"Absolutely," Shepard said.

"That is not your decision to make!" Jonah said.

"Actually, it is," Shepard said.

"She's my wife!" Jonah said.

"We're aware," Shepard said.

"Hey," Graham said, tossing the book and placing the thumb drive in his front pocket, "I think it would be best to continue this conversation elsewhere."

Shepard nodded. He placed his gun back in its holster. Graham propped his wounded hand on the other wrist and the two walked through the bullet-torn study toward the broken doorway. Jonah stood over Santiago's body, fuming with anger.

"If anyone has a right to kill Barbara, it's me!" Jonah shouted.

"Kid, the line to kill Barbs started long before you said 'I do,'" Shepard said.

MIEA VERDADE

KANSAS CITY, 2013

"You OK, kid?" Shepard asked.

"Stop asking him that," Graham said. Shepard stared at Graham's blank expression. "It's a silly question."

They both looked at Jonah, bent over in the backseat of a navy-blue Sudan. The car was parked on a green hill in front of a dark-gray marble tombstone with a statue of a cloaked angel covering her face with her hands. It was one of hundreds of tombstones in a large gated cemetery. A dark overcast sky shadowed a procession of cars cruising through the black iron gates.

"I'm fine," Jonah said, rustling his long blond hair. His bangs dangled over his left eye.

"You don't look fine," Shepard said.

"I'm fucking fine, all right?!"

Shepard held his hands up. Jonah took a deep breath and straightened his tie.

"No," Shepard said, tousling Jonah's hair. "Clean but disheveled. You're not a physicist. You're a wise guy's illegitimate child."

Jonah nodded. The procession stopped midway up the hill. Cars parked on the street across from a burial site arranged with black folding chairs. "When you go down there, you get his attention. You don't walk up to him. You don't make a scene. You wait for him to notice you."

"What if that doesn't happen?" Jonah asked.

"It will," Graham said. "If there's one thing about Mayada, he needs to know everyone around him."

"It's one o'clock," Shepard said, looking at his watch. "We ordered the hit to be around one-forty-five. That should give you enough time."

"I can't believe you guys hired a hitman," Jonah said, shaking his head.

"If you're gonna hit a guy," Graham said gesturing with air quotes, "you hire a hitman, right?"

"Only thing is, he's the one getting hit," Jonah said. Graham and Shepard laughed. "Not much of a conscience you guys have, do you?"

"Listen," Graham said, catching his breath, "we all want to find her. But she has disappeared off the face of the earth, and finding her is going to take resources. Resources that we don't have. We've been doing jobs for Mayada for what, about three years now? He trusts us. Now, our next heist involves taking something from our previous employers that they're going to move heaven and earth to try to get back, and when that happens, we need an inside man."

"We're robbing 7721?" Jonah asked. The two nodded. Jonah shook his head and whispered, "Shit." He closed his eyes and asked, "What are we stealing?"

"If we told you what it is, you wouldn't believe us," Shepard said.

"This is bullshit!" Jonah said, sinking his head in his hands, "You got me playing some phony-ass mobster's prodigal son...."

"Think of it as a school play. You did high school theater right? Of course you did." Graham said.

"And now you got me killing a guy who has nothing to do with this!" Jonah shouted.

"You want us to call it off?" Shepard asked. "Find a way that doesn't involve taking an innocent life?"

Jonah scoffed, shaking his head.

"Is that your point?" Jonah asked with sarcasm. "Since he kills, this isn't wrong?"

"Exactly," Shepard said. "Not only that, this piece of shit has a thing for little girls. He posts pictures of what he likes to do to them on the black market. Want to see?" Jonah turned his head. "You sure? Might I remind you that you asked for this. All you had to do was point in a direction and go on with your life but no, you wanted revenge. This is it. The bad, the worse, and the fucked-up."

"It's time, kid," Graham said while glancing at his watch. "Break a leg."

Jonah got out of the car and walked toward the funeral. He stood in the back, watching as the priest made a feeble attempt to comfort a somber crowd. Mayada was sitting at the front, wearing a dark charcoal suit and gray tie, his arm around a sobbing old woman dressed in black. He looked up for a moment and saw Jonah's scuffled appearance: A black suit that was two sizes too small with a dingy white shirt and a faded multicolored tie. Jonah adjusted his dark black shades and locked eyes with Mayada. He stared at him and pulled a cigarette from his ear before walking away.

"I'll be back, hon," Mayada said. He looked to his wife. "Here, comfort your sister-in-law." Mayada got up from his seat and walked down the aisle. His security quickly caught up with him. "It's fine. It's fine," he said. He leaned next to one of his guards and asked, "Thought I told all the guys this was a family affair? Blood only."

"I don't think he works for us," the guard said. "Never seen him." He looked at Jonah standing by a large oak tree on the other side of the street. Mayada started to walk across the street.

"Sir?" the guard asked, ready to unholster his pistol. Mayada held up his hand and shook his head.

"You mind if I bum one of those?" Mayada asked. Jonah nodded and gave him a cigarette. "My wife is trying to get me to quit." Jonah gave a smirk and nodded. "You seem kinda young to be doin' this shit."

"I'm older than I look," Jonah said.

"It's funny," Mayada said. "I thought I told you guys this was for family only."

"I didn't work for him," Jonah said, lighting up another cigarette.

"Then why the fuck are you at my brother's funeral?"

Jonah laughed. He took a large drag and blew smoke in the air.

"Did he ever tell you about Diane?" Jonah asked.

Mayada squinted his right eye. He looked down at the ground and paused before a flash of enlightenment came across his face.

"I'll be dammed," Mayada said. "You look just like her."

"Yeah, I get that a lot," Jonah said.

"What's your name son?"

"Ares."

"Ares?" Mayada chuckled. "What's Diane doing with herself these days?"

"Same thing my father is doing. She's dead. Cancer."

"Shit," Mayada said shaking his head. "If he knew…"

"Why would he? He hasn't seen me or my mother in twenty years."

"Now," Mayada said, straightening his shoulders, "this isn't going to be a problem, is it? Cause if you're looking for money…"

"Money?" Jonah scoffed. "Mr. Mayada, I'm paying my respects to my father. This'll be the last time you ever see me."

"I see," Mayada said, nodding slowly. He took a deep sigh and looked back at the funeral. "Listen, stick around. OK? We should talk."

Jonah looked at Mayada and nodded.

"OK," Mayada said as he started to cross the street. A black SUV cruised down the narrow cemetery road and stopped next to the funeral. Techno music blasted from the trunk subwoofers causing the wood funeral chairs to vibrate.

"What the fuck?! The balls on this one!" One of the guards said. He walked over to the SUV and banged on the tinted window. "Hey, asshole! Get the fuck out!"

There was no response. The guard continued to bang against the black door of the SUV. Three holes appeared in the driver's window. The guard held his chest and gasped for air. Two in the neck and one in the face. The driver, dressed in gray jogging pants and a gray pullover hoodie with white sneakers, stepped out of the SUV holding a machine gun. Before Mayada's second guard could draw his pistol, a hail of bullets ripped through his torso. Mayada was frozen. He watched the gunman point the machine gun in his direction. Mayada slammed his eyes shut and braced his body. Three gunshots sounded off through the cemetery. When Mayada opened his eyes, he ran his thick fingers across his unscathed, chubby frame. The gunman was on the ground, motionless. Mayada slowly looked behind him to see Jonah, holding a Glock at an angle, puffing away at his cigarette.

A muzzled thud pounding against Rosa's door startled her. She rose from her couch cautiously. Wearing an old gray T-shirt and knee-length black basketball shorts with blue streaks, Rosa shook the back of her damp, long curly brown hair. She stepped across the carpeted floor and looked through the peephole of her door, through which she saw the distorted image of Jonah. She sighed with relief and frustration, flinging loose the padlock. He was still in his mobster apparel—dark slacks, white oxford shirt, and black tie. She opened the door, giving Jonah a rigid posture with her arms folded and a cold stare. She let out a loud sigh before turning her head and walking away.

"Nice to see you, too," Jonah said, closing the door.

"Did you get it?" Rosa asked as she tied her hair back with a rubber band.

"Yeah, we got it."

Rosa turned around to face Jonah, her arms still folded. She glanced down at the sling on his arm.

"And?" Rosa asked.

Jonah walked over to an old leather two-seat couch and sat down.

"That's all I have," he said, placing his feet on a brown coffee table.

"They didn't tell you anything? What this Blackout is?"

Jonah shook his head.

"They did manage to kill a Wolf, though," Jonah said.

"I thought those guys were unkillable."

"Yeah."

Rosa sat on the coffee table and leaned forward.

"Jonah, have you ever thought these guys are feeding us a bunch of bullshit?"

"Those two trained me, you know?" Jonah said, sitting up. "They only had two years, so they kept it simple—how it's not about the knowledge when it comes to fighting. It's the experience that counts. First it was the bar fights. Taunting bouncers, drunks. Then we escalated to underground Vale Tudo. I think I've fought over three hundred opponents, all walks of life, shapes and sizes." He leaned forward in his seat, staring down at the coffee table. "I've never seen anything like him."

"What do you mean?"

"He threw me, Rosa. I remember going for my gun and the next thing I know I'm crashing through a fucking door."

"What are you saying? These Wolves have like superhuman strength or…"

"I'm saying whatever this is, whatever the Blackout is, none of it is bullshit," Jonah said as he rubbed the left side of his abdomen.

"Then why won't they tell us anything?"

Jonah rose from the couch and walked into Rosa's eggshell-colored kitchen cubicle.

"Because they don't trust us."

"You mean they don't trust *me*."

"They definitely don't trust you," he said, grabbing a glass from the cupboard. Rosa's eyes widened. Her mouth half-opened.

"Why not?" she asked, holding up her arms. "If it wasn't for me…"

"You're not helping your argument," Jonah said as he filled his glass with water. "The fact that you helped us is the exact reason why they don't trust you."

"I don't understand."

"My God, you can't be this obtuse," Jonah murmured to himself as he scratched his head. "The deal you had with them, Ms. International Banker, Ms. Linguist, was what?" Rosa was silent. She turned her face away from Jonah. "Speak up, Rosa" Jonah said, raising his voice. "Make these embezzlement charges go away. That's why you're here—because you're a thief." Jonah chuckled. "So, when you sit there and ask yourself why don't they trust me," he said in a high-pitched voice, attempting to mimic Rosa, "put this in perspective, hon: We're sleeping together, and I don't even trust you!"

"You're a fucking asshole, Jonah," Rosa said, holding up her middle finger. "And if that's the case, why the fuck are you here?"

Jonah sighed, staring at the plastic flooring.

"Because…you can't help who you're attracted to." Rosa

walked toward Jonah with purpose, grabbing the hem of her T-shirt and pulling it over her head. She pinned him against the wall and wrapped her thigh around his, pulling the back of his blond hair as she kissed him violently.

❦

Shepard sat at Graham's small oval wooden kitchen table sharpening Santiago's knife. He would periodically look across the table at Graham, who was wearing a white tank top as he cleaned his nine-millimeter with one hand, the other sutured and resting under an ice pack.

"You didn't answer Jonah's question earlier," Graham said.

"Yeah? What's that?"

"How did you kill Santiago?"

Shepard glanced at Graham for a moment before returning his focus to the knife.

"You too?" Shepard asked.

"Santiago was a Wolf, Shep. A Wolf."

"I'm aware."

"When we devised that plan, we both knew it was a Hail Mary."

"Even a Hail Mary can be successful," Shepard said looking down the shaft of Santiago's knife.

"The things I've seen Santiago do, turning the lights off shouldn't have been enough to…" Graham paused for a moment. "Shep," he said, squinting his eyes, "is there something you want to tell me?"

"For Christ's sake! What, Graham? I started 7721 with you, remember?"

The room was quiet. The two shared a tense stare. Graham sighed, relaxed his furrowed eyebrows, and closed his eyes.

"You're right," Graham said, shaking his head. "Shit. Hysteria is contagious today, I guess. So, what now?"

"That's a good question. They have no idea we're still alive, which means..."

"They have no idea that Barbara is still alive."

"Exactly," Shepard said, placing Santiago's knife back in its sheath. "Which means when Ashcroft finds Santiago and no Blackout, they're going to rationalize that only another Wolf could kill Santiago." Graham nodded. "They find Barb, we get all of them."

"That plan is sound," Graham said with sarcasm.

"Yeah, as sound as the Mad Hatter."

Graham turned and was about to walk away when he stopped and asked, "Who is she?"

"Who?" Shepard asked.

"Fuck you," Graham said. "You know who. The barista you go visit once a week. What's her name?"

"Trish," Shepard sighed.

"Trish," Graham nodded. "Nice name. A new fling?"

"It's none of your business."

Nightmares

Jonah opened his eyes and arched his back as if he were being brought back to life. He rotated his head back and forth, trying to stretch out his sore neck.

"Honey," he mumbled. The words sounded muzzled; a thick sock was crammed in his mouth. He was bound, sitting on his gray couch in the living room.

He looked across the glass coffee table and saw two figures sitting in chairs across from him, motionless. When his eyes came into focus, Jonah gave a guttural cry. His mother sat in a chair with her throat slit from ear to ear, her eyes still open, staring in fear at her dead husband. Mr. Hayward's head was cocked to the side with his jaw dangling only by skin. His neck had been snapped. Both of his parents were sitting in a pool of blood, each two large incisions down the flanks of their abdomens. Jonah heard a shriek coming from his left. He looked over and saw Carol covered in blood, straddling Brent.

"Hold still!" Carol shouted. Brent squirmed and grunted as Carol's hands bored inside his abdomen. The two struggled until Carol let out a sigh of relief.

"Got it," she said. Carol took out Brent's second kidney. She clamped the artery, wrapped the organ in gauze, and dropped it in an ice-filled cooler. "So I guess that's it."

She looked Brent in the eyes, rubbing his spiked hair. He was delirious from the pain and blood loss. Every time he tried to speak, all he could muster was a high-pitched groan.

"I never liked you," Carol said softly. "You did things just to annoy me. I'm not gonna kill you. And just so you know, it's *because* I don't like you that I'm not killing you. If you survive this, enjoy dialysis." She caressed Brent's face, smearing blood over his cheek.

Jonah grunted again, this time catching Carol's attention. She stood up and walked around the coffee table toward him.

"I didn't want you awake for this," she said. She quickly wiped the tears from her face and stuck her hand out. "My real name is Barbara." Still bound, Jonah stared at her bloody hand. Barbara examined her hand and chuckled.

"You're probably confused," she said sitting down next to Jonah. "I'll catch you up. Your father killed me... well, tried to, obviously." She unbuttoned her dress pointing at four bullet scars going down her cleavage. "You were always curious, remember?" She leaned over and picked up her kitchen knife. "It was love," she said, mounting his lap and whispering in his ear. "I mean, I love you, Jonah." Jonah closed his eyes and shuddered at her touch before letting out an agonizing growl. He could feel a sharp ripping pain going down his side. "I love you so much I can't kill you. I'm gonna charge the black market extra for your kidney, cause that's how much you mean to me."

Jonah looked down and watched Barbara cut through his flesh, stopping the incision at his pelvis.

⚛

Jonah flung himself up in his bed and grabbed his sweating face with his trembling hands. He looked down at his damp gown. His wound was oozing blood. It was an empty hospital room with a single window allowing only a sliver of light in front of the bed. The door was shrouded in darkness.

"Hello…" a voice said. His words echoed.

"The nightmares will subside," another voice said.

"Who said that?" Jonah asked, startled.

"Just us."

Two shadows appeared from the entrance. Their dress shoes tapped against the tile and echoed through the room. Like a child, Jonah grabbed his white cotton sheets and drew them close.

"Stay away!" Jonah shouted.

"Kid, relax, we're on your side."

"What do you want?" Jonah asked.

"We want to kill the monster who did this to you."

"What are you? CIA? FBI?" Jonah asked.

"Why don't we just leave it at the enemy of your enemy."

"You have no idea what you married, kid."

"Listen, tell us what you know and we'll take care it."

"You," Jonah said, pointing at one of them, "come closer." The figure stepped into the light, his one blue and one green eye gazing down at Jonah, his expression emotionless. He wore black slacks and a black button-down shirt with his sleeves rolled up.

"So…" Jonah said, catching his breath. "You hunt demons?"

"Yeah, I hunt demons," Shepard said.

Jonah laid in bed, clutching the sheets. His shaking hands, wavering eyes, and fast shallow breaths melted away. His breathing deepened, his arms became tense. He locked eyes with Shepard.

"OK then," Jonah said with clenched teeth. "Teach me how to kill a demon, and I'll tell you about a bitch named Barbara."

Show-and-Tell

Jonah opened his eyes. He let out a slow, labored sigh and wiped the cold sweat dripping from his light-blond hair onto his forehead. Rosa was sitting up, her naked body leaning against the bed frame. She had her arm resting on her leg as she leaned in to take a puff from her cigarette. Jonah pulled himself up from the white sheets and scooted his body against the bed frame. They sat silent until Jonah's cellphone started to buzz, shaking on the nightstand. He cleared his throat and picked up the phone.

"Yeah? OK, I'll be right there," Jonah said.

"Who was that?"

"Shepard, they just reached Mayada mansion." Jonah put on his underwear and stood up. He picked up a stray T-shirt from the floor and wiped the sweat from his body. Rosa looked down at the soaked imprint he left behind.

"That dream again?" she asked, flicking her cigarette ash on the carpet floor.

"Every night."

"You plan on telling me?" Rosa asked.

"Tell you what?" Jonah said, scouring the bedroom for the rest of his clothes.

"Who she is to you."

"Who's who to me?" Jonah asked. Rosa chuckled. "What?"

"Don't do that."

"Do what?" Jonah asked as he put on his jeans.

"Who is Barbara?"

"She's my wife."

Rosa gasped as if the wind had been knocked out of her, then took another puff from her cigarette. Jonah picked up his dark-blue polo shirt and white tennis shoes. He walked back over to the bed and continued to dress. Rosa remained quiet and stared at the circles of smoke spiraling into the air.

"You coming?" Jonah asked while tying his shoes.

"Do you still love her?"

"Madly," Jonah said. Rosa folded her arms and narrowed her eyes, hoping that he would look back at her. Jonah picked up his cell and glasses from the nightstand. "I'll see you down there," he said, walking to the door.

"Fuck," Rosa said under her breath. "They're gonna kill her, you know."

"Not if I kill her first."

"What?"

"If your spouse killed your best friend and parents in front of you, then ripped out your kidney, you'd want first dibs, right?" Rosa couldn't respond. She could only stare at Jonah with a gaping mouth and wide eyes. "Exactly."

⁕

"General," a soldier said, saluting Ashcroft.

The general paced Mayada's upstairs hallway. He was wrapped in his black trench coat, a giant black star embroidered across the left lapel. Ashcroft's light-blue eyes wandered through the hallway until stopping at the broken door of Mayada's study. He rubbed his black Isotoners across his auburn-and-gray stubble. Ashcroft walked into the study and let out a slow, labored sigh at the scene in front of him. Two men in dark suits hovered over Mayada's corpse, one taking photographs and the other scraping his fingernails. He walked over to Bradshaw, who was kneeling down, examining Santiago.

"That's our lead?" Ashcroft asked, pointing at Mayada.

"It would appear so," Bradshaw said.

"Shit," Ashcroft said softly, looking down at Santiago shaking his head.

"He was stabbed," Bradshaw said, standing up and wiping down his blue military uniform. "One strike."

"Yeah."

"I think..."

"Where's the Blackout, Colonel?" Ashcroft asked, rubbing his forehead.

"About that," Bradshaw said walking to the bookshelf. He pulled *The Old Man and the Sea* from the shelf and opened it. "I'm guessing it was in here."

Ashcroft let out another labored sigh.

"Sir," a soldier said, walking into the study. He was wearing an orange hazmat suit with the top wrapped around his waist. "The preliminary results on the blood on the victims downstairs as well as Santiago's just came in. Turns out to be an aerosol neurotoxin that..."

"Let me guess," Ashcroft said. "It doesn't exist."

The soldier winced at the comment.

"Yes, sir," he said. "How did you..."

"Move on, doctor," Ashcroft said.

"Before Mayada was shot, his blood work came back positive for one of our...um...persuasion chemicals," the doctor said.

"You mean one of our methods of torture," Ashcroft said folding his arms. "It's fine, doctor. We're all big boys here."

"Yes, sir," the doctor said. "I believe your field operatives call this one 'the lake of fire'?"

Ashcroft chuckled and said, "Good choice."

"We'll get you more information as it comes, sir," the doctor said. He saluted Ashcroft and walked out of the study.

"Excuse me," a voice said as he tapped on Ashcroft's shoulder. He turned around. It was one of the men taking pictures of Mayada. He was of short stature and wearing square-cut glasses. He rubbed his thick goatee and studied Ashcroft from head to toe. "You must be the Black star general." Ashcroft squared his shoulders and placed his hands behind him. He stared down at the young man. "I just finished my investigation and thought I might tell you my findings before I take my leave."

"Take my leave?" Bradshaw mumbled to himself. "Who the fuck is this guy? Shakespeare?" Ashcroft glanced at Bradshaw over his shoulder before focusing back on the short-statured agent.

"It would appear your um…I'm sorry, your Wolf? Uh…your guard?" The young man sighed. "You have so many code names for these people I don't know how you keep track. I'm inclined to believe he was doing his assignment, which I assume you sent him on, and he was stabbed. Most likely by the gentleman he was torturing."

Ashcroft remained silent.

"What?" Bradshaw asked, squinting his left eye. "So, who shot Mayada?"

"Your guy, of course," the agent said with an attitude.

"His bullet wounds are on his left side," Bradshaw said, pointing at the door, "which means someone from the door…"

Ashcroft raised his hand an inch in front of Bradshaw's face.

"Now that's some deductive reasoning, Detective," Ashcroft said. "Where did you learn to think like that, young man?"

"Harvard, sir," he said.

Ashcroft smiled.

"Best Ivy league nursery in the country," Ashcroft said slapping the young man's shoulder. "Who do you work for son?"

"The senator's office," he said. "I answer to him. I thought I would give you the courtesy of telling you my thoughts and what I am going to present to Senator McCray in my formal write-up."

"Sounds good, agent," Ashcroft said.

The young man nodded and walked out of the study.

"Fucking moron," Bradshaw said. "You don't agree w—" Ashcroft gave Bradshaw an intense stare. "Of course you don't. Then why…"

"Because that report will keep McCray off our backs," Ashcroft said, kneeling back down next to Santiago. "At least for now."

"Obviously, whoever did this has the Blackout."

"You know who." Ashcroft said in a monotonic voice.

"Sir, she's dead."

"You expect me to believe she just fell out of a chopper?"

"Yes, from two hundred feet. She and two others fell off the chopper that day. Even if she were alive, the fall alone would have killed her."

Bradshaw walked over to the bookcase.

"You don't know her. You never did."

"Believe me," Bradshaw said wiping the dust from the worn pages of the novel. "I knew her."

"No, you don't," Ashcroft said, running his index finger across Santiago's black hair before standing up. "You may have fucked her and fucked her over. But if you really knew her, I shouldn't have to tell you to leave no stone unturned until you find her carcass or make one."

"Sir, you're asking me to begin a manhunt for a corpse."

"Not a corpse, Alan, a sociopath."

"Do you want me to dig up the rest of 7721 while I'm at it?"

"No, Colonel," Ashcroft said annoyed. "Unless you're going to tell me that you failed to confirm Shepard Black's death as well."

"No, sir. I watched them bury him myself."

"Good." Ashcroft reached into the inside pocket of his black trench coat and pulled out a maroon Blackberry. "And since we don't know where she is, and since you believe she's still dead, I'm calling our investor for assistance."

"General," Bradshaw said. "I don't think that's necessary."

"Hello?" Ashcroft asked. "Patch through to the WNB."

Bradshaw shook his head. He closed the book and placed it back on the shelf.

"Yeah," Ashcroft said. "It's me. We need to talk."

⋐

Knock-knock. Jonah stood outside the front door of Shepard's apartment, looking over his shoulder. He could hear footsteps echoing from inside, getting closer until the door was unlocked and opened.

"Yo," Shepard said.

"You just open the door without checking to see who it is?" Jonah asked.

"I just called you," Shepard said, shrugging his shoulders.

Jonah looked around. It was an old ballet studio that Shepard must have renovated. Jonah stared at his many reflections in the mirrors that lined the walls on opposite sides. Each step they took echoed throughout the high-rise ceilings. Shepard had arranged the long empty studio into four corners. In the far-left and right corners were the bathroom and kitchen. In the corner next to the door was a punching bag hanging from the ceiling and weights racked next to a rusty bench. On the other side of the door was a gray walk-in cage. Guns, knives, and explosives hung on the walls of the cage with a king-size mattress and nightstand in the middle. Jonah strained his eyes to see the spine of the book on the nightstand. It was *Alice's Adventures Through the Looking Glass.* They walked to the living room area in the middle of the space, which featured a leather sofa in front of a sixty-inch high-definition TV mounted on a wooden wall propped in the middle of the studio. Graham was sitting on the sofa holding a small controller plugged into a laptop. His eyes were fixed on the TV.

"So how often do you pretend you're Kevin Bacon in here?" Jonah laughed nervously.

Shepard scoffed and said, "If I was going to pretend I was anyone, it would be Michael Jackson from *The Wiz.*"

"What?" Jonah asked, rubbing his chin. "You mean *The Wizard of Oz?*"

"No," Shepard said sighing. "*The Wiz.*"

Jonah stared at Shepard blankly.

"*The Wiz?*" Shepard asked. "Diana Ross? You mean…" In that moment, Shepard realize the young man was clueless. "Forget it."

"What am I looking at?" Jonah asked, staring at the TV.

"Mayada's study. Or at least it should be," Graham said, slowly adjusting the cursor. The screen was black but distant, muffled voices were audible.

"I'm not seeing anything," Jonah said.

"Give me a minute," Graham said.

There was another knock on the door. Shepard traversed the lengthy loft again. When he came back to the living room area he was with Rosa. Her curly brown hair still had water dripping from it.

"Have a seat," Shepard said.

"I'll stand, if you don't mind," Rosa said.

Shepard took in a deep whiff and said, "Is it me, or does it smell like oranges in here?"

"Yeah," Graham said, sniffing as he focused on the TV screen.

"So, what am I looking at?" Rosa asked impatiently.

"Hold on a sec," Graham said. Everyone in the room sat quietly, staring at the black screen. Then a flash of light appeared on the TV. The light faded to a clear image of General Ashcroft. Graham smiled, waving his fist at the TV. "Got it!" he whispered.

"Who is that?" Rosa asked.

"Shh!" Graham and Shepard said in unison. They watched Ashcroft kneel next to Santiago's body.

"I don't see her," Graham said.

"Obviously," Bradshaw said from the screen. "Whoever did this has the Blackout. The question is who?"

"You know who," Ashcroft said in a monotone voice.

"Sir, she's dead," Bradshaw said.

"Shit," Jonah said, grabbing his head. "If they don't know where she is, how the fuck are we going to find her?"

Shepard took a deep sigh and kept his eyes fixed on the screen.

"Black!" Jonah shouted at Shepard.

"Dude," Shepard said raising his voice. "Shut the fuck up."

"Unless you're going to tell me that you failed to confirm Shepard Black's death as well," Ashcroft said.

"No, sir," Bradshaw said. "I watched them bury him myself."

"At least they still think we're dead," Graham said as he stared at the screen.

"Hello?" Ashcroft said. "Patch me through to the WNB." Ashcroft looked at Bradshaw and said, "I'll talk to the broker. In the meantime, clean up this mess."

"WNB?" Shepard asked, tilting his head and staring at the floor.

"World National Bank," Rosa said.

"That's the bank you used to work for, right?" Graham asked.

Rosa nodded. They watched Bradshaw close the book, causing the screen to go black. Ashcroft's and Bradshaw's voices became muzzled and unintelligible.

"That's all I got," Graham said. The entire room stared at Shepard as he scratched his clean-shaven face.

"Looks like we're going to London," Shepard said.

Jonah shook his head.

"That's a fucking joke, right?" Jonah asked.

"OK, my dude," Shepard said. "You tell me the part in this feed where they give us Barbara's whereabouts."

"Well, they certainly didn't say she was in London, so why are we going?" said Jonah.

"Kid," Graham said, "as of now it's the only lead we got."

Jonah walked away from the living room area and started to pace the width of the studio.

"Rosa," Graham said. "Can you get us access inside?"

"I still have my access cards," Rosa scoffed. "But I'm sure as shit not going back there."

"We need to get intel on who's working directly with the Blackstar general," Graham said.

"No doubt," Shepard said.

"Guys," Rosa said, annoyed. "Fucking meet me halfway here. We went from a small heist in Iceland, to umm…mass murder, to dealing with people who belong in a fucking James Bond movie!"

"Calm down," Shepard said. "What would you like to know?"

"Um…OK," Rosa said, surprised. "For starters, you could expound on who these Wolves are that you keep talking about, and who the hell is this bald guy wearing the black trench coat."

"Fair enough," Shepard said, looking at Graham. "What do you know about the word *transparency*?"

"That our little group here doesn't have enough of it," Jonah said.

"That's the perfect definition," Shepard said, pointing at Jonah. "You give just enough information so that others can leave you alone and you can do your job." He placed his hands in his black slacks, walked up to the flat screen, and stood next to it. "Transparency doesn't mean I tell you everything. There's a reason why politicians use that word as opposed to honesty or truth. It basically means I tell you what I *want* you to know."

"Can anyone here tell me how many independent intelligence agencies there are in this country?" Graham asked.

"Twenty-something, I guess," Jonah said.

"What if I were to tell you that number is much higher?" Shepard asked.

"Wouldn't surprise me," Jonah said. "Though it couldn't be that much…"

"Over eight hundred." Shepard said.

Jonah paused. He stared down at the tan hardwood floor, confused.

"That's impossible," Jonah said. "That means that…"

"We're watching everyone," Shepard said. "You see, this thing called democracy comes with a price. The Cold War never ended, assassinations haven't stopped, we just neither confirm nor deny. We've become transparent."

"Fuck my life," Rosa said, straining her voice. "He's about to tell me something I don't want to know."

"Probably," Graham said.

"This network doesn't have a name," Shepard said. "They exist only as numbers on a spreadsheet for funding purposes."

"What's the number of the group you guys used to belong to?" Rosa asked.

"7721," Graham said.

"It's true that we all work independent of one another, but we all answer to that man," Shepard said, pointing at the black screen.

"His name is James Ashcroft, our current Blackstar general," Graham said.

"Blackstar?" Rosa asked.

"You know how you were taught in school that government is decentralized, and there are checks and balances in place to make sure that some narcissistic, racist, piece-of-shit billionaire doesn't take office and start a totalitarian government?" Graham asked.

"Yeah," Shepard, said laughing. "That's some bullshit. Look at the last election. No. He's your check and balance."

"I don't understand," Rosa said.

"The Blackstar general is the overseer of all covert operations," Shepard said. "The rank was created during the Cold War in the fifties. That man has the authority to assassinate heads of state, wipeout entire countries if necessary."

"Don't you need an act of Congress for that last one?" Jonah asked.

Shepard gave Jonah a sardonic grin and said, "Once again, kid, transparency."

"And the Wolves?" Rosa asked.

"Ashcroft's personal bodyguards," Shepard said. "They follow three rules. One: Protect the Blackstar general with their life. Two: Follow the orders of the Blackstar general alone. Three: Kill anyone that poses a threat to him."

"What makes them so strong?" Jonah asked.

"That's the mystery," Shepard said, sighing. "No one really knows."

"Shit! What the hell did I get myself into?" Rosa asked with a nervous laugh. "So, these Wolves are some super-soldier military experiment?"

"I'm saying I don't know what the hell they are," Shepard said. "I'm saying that men have shattered their hands hitting their faces. One of them can take out an entire platoon. I can say all of this, because we've seen it."

"How many are there?" Jonah asked.

"There were three of them," Shepard said. "They killed Sean years ago."

"That's before we joined the 7721," Graham said. "They say he went rogue or something."

"Good for him," Jonah said.

"Santiago's dead," Graham said, looking at Shepard.

"He got cocky and we got lucky," Shepard said.

"That just leaves her," Graham said.

"You mean my wife?" Jonah asked.

Graham nodded.

"Of the three, Barbara is the most dangerous," Shepard said. "Which is why when we find her there is no room for brash moves." He glanced at Jonah and continued. "Rosa, why do you think Ashcroft has your bank on speed dial?"

Rosa shrugged her shoulders and said, "I don't know. Maybe he has an account with them."

"What are you thinking?" Graham asked.

"The World National Bank has its main offices in London, right?" Shepard asked. "Perhaps he needs outside resources to finance something. Something big."

"McCray," Graham said. "The new steward of the Blackout."

Shepard nodded and said, "If Ashcroft is up to something that he doesn't want the senator to know…"

"He's going to need to get his money elsewhere," Graham said.

"Who?" Rosa asked.

"Senator McCray," Graham said. "Ashcroft can't buy a pack of gum without his approval."

"The World National Bank?" Jonah asked with a confused expression. "They build wells in Africa. They finance third-world hospitals. They are completely nonprofit."

The entire room looked at each other before erupting in laughter.

"What?" Jonah asked.

"May I," Rosa asked, catching her breath.

"By all means," Graham said wiping the tears from his eyes.

Rosa looked at Jonah with pity and sighed.

"Wow, you were raised middle-class," Rosa said. "Didn't have a care in the world growing up, did you?"

"The fuck that's supposed to mean?" Jonah asked.

"Jonah, think about it," Rosa continued. "When in the history has anything nonprofit been called a bank?"

Jonah stared at Rosa with a blank expression.

"Bingo," Rosa said. "The World Bank makes its real money off of funding third-world countries. They hide behind the pretense of funding these governments to make the world a better place. The public sees the WNB funding schools, building infrastructure. Countries that have vast resources with an unstable government. When civil war breaks out, the bank supports a side. When that side wins, the bank forces the new acting government to take a ridiculous high-interest loan. The kind of loan that'll keep you and your subjects indentured servants for a hundred fucking years."

"So just don't take the loan," Jonah said.

"Heads of state have tried that," Rosa said. "They end up assassinated."

"And I'm sorry," Jonah said, shaking his head. "How do you know this?"

"Because I translated for those economic hitmen for eight years."

"That's how we tracked her," Graham said. "We needed a linguist. A good one who could get us in and out of the American embassy in Iceland."

Rosa looked at Shepard and said, "The World Bank is tied to America by the hip. They wouldn't think to…"

"Maybe not the bank, but a group within," Shepard said.

Rosa folded her arms, tapping her left shoulder.

"It's possible," Rosa said.

"London it is," Shepard said. "Gonna need you on the field for this one, Rosa."

"What?" Rosa grimaced. "No. I am done with this field bullshit or whatever you secret spy people call this."

"That wasn't a request," Shepard said.

"Yeah," Graham said, nodding. "You and the kid. Just like in Iceland."

"I'm wanted for fucking embezzlement, Shepard!" Rosa said.

"So, we'll put a wig on your head," Graham said. "Quiet mouse like yourself, whole job was to speak only when spoken to? They barely remember you."

"You don't understand!" Rosa said. "I walk through that door, they'll put a bullet in my head."

"Don't be so dramatic," Shepard said, "How much you steal? A couple hundred thou? Petty larceny. Handcuffs at best."

Rosa shook her head, mouthing, *Bullshit.*

"So how many Jackals are on staff at the WNB?"

Rosa scoffed and said, "You watch way too many movies. There is no—" Rosa stopped talking when Shepard's head tilted, and an expression of disbelief came over his face. "E-Eight." She said with a soft, embarrassed tone. "I think there are eight."

Shepard closed his eyes and shook his head.

"Care to tell us about the Blackout?" Jonah asked.

"Sorry, kid," Shepard said, walking away from the living area. "That concludes today's segment of show-and-tell."

Jackals

"Talk about what, exactly?" He had a thick, raspy voice with a cockney accent. "I'm afraid I'm in the middle of somefin. Call you back, all right?" He rolled his dark-brown eyes. "Yes. I do realize the brevity of the situation, but ours is the long con, right? And as I said before, I'm busy. Wha-ever it is can't be that dire, right?"

He looked up at the glass ceiling, condemning its gaudiness. The room was lined in black velvet with tarnished gold plating lining the wall fixtures, including the windows and the sliding doors that led to a worn cement balcony. The room was dimly lit by a chandelier swaying on creaking metal hinges. Seated at a large circular table made of bog wood, a man with coarse facial features and thick eyebrows sat across from him. A scar ran down the left side of his rugged face, illuminated in bright orange when he lit up his Cuban cigar. Behind him were soldiers dressed in olive-green uniforms with pistols holstered at their sides. One of the soldiers were standing at ease by the table. The man seated had on a similar uniform with a red sash that separated him from the other soldiers behind him.

"Mr. Sayf," said the soldier standing next to the table. "This is very disrespectful to the prime minister."

"Ashcroft," Sayf said. "I have to go." He pressed END on his cellphone and placed it back in the side pocket of his dark-blue slacks. "Sorry about that."

"It's not a problem," the prime minister said. "My brother Nico can be a bit overprotective of me. Would you like a glass of cognac, Mr. Sayf?" His heavy eastern European accent echoed softly through the black-and-gold banquet hall.

"No, thank you, Minister," Sayf said, leaning back in his seat. He adjusted his dark-blue tie, which nicely complemented his light-blue dress shirt. "I think our discussion will require me to keep my faculties intact."

"You know," the prime minister said, "man who won't drink is a man not to be trusted."

"Well," Sayf said, clearing his throat, "you trusted me and my organization to finance your grab for power. You trusted us to supply your armory and you've managed to…"

"How can I help you, Mr. Sayf?" the prime minister asked, annoyed.

Sayf cleared his throat again. He pulled out his smartphone and placed it on the table.

"Let's see here," Sayf said as put on his reading glasses. "Five years ago, you and the other generals threw this country and its people into a civil war. To make matters worse, the Russians were invading your lands. Perfect timing, eh, Prime Minster?"

The prime minister groaned.

"What an annoying black man you are," the prime minister said. "I am aware of our countries' history. After all, I wrote it. What is it that you want?"

"Black man?" Sayf said, chuckling quietly to himself. "It should be quite obvious as to why I'm here. You owe us money, Mr. Minister."

The prime minister laughed.

"The agreement," the prime minister said while puffing away his cigar. "Remind me of it."

"Certainly. The WNB allotted to your country a five-hundred-billion-dollar loan with one-percent interest. Now ten percent of the principal plus interest is expected to be paid annually. Which means we expect at least fifty-five billion dollars a year."

The minister looked over his shoulder and glanced at Nico.

"We'll pay it when we pay it," the prime minister said.

"It's been three years," Sayf said. "And you'll never have it, mate."

The prime minister's lips flattened and his eyes bulged.

"What do you mean, 'never'?" the prime minister asked, deepening his tone. "If the will is mine to get you this money, I can."

"Let me simplify this for you," Sayf said wiping his eyes. "Let's say each country is a person and they have a job. And we base each person's job on their income, which would be the gross domestic product. That means countries like Great Britain and China are the doctors and lawyers of the world. They make a shit-ton of money, because they are needed in the current world order. If I were to give Slokrania a job based on its GDP, you would be, at best, handling the money at some cash register at some shitty supermarket. You make only twelve quid an hour, but you have high hopes and borrowed a hundred thousand pounds from the bank for a house. But you only make twelve fucking quid!" Sayf chuckled. "Which means you could work night and day, every day, and you will never have enough money to pay off that loan, and that is when the bank comes to rip the house from under your bare Slokranian feet." Sayf leaned forward in his seat and rested his arms on the table. "We'd like our money. Today, if you don't mind."

The prime minister's laugh shook the banquet hall. He coughed on his saliva and spat it on the floor before gaining his composure.

"These darkies," the prime minister said, staring at Nico. "You all are comedians, yes?"

"If I were you, minister," Sayf said. "I would look closely at this darkie's face. This is not a laughing matter."

The prime minister leaned back in his seat and placed his cigar gently over a glass ashtray.

"I don't pay," the minister said.

"Come again?" Sayf asked, pointing to his ear.

"This that you ask is extortion. Where was your bank when we kept the Russians from invading our borders? Sure, you supplied us with weapons, but none of her majesty's service gave their lives. It was Slokranian sacrifice and my military brilliance that defeated…"

"Is that what you think that was?" Sayf laughed. "There is no way a head of state could be this thickheaded," he mumbled. "That was just a dog-and-pony show for the world."

The minister clenched his fists, taking deep and deliberate breaths through his nose. Nico and the soldiers behind him could feel the minister's rage fester.

"Listen," Sayf said. "No one likes this place. It's the fucking cesspool of humanity. To be honest, if the Russians took over, it would be irrelevant. The world would simply keep turning. The fact of the matter is Slokrania has land that is perfect for another pipeline. To be frank, her majesty couldn't give a shit what happens to this place, but the World National Bank saw opportunity. You see, Mr. Prime Minister, if I was to…" Sayf paused and chuckled before continuing, "randomly, and let me emphasize that word—*randomly*—pick one of the warlords to come to power and unify this country, we could all profit. Us, the Russians—hell, even the Yanks. They're all in on it, mate. You see, Mr. Minister, your military brilliance has nothing to do with it. I could have easily appointed a pig to do your job."

The prime minister's eyes were blood-red. His veins pulsated on the sides of his head as Sayf continued.

"A massacre, which is *exactly* what a real war between you and Russia would be, would cost money. Military costs, occupancy, upheavals—none of this is cost-efficient. It would take decades for the Kremlin to recuperate their financial losses. But our strategy would mean minimal loss and a piece of the pie."

The minister's thick, burly fist trembled and shook the entire table.

"Sorry to bust your bubble, prime minister," Sayf said, laughing. "It seems you were so concerned about being the bitch, when in reality the Kremlin has been fucking you this whole time."

The prime minster slammed his hands on the table, cracking the wood.

"You black devil!" the prime minster shouted.

"And here we go with the racism...."

"You think I have no control of my country?" the prime minister asked. "What do you know of being royalty when you come from line of slave?! To world I may be just as you say 'a dictator,' but here I am God!" The prime minister shoved his finger into his chest. "I show you I am God."

"How so?" Sayf asked.

The minster stood with his hands on the table, leaning forward.

"In your near future, you will leave here and have an accident."

"Really?"

"That's right," the prime minister said, smiling. "First, you will leave palace gates. You'll turn down a bad alley and be visited by five unscrupulous men. Men of the Aryan brotherhood. My kind of men that will find your complexion offensive. They will beat you within an inch of life before cutting out your tongue and cramming it down your throat."

"Now that sounds like a nasty fate," Sayf said, sighing.

"But don't worry, we make sure body gets back to England." The prime minister sat down in his seat with his arms folded. He waited for the guards to grab Sayf and drag him away but no soldier, including Nico, budged. The prime minister frowned at the fact that Sayf was still in his seat. He blinked five times in rapid succession before looking over his shoulder at the guards standing like statues behind him.

Sayf took off his glasses. He pulled out a headset and inserted the earpiece.

"Uh, Nico?" Sayf asked.

"Yes, Mr. Sayf?" Nico asked.

"I think I'd like to have a go at that cognac," Sayf said. "Neat, if possible."

Nico nodded and gestured for the servant to bring Sayf a glass.

The prime minister breathed violently and clenched his teeth watching his servant pour his cognac in a stemless glass. He placed it in front of Sayf.

"Cheers," Sayf said. He took a sip and nodded at the prime minister with approval.

"What the hell is going on?" the prime minister shouted.

"Brother," Nico said smugly, "you will be mourned."

The prime minister jerked his head back and shouted with a shaky voice, "This is treason! You will pay! All of you!"

"Charlie," Sayf said into his headset. "Pop the knee." A few seconds later, a bullet bore a hole in the glass window leading out to the balcony. It ripped through the prime minister's knee and disintegrated against the hardwood floor. The prime minister collapsed. He looked down at his mangled knee and screamed.

"You black jackal," the prime minister murmured.

Sayf got up from his seat, cupping the glass of cognac. He walked toward the prime minister and kneeled down next to him.

"Let's not be so melodramatic," Sayf said. He sat in the prime minister's seat, picked up his lit cigar, and took a puff. "Do you know what heads of state have in common? Narcissism. Kim,

Saddam, Mussolini—you all think that your rise to power was some sort of divine intervention. That somehow all of your lying, killing, and plundering was all a part of some act of God. It's a weakness, you see. One that makes you think you're invincible, that somehow the rules don't apply."

The prime minister wrapped his hands around his knee and squeezed to try to stop the bleeding.

"It's like you said, you think you're God," Sayf said.

"Get on with it!" the prime minister shouted.

Sayf took another puff of the cigar and leaned forward in his seat, hovering over the minister.

"Is that what you want?" Sayf asked.

The prime minister's face lightened. He looked up at Sayf from the floor with glazed eyes and a half-open mouth.

"What are you talking about?" the prime minister asked.

"It's a simple enough question, Prime Minister. Do you want to die today?"

"What?" the prime minister asked again.

"What are you talking about?" Nico asked.

"The men in this room," Sayf said, pointing at the soldiers standing at attention, "they love you. Of course, not as much as a million pounds in each of their bank accounts, but enough to follow you into battle. Even with money, that type of loyalty cannot be reproduced."

"They betrayed me!" the prime minister shouted.

"Minister, everyone has a price," Sayf said. "I'd push her majesty herself off a fucking bridge if you named the proper terms. The fact of the matter is that your men want you to lead."

"What the fuck is happening?" Nico asked.

"Nico, take one more step and you will be joining your brother," Sayf said.

Nico exhaled sharply and froze. His hand drifted to his holster.

"I wouldn't do that, Nico," Sayf said.

Nico sighed and placed his hands on his thighs.

"Wha…what are you getting at, Mr. Sayf?" the prime minister asked.

"I'm saying that tomorrow's headlines can read one of two ways," Sayf said. "But I need you to understand going forward that you are not God, and that piece-of-shit dictators like yourself are a dime a dozen. The lot of you are just crabs in a bucket."

"I assume you are God in this relationship?" the prime minister asked.

"Well, I'm certainly not God now, am I?" Sayf asked. "Let's just say I'm the guy holding the bucket."

The prime minister looked down at his leg and then the pale expression of fear on Nico's face. The prime minister panted before finally nodding his head.

"Wait!" Nico shouted.

"Charlie," Sayf said in his headset. "If you don't mind."

A second bullet ripped through the window seal. The blast cracked open Nico's skull, splattering blood and brains on the floor. The prime minister took a deep breath and stared at his brother's body twitching its last moments of life.

"Now," Sayf said. "Our money?"

"You'll have it," the prime minister said.

Sayf's cellphone buzzed.

"Shite," Sayf said to himself. He stood up from the prime minister's seat. "Gentlemen, for God's sake, help your leader and someone call a fucking doctor."

Sayf grabbed his phone and placed it next to his ear as he strolled toward the other side of the hall.

"Ashcroft," Sayf said, annoyed. "Problem? What kind of a problem?"

"The Blackout has been taken," Ashcroft said.

"What do you mean taken?"

"Sayf, this is not the time. She killed Santiago."

"Santiago? Who?"

"Barbara!"

"I thought she was dead."

"So did I."

"Correct me if I'm wrong, but you had three of those mad dogs?"

"Yes."

"And of the three, the bitch was both the craziest and strongest?"

"Yeah," Ashcroft said sighing.

"Shit, sounds like a job for the Blackstar general and his shadow army, wouldn't you say?"

"Marcus, my hands are tied. Only a few are aware of our plans, and McCray knows that I was outsourcing the maintenance for the Blackout, which means that once it's retrieved, it will never leave the pentagon."

"What do you want me to do about it?"

"What do you think?" Ashcroft asked, sarcastically.

Sayf laughed.

"The psychopath? You want me to track her? With what? A pocket knife and compass?"

"Cut the bullshit, Marcus. I know who you are. Find her and get the Blackout."

Sayf sighed and placed his cellphone back in his pocket.

"Mr. Minister," Sayf shouted. Delirious from blood loss, the prime minister opened his eyes and focused on Sayf's blurred image. "I assume during your ascension to power you surrounded yourself with some sort of commando bunch. A Gestapo, kind of assassinations genocide squad. We developed countries refer to them as special forces. Mind if I borrow them?"

THE UPSIDE DOWN

Knock. Knock.

"Yeah," Senator McCray said.

Ashcroft walked through the door.

"Senator?" Ashcroft asked.

"Come in, James."

Ashcroft closed the door behind him. He examined McCray's dark, burgundy-colored office. Water oil paintings of lions adorned his walls. McCray, sitting behind his oak desk reading a stack of documents, adjusted his thin wire glasses. He looked up and gestured for Ashcroft to have a seat.

"Interesting decor," Ashcroft said, sitting down.

McCray didn't respond.

"Are you looking at the crime scene?" Ashcroft asked.

"Yeah."

"I take it your investigators filled you in on our findings?"

"That they did," McCray said with a sigh.

"Your aids are..."

"Dumb as shit?" McCray sneered. "Damn straight. I fired

their asses this morning." McCray threw the stack of papers in his hand on the desktop.

"Fifteen years in the DA's office, I've never heard of a theory this moronic," McCray said.

Shit, Ashcroft thought to himself.

"I see," Ashcroft said. "So, what do you think happened?"

"Definitely not this bullshit. Santiago gave Mayada this torture serum? This stuff makes you feel like you're on fire and somehow he was able to overcome this and stab Santiago with his own knife?" McCray took off his glasses and tossed them on the desk. "Mayada was a badass. A John Gotti of the twenty-first century. He wasn't bad enough to do this. Whoever did this also has the Blackout, I'd imagine." Ashcroft leaned forward in his seat, placed his head on his hands, and nodded in agreement.

"Ashcroft," McCray said, raising his voice.

"Yeah?"

"Here's the part where you tell me something that isn't bullshit."

Ashcroft sighed and said, "We think it's Barbara."

"Barbara? The Wolf?" Ashcroft nodded. "I thought she was dead."

"So did I. Bradshaw told me a few months ago. He never confirmed the kill."

"Son of a bitch," McCray said, hopping out of his seat. "Do we know where she is?"

"No, sir. But I can assure you we are looking."

"I don't want your assurance, James!"

McCray walked over to the front of his desk and sat on the edge. He took a deep breath. "You're telling me your psychopath science experiment has ran off with the most dangerous piece of technology in mankind's history and all you can say is..."

"Sir, we are on it. My men and I are going to..."

McCray held up his right hand. He flapped his fingers and

thumb together to mimic Ashcroft talking. They both shared an uncomfortable silence as McCray walked back to his seat, shaking his head.

"Don't try to politic me, general," McCray said. "The reality is that while trying to save a buck you lost a weapon more destructive than a thousand nukes!"

"I didn't take lectures from your predecessor and I damn sure won't be taking any from you," Ashcroft said sharply. Ashcroft straightened his back and squared his shoulders in his seat. He gave McCray a stare so callous, the seasoned politician glanced away.

"Fine," McCray said with a smug smile. "But I need some straight answers."

"What would you like to know?"

"Let's start with the Wolves. How many are there?"

"There were three."

"Are the stories true?"

"The ones about the full moon? That they can sprout wings and lift cars? No."

"Don't insult my intelligence, General," McCray said, annoyed. "You know what I'm talking about." Ashcroft smirked and nodded.

"Yeah," Ashcroft said. "It's true. Do you know how they got the nickname 'Wolves'?" McCray shook his head. "Watching a pack of wolves on the hunt is quite elegant. They are a unit. Loyal to their common duty even if it means entering the gates of hell. A wolf is nature's soldier." A sparkle flashed across Ashcroft's eyes. The general sat back in his seat and crossed his legs. "They were orphans, you see. I trained them from the time of their first treatment. The hormones affected each of them the same. Increased speed, awareness, bone density. It also seemed to bring out their natural talents."

"Such as?" McCray asked.

"Santiago was the smart one. Calculating every move. He was loyal. Right down to the end."

"And Barbara?"

"Unstable. The treatments gave her twice the physical attributes as the other two, but her mind was lost. We had to keep her on a tight leash."

"You knew she was unstable this whole time?" McCray asked, scratching his jaw.

"The madness is what makes her so dangerous. And in that madness was a monster that kills without prejudice. That raw power is harnessed, not disposed of."

McCray scoffed and said, "Until she goes off the fucking deep end." McCray closed his eyes and sighed. "And this Sean?"

Ashcroft nodded slowly and flashed half a grin.

"Sean was the leader. The glue that kept my guard honest." Ashcroft smiled again. "I remember when he was a kid, must have been his fourth treatment. He told me for his thirteenth birthday he wanted a baseball with a catcher's mitt. It was only my third year in this position. Upstead forbade it. But I thought, he's just a kid. So, I bought him a couple of catcher's mitts and a baseball, but the three of them lived in a lab, and there was no room to throw. So, every Sunday morning like clockwork we'd sneak out of the lab, go to a nearby park and toss the ball. You know, he kinda threw like Ken Griffey."

"You befriended the little black boy," McCray said with sarcasm. "I can hear the violin."

"Yes," Ashcroft said, raising his voice. "Sean was black, we both happened to like baseball, and no, I have not seen *The Blind Side*. Can we move on?"

McCray held his hands up and gestured for Ashcroft to continue.

"For close to a year those Sunday mornings were sacred. Then one morning, he held the ball in his hand and gave me this look.

There was this fire in his eyes. Rage from the pit of his stomach. The last time I saw that kind of animosity was in Desert Storm. The intent had me frozen. When he wound up to throw, I swear I had heard a rifle being loaded. Is this it? Has this all been a ploy to take me out and escape? I thought those were going to be my last thoughts, because when he released that ball, I didn't see it." Ashcroft caressed his left cheek. "The hormones had kicked in. I can still feel the heat of that throw. Felt like the damn ball was on fire. Sean was kneeling on the ground shivering. Sean, I asked, why? He raised his throwing hand and pointed. When I turned around, about five meters from the road on the other side of the street was a man with a M40. The baseball that I thought was intended for me was imbedded in my assassin's forehead. Turns out he watched me every Sunday for months before making his move. It's not old age that kills you, Senator. It's the monotony. From that moment I knew that child would protect me as a son would protect his own father."

"I think that should be the other way around, right?" McCray asked. "Why'd you kill him?"

"He betrayed me."

"What did he do?"

"Fell in love."

&

"What time is it?" Morgan asked Charlie with a thick Irish accent.

They were standing in front of a rusted gray metal hangar at the Slokranian airport. Even wrapped in black winter coats with fur hoodies, the cold was bone-chilling. Warm air steamed from their nostrils with each breath.

"Wha?" Charlie asked. He placed his rectangular black metal briefcase on the concrete ground.

"The time."

"Almost midnight," Charlie said, looking at his watch. He

shook his head as he rocked his body back and forth to generate heat. "Hurry up, chief."

"Cold, are ye?" Morgan asked, grinning. "Ain't ye a marksman?"

"Fuck off! Who was the one perched on the roof for four hours waiting for the chief's order?"

Morgan chuckled and asked, "So which one ya kill?"

"Nico got it."

"Tough break, little bro," Morgan said, rubbing her hands together. "Wait, why didn't you stay?"

"What you mean?"

"What if that neo-Nazi piece of shite killed the chief anyway?"

"What ye want me to say?" Charlie asked shrugging his broad shoulders. "He told me to leave."

"That don't mean you do it!"

"Enough with the chastisin'! You're worse than me fuckin' ma!"

Morgan sighed, shook her head, and the two shared a brief moment of silence.

"If they did kill 'em, what are we gonna do about it?" Morgan asked as she pulled her short hair behind her ear.

"Do about it?" Charlie asked, laughing. "Not a bloody thing, yeah?"

"I'm inclined to agree. The chief would want it that way."

A string of paired lights appeared in the distance.

"You see tha?" Charlie asked. The convoy was approaching fast. "You think they're coming for us?"

Morgan didn't respond. The two stared at each other for a split second before Charlie kneeled down and popped open his briefcase. He seamlessly locked, loaded, and popped the scope on his rifle. Morgan took a knee in front of Charlie and pulled out an automatic pistol from her hip holster. Charlie rested the shaft of his sniper rifle on Morgan's shoulder and gazed through the scope. The headlights of four camouflaged Hummers appeared through the green night-vision scope.

"Looks like quite the welcoming party," Charlie said.

"Neo-Nazi shites!" Morgan said, snarling her lips. "We'll come back for the chief's remains when we have reinforcements. Can you take out the front tires?"

"On it."

A fifth vehicle came over the horizon. It was a Lincoln Town Car. Through the windows he could see a dark-skinned figure smoking a cigar. "Hold on. It's the chief! He's in the back of a limo sucking on a fucking stogie!"

Charlie put the safety back on his rifle and placed it on top of the black case. Morgan holstered her weapon. She stood up and placed her hands on her hips. The five-car convoy came down the deserted road and disappeared as they drove along a tall barbed-wire fence.

Moments later the convoy appeared in front of the airport hangar. The doors to the Hummers popped open. Soldiers, each wearing fatigues and thick black army boots, hopped out of each vehicle. Some of them wore thin black sweaters with yellow swastikas sewn onto the sleeves. Others were shirtless, wearing only bulletproof vests, racial epithets covering their pale white arms. They each pulled black duffle bags from the Hummers, tossing them over their backs. Heavy metal music was blasting from the stereo as the rambunctious soldiers pushed and shoved each other.

Charlie wrinkled his nose and shook his head. "Wha the fuck is this?" he muttered. "Some mosh-pit version of GI Joe?"

The driver got out of the Town Car, walked to the passenger door, and opened it. Sayf stepped out. He took one last puff of his cigar and put it out on the ground. The heavy metal was turned off and each soldier stood at attention. As he walked past them toward Morgan and Charlie, each of them glared at him with disdain. Sayf glanced at one of the soldiers who quickly looked away.

"Charlie, Morgan," Sayf said.

"Evening, chief," Morgan said.

"Good to see you're still alive, chief," Charlie said. "Want to explain why the scum-of-humanity brigade is behind ya?"

"Easy, mate," Sayf said, turning around pointing at his new military ensemble. "These are our new comrades." He walked by Charlie and patted his shoulder. "Trust me, they stink worse than they look."

"What are we to do with them?" Morgan asked.

"We're going on a hunt," Sayf said.

"Who?" Charlie asked.

"Turns out Barbara has stolen the Blackout," Sayf said.

"Barbara?" Charlie asked. "You mean the Wolf?"

"They said she was dead and gone," Morgan said.

"I don't know," Sayf said, turning around to face his Aryan army. "Chickens come home to roost. You two know as well I that the Blackout is the key to our future endeavors. Without it we might as well plan for a long, prosperous future of sticking up Third World countries."

"Well, I got the intel that ye asked fer," Morgan said. "I did some diggin' into unsolved American homicides over the past five years. An older couple and a young man from Ohio were found dead with their kidneys removed."

"So?" Charlie asked.

"Here's the thing," Morgan said. "The kidneys are missing. Whoever took 'em out, took 'em."

"Names?" Sayf asked.

"A condo owned by a Jonah Hayward," Morgan said. "His father, a Jo Hayward, was a special-ops helicopter pilot. I cross-referenced that name with members of Ashcroft's Blackout outfit and it matched."

"Shit," Sayf said, scratching his chin. "He must have been a pilot for 7721. Question: If I want to sell an organ and get out of the country at the same time, where would I go?" Morgan and Charlie stared at Sayf with blank expressions. "I think we're headed to Thailand."

"I have no qualms with that, chief," Charlie said staring at the Slokranian commandos. "But why the fuck are we bringing 'em along?"

"Ashcroft is tied up at the moment," Sayf said. "We need the extra manpower. Where we're headed is the…" Sayf paused. He walked up to Charlie and held up his index finger. "Before we go on, I need to ask somefin really important. Did you open that Netflix account I got you?"

Charlie shifted his weight and folded his arms. "Aw, c'mon…"

"Answer the bloody question!" Sayf shouted.

Charlie looked away from Sayf like a scolded child.

"No," Charlie said quietly.

"Why not?"

"Aww for Christ's sake, chief," Charlie said, shaking his head. "I dunno."

Sayf pointed at Morgan and asked, "Your Netflix account?"

"I-It's amazing, chief," Morgan said, smiling. "Very thoughtful gift."

"You see?" Sayf said staring at Charlie. He glanced at Morgan and said, "Anytime, luv. You're welcome."

"Sorry!" Charlie said, staring at the ground. "I just want to watch the news and a little footie! It shouldn't be a fucking crime that I'm not into TV."

Sayf held up his hands and said, "Wait." He turned around. "Oi!" He shouted to his new militia. "By a show of hands, who here has a Netflix account!" The entire group of commandos raised their hands. Sayf looked at Charlie. "Good! Cause the reference that I'm preparing to use should be understood by all of you, except my esteemed colleague here."

Annoyed, Charlie turned away blowing out winter vapors.

"The journey that we are about to embark on isn't the typical war zone," Sayf said. "It's the fucking Upside Down! We are on the hunt, gentlemen. Hunting a monster. And her name is Barbara."

The Slokranian commando's chuckled and snorted. Their eyes teared, smudging their rosy, dirty cheeks. Each time Sayf had thought they had settled down, a new wave of laughter would take over.

"That's right," Sayf said. "Laugh it up."

A young soldier with a buzz cut pointed at Sayf. A black swastika was tattooed on the tip of his index finger.

"No wonder they were slaves for so long," he said in Slokranian. "The monkey fears woman!" The crowd laughed again.

"It isn't a gender I fear," Sayf said in Slokranian. He strolled up to the soldier who was stunned by his fluent Slokranian tongue. "It's the monster that is in her." He walked past the soldier and continued in English. "Let's be clear, shall we? I don't like you any more than you care for me. But you are a necessary evil. So, I am only going to say this once: If you do not take this woman seriously I promise you will be no more than a broken carcass rotting on the streets of Bangkok!"

Sayf stopped. He turned to face the chest of a giant—six-foot-eight and built like a tank. On his wide forearms were tattoos that told the story of the Third Reich. Sayf tilted his neck back and glanced at the Slokranian's blue eyes before walking back toward the soldier with the buzz cut.

"Just remember," Sayf said to the buzz cut soldier in Slokranian, "*you* are this monkey's slave. Boy."

The soldier rapidly blinked his eyes. His face turned flush. He clenched his stained cavity-riddled teeth and snarled.

Sayf looked around at the rest of his skinhead army glaring at him with resentment and hate. He felt the heat of anger, smiled, and said, "Right then, let's do this."

Xe4f145d106s2

An older bronze-skinned man sat at a small table for two on a crowded patio outside a coffee shop. Waiters wearing white dress shirts wiped the beads of sweat from their foreheads as they hustled between tables. The man sipped his iced coffee and wiped his gray beard with the back of his hand. He sat at a table in the middle of the patio, watching intently as customers walked through the glass entrance to the patio. Moments later, he saw a younger man wearing glasses, tan khaki pants, and a charcoal T-shirt. An army-green bag was strapped around his shoulder. He surveyed the area until he saw the gray-bearded man waving at him. The young man walked over and sat down.

"Mr. Zaidi?" he asked. His voice was American.

"I need to know," Zaidi said.

"What's that?"

"That you are not one of them."

The young man raised an eyebrow and asked, "That I am not one of who?"

"No," Zaidi said, staring into the young man's eyes. "You

can't be," Zaidi picked up his cup. His hands shook as he sipped his iced coffee. "I need for you to tell my story. Are you ready?"

"Hold on, Mr. Zaidi," the young man said, holding up his hands. "You called the embassy looking specifically for a reporter. I must admit I was a bit reluctant coming out here, because the story is a bit odd."

"What's so odd about it?" Zaidi asked sharply.

"For starters your nationality is…"

"Egyptian."

"And somehow you are being detained by the North Korean government?"

"That is correct."

The young man scrunched his face, shaking his head.

He sighed and said, "And you're a scientist who has discovered…"

"Look!" Zaidi shouted, slamming his palm against the iron patio table. "I don't have time for this! They gave me an hour to sit outside and enjoy one cup of coffee before I am locked up back in that godforsaken lab! Please—you have to help me."

The young man sighed. He took out a tape recorder and placed it on the table.

"No recorders," Zaidi said.

"Why not?"

"This is protection for yourself," Zaidi said.

"OK, Mr. Zaidi, what exactly do you want?"

"I am a physicist, you see. Years ago, I was working on a mathematical equation that would be able to pinpoint an electron in time and space."

The young man rolled his eyes and took off his glasses.

"Mr. Zaidi," he said. "I believe you're referring to quantum mechanics. It already exists. People have been doing this for years."

"No, you don't understand," Zaidi's eyes widened. "It's more than just moving electrons from one place to another." The reporter squinted his eyes. "We applied the equation. At first it was small elements—hydrogen, nitrogen. Then we got bolder, moving bigger elements like radon and tungsten."

"What are you saying?" the reporter asked in a condescending tone.

"I am saying that in my lab I can transfer atoms from one place to another."

"You mean teleportation?" He let out a sharp exhale and picked up his bag. "You know, I need to tell my secretary to start screening my calls."

"What?"

"Thanks a lot, Spock, for wasting my time," he said as he stormed off the patio.

Zaidi sunk back into his iron patio seat, his body slumped over, almost lifeless.

"Now that is a tough sell," a voice said.

Zaidi looked over his shoulder. All he could see was a man with dark-brown hair sitting with his back turned to him. He was wearing a light-blue shirt, sipping on what appeared to be a cappuccino. "Teleportation? If I hadn't seen some crazy shit in my life, I'd call bullshit too."

Zaidi stared at the back of the man's head.

He adjusted himself in his seat and asked, "How did you…"

"Turn back around, Zaidi," he said. Zaidi turned his body so the two men faced away from each other.

"Who are you?"

"That's not important. Just what did you expect to get out of meeting a reporter?"

"I-I don't know," Zaidi said shamefully. "But someone needs to know my story! A power like this could…"

"Easy, Zaidi. Keep your voice to a whisper. We have this entire restaurant bugged. You have my ear. Tell me your situation and maybe we can help each other."

A waitress walked by Zaidi and stopped at the table behind him.

"Excuse me," the waitress said. "I think you dropped a contact."

"Thank you, but I don't wear contacts," he said.

"Oh! That's so cool," the waitress said with a pleasant French accent.

Zaidi could hear her refill his drink. She strolled past Zaidi and smiled at him before stepping back into the coffee shop.

"Zaidi, you were saying," he said.

Zaidi looked down at the table and sighed.

"Who are you, CIA? Interpol?" Zaidi asked.

He scoffed and said, "You definitely don't want to talk to those guys."

"Fine." Zaidi took a sip of his water. "I am a physicist. I had been working on an equation for a very simple theory, which I knew would take years to execute. Can you transfer matter from one place to another?"

"You're referring to teleportation."

"That is such a crude term," Zaidi said, grimacing. "Teleportation is simply moving matter from one place to another in the form of energy. It has no data behind it. Television whores that word out, because it can describe to the layman what is happening without being too complex. It's no better than magic. You see, in order to move matter, you have to move protons and neutrons, which is relatively easy—but the electrons…" Zaidi could feel the excitement swelling inside him. He patted his hand against the tabletop. "The fucking electrons. That's the problem. They are like planets rotating around the sun. Faster than the speed of light. So fast it's as if they can disappear and reappear. Even with quantum equations, we still can only hold them to a quadrant of space and time, not one specific destination."

"Agreed. It's impossible."

"You don't believe me, do you?" Zaidi asked, irritated.

"Zaidi, I'm not here to believe or condemn. I'm only here for the truth."

"When you are shooting a moving target, Mr. ..."

"Black."

"When you are shooting a target, you don't shoot where it has been, but where it is going. Right? My equation has done just that. I know what their next move is. I know where the electrons move next. With this information I can convert atoms into radio waves and transmit them from one place to another."

"The Swedes can move charges, but you're saying you can move matter?"

"Exactly."

There was a pause between the two men.

"Where is your lab?"

"It's on the outskirts of town," Zaidi said, looking on both sides of him. "Me and my family are held captive there."

"Listen to me very carefully, Zaidi. I can help you, but I've got to see your equation in action."

"That won't be possible."

"Why?"

"The facility is heavily guarded. They allow me to leave for a couple of hours in the morning to…"

"We're aware. You've been coming to this coffee shop for weeks. You've become good friends with your security detail who waits for you around the corner while you clear your head."

"How did you—?"

"Let's just say a renowned Egyptian physicist shopping for groceries with known North Korean extremists in Brussels caught our attention. Your friends aren't the brightest, are they?"

Zaidi snickered and said, "No. They are not." He looked down at his gold-plated watch and said, "My time is up. I must go now. How do I…"

"Don't worry," Shepard said. "Be ready to show me your toy tonight."

∽

Eleven-thirty. Zaidi thought to himself as he stared at a digital watch mounted on the wall. He was dressed in a blue hazmat suit, standing in a bright white room at a computer station that folded out of the wall. He typed equations onto a black prompt screen.

"Ahmed! That is not correct!" A researcher shouted in Egyptian. She walked past Zaidi holding a long metal vial with red initials *Hg* written on the front. "McFarlane never did a Spider-Man comic!"

"What are you…" Ahmed laid flat under a cylindrical metal stand, connecting wires. He finished, stood up, and stretched out his thin frame. "Don't say that out in public! You sound like a stupid bitch!"

"You're the stupid bitch!" she shouted. "He never did a…"

"Eshe," Ahmed said, adjusting his black hazmat suit. "The man had a whole life before *Spawn!*"

"That's bullshit!" Eshe said, jabbing Ahmed in the chest with her index finger. "And you know why? Because I didn't have a life before I read *Spawn*. So how the hell could he?!" Ahmed closed his eyes and took a deep breath.

"Are you crazy?" Ahmed asked, taking a step back. He looked down at his hazmat suit. "You could have ripped it!"

"Good!" Eshe shouted. "Maybe a little radiation will make you smarter!" The two went on arguing behind Zaidi until he finished typing on the fold-out computer and slammed it back into the wall.

Zaidi walked past both of them and said, "I curse the day I bought you your first comic books."

He walked out of the white room into a long, narrow space that housed wooden workbenches and computer monitors. On the other side was a black painted room lighted by purple UV lights. Two thick fiberglass windows were placed so that the black and white rooms could be viewed. He plopped his body in front of a monitor closest to the glass door leading to the white room. He glanced at Ahmed and Eshe, who continued their squabble.

Zaidi pressed the intercom button and said, "Everyone, we needed to be ready to go five minutes ago. If your conversation is not one that is in the collegiate spirit of making this experiment successful, SHUT UP AND GET BACK TO WORK!" The entire group quieted and worked in silence. Zaidi sighed and rubbed his eyes.

"Are you OK?" asked one of the young researchers in the narrow computer room. He stood up and walked toward Zaidi. His white lab coat swayed against his blue jeans. His T-shirt read RAMEN on the front.

"I'm fine, Bennu," Zaidi said. "And how are you, my son?"

"Scared," Bennu said. "Are you sure this is safe?"

"This is our only chance of getting out of here."

"By giving it to the Americans?"

Zaidi stared at Bennu. He looked down at the LCD computer screen and sighed.

"It is the lesser of two evils."

There was a knock on the door. Zaidi looked through the small square window. He lowered his head and grunted while opening the door to let in one of the guards. He stepped into the lab wearing an army uniform and carrying a pistol holstered to his side.

"You and your team done for the day?" the guard asked.

Zaidi frowned at the guard.

"You say things so politely," Zaidi said with a sarcastic smile. "As if we had a choice in the matter."

"I am just following orders," the guard said. "I was told to treat you with respect as opposed to force."

"You don't think this is force?" Bennu asked, balling his fists.

"Bennu, enough," Zaidi said. Zaidi then looked at the guard and said, "We have a few other projects to conduct before we can call it an evening, so just lock us down."

"Very well," the guard said as he walked toward the door. "The fridge should still have some food if you and your team become hungry."

"Thank you," Zaidi said.

The guard closed the door behind him. Zaidi and his team could hear the dead bolts lock the door shut.

"This is a waste of time!" Bennu said. "Do you see how heavily guarded this place is? Even if he is CIA, there is no way…"

Knock-knock. Bennu and Zaidi looked at each other. Zaidi walked to the lab entrance and placed his hand on the doorknob. It was unlocked. When he opened the door, the guard wearing a metal band on his arm walked into the lab. A red light flashed in the middle of the metal band. His patrol hat shadowed his eyes. All Zaidi could see was the sweat trickling down his face.

"Is there a problem, sir?" Zaidi asked.

"Not at all," Shepard said, walking behind the guard.

Zaidi stared at Shepard with his mouth agape.

"This isn't possible," Zaidi said, scanning Shepard from head to toe. "There are cameras everywhere."

"Poorly placed cameras," Shepard said. "You could smuggle an elephant in here, there are so many blind spots." He walked over to the guard and patted him on the shoulder. "My friend here was my eyes. Isn't that right chief?"

"Y-You," the guard uttered.

"What's that, chief?" Shepard asked. He grabbed the guard's neck and said, "Speak up."

"You said you would let me go," the guard said.

"I did, didn't I?" Shepard asked. Shepard pulled out a small black detonator from his pocket. "I am gonna let you go. But not the way you think." A look of confusion came over the guard's face. "The thing is, you're at war right? You can't hold it against me for shooting at you if we're both on the battle field." The guard's dark-brown pupils shook back and forth, staring at Shepard with terror. "I am gonna let you go, but back to your ancestors." Before the guard could grab Shepard's wrist, he had already pressed the top of the red detonator. The flashing red light on the metal brace switched to solid blue.

The guard grabbed his chest. Each breath became labored, and he dropped to his knees. The guard looked up at Shepard's blank expression. His face was red, and his eyes looked as though they were going to pop out of their sockets. With his final breath, the guard keeled over, frozen in agony.

"What the hell have you done?" Zaidi asked, his voice wavering. "This man was on duty. He will not return to his post, and they will kill us."

"That is not your concern," Shepard said. "This is an audition, Zaidi. You wanna get out of this? You gotta make it to Hollywood."

"What?" Zaidi asked, squinting his eyes.

Shepard looked up and said, "Not big on pop culture, are we?" Shepard asked while scratching his head. "What I mean is that you have twelve hours to impress me."

Zaidi took a deep breath and nodded.

"I can do it in one," he said.

⁋

Shepard put on a blue hazmat suit and walked into the white room. Ahmed was at the foldout computer station, typing his calculations onto the screen. He closed the screen and approached Shepard.

"There are two rooms that make up my lab," Zaidi said. "This is the white room."

He pointed across the room to a window.

"That is the dark room," Zaidi said.

In the middle of the white room was a massive cylindrical creation made of metal and plastic. In the middle of it was an opening that gave off a blue light. Zaidi stepped past Shepard, holding a metal vial with *Hg* etched on it.

"What's that?" Shepard asked.

"That is the transmetric device," Ahmed said. "We use it to make the jumps."

Zaidi opened the vial. He turned it upside down. Five metal cubes the size of dice fell into Zaidi's hand. He quickly placed them into the cylindrical opening. Moments later, each of them melted into liquid puddles.

"Don't be too shocked by what you just saw," Ahmed said smugly. He took his index finger and drew an infinity symbol with the puddle of mercury.

"Mercury liquifies at room temperature," replied an annoyed Shepard. "You're not the only who took introductory chemistry."

"Let me explain to you what is about to happen," Zaidi said. "The transmetric process is all about accuracy and precision. In order to move matter from one place to another, we must have the exact weight number of protons and neutrons. That's the easy part. The electrons have always been the issue, because they move."

"That's where your equation comes in?" Shepard asked.

Zaidi nodded.

"We take a magnet, one similar to that of a magnetic resonance imaging machine, and turn it on, giving out a positive polarity. The electrons in the element will be attracted and forced to orient in the direction that I choose. The software my engineers designed will utilize my equation to predict the electrons' next move."

"What if the electrons don't move in the direction that you want?" Shepard asked.

"These are electrons, Mr. Black," Zaidi said. "Not people."

Eshe walked into the white room, humming a pop song, off-key. She bobbed her head from side to side, her dyed purple locks swaying against her jet-black hair. Her worn sneakers rubbed across the floor. Shepard looked at the young girl's black T-shirt that read JOURNEY on the front. In her hands was a thick black metal box about the size of a basketball. She placed the box on the metal table.

"What you got there?" Shepard asked.

"We call it the black vault," Eshe said.

She looked at Zaidi with a *Who is this guy?* expression.

"This is Mr. Black, Eshe," Zaidi said.

Eshe stared at Shepard for a brief moment and walked back to the monitoring room.

"What is the, um, black vault for?" Shepard asked.

"This isn't magic," Eshe said, staring at Shepard. "To make something disappear and reappear takes a lot of fucking energy and will produce a shitload of radiation…"

"Eshe," Zaidi said, pointing his finger. "Language, little one, Yalla."

Eshe glanced at Zaidi and rolled her dark brown eyes.

"So the jump requires two boxes to be present," Eshe said. "Otherwise you get radioactive sludge."

She walked through the monitoring area into the dark room, where she placed the box on a metal stand.

"It's time, Mr. Black," Zaidi said.

He motioned for Shepard to follow him. They walked into the monitoring room, locked the doors, and helped each other unzip their hazmat suits. Shepard looked around at the young researchers. All nine of them were having random conversations about video games and anime. He walked over to Zaidi, who was sitting at a computer in the front of the white room.

"How old are these kids?" Shepard whispered to Zaidi.

"Eshe's the youngest, thirteen."

"Hmm…" Shepard said with a raspy voice.

"Are you ready, Bennu?" Zaidi asked in Arabic.

Bennu nodded and said, "Engage!"

"That's not the meaning!" Eshe said slapping the back of Bennu's head. "We are not jumping to light speed!"

"Well, theoretically we are," one of the children responded.

The entire room erupted in a heated argument. Zaidi stared at the computer screen and shook his head.

"What are they arguing about?" Shepard asked.

"Nothing," Zaidi said.

Zaidi slammed his fist against the tabletop of the computer station. After the fifth knock, the noise subsided.

"This is exactly why I hate science fiction!" Zaidi shouted. "Why are you children so enthralled by some random person's imagination? It is fiction! Just that. Nothing more."

He looked at Bennu and pointed his finger.

"If you downgrade my research again to that non-sense, by God's name I will strangle you with my bare hands!"

Bennu settled back in his seat and continued typing. He cleared his throat and said, "Telemetric system is online."

The computers in the back room made a high-pitched noise that continued to increase in intensity. Shepard winced at the sound. He held his hands over his ears. Shepard looked around, wondering why he was the only one who was bothered.

"This motherfucker," he mumbled to himself.

Zaidi and his children had clear noise-canceling buds crammed in their ears.

Small electrical charges bounced around the cylindrical structure in the white room. On Ahmed's computer screen, a group of letters slowly appeared.

"Xe4f14," Ahmed said. "5d10 and…6s2." He typed feverishly on his keyboard. "Send it to the black room."

He nodded and looked at Bennu, who took over Ahmed's aggressive typing. A low-pitched sound started in the black room. The metal box started to vibrate. The vibration became an intense low rumble that shook the entire monitoring room.

"Almost there," Benuu murmured as he pegged away at his keyboard.

Shepard's green and blue eyes glanced at the lights fading in and out.

"Xe4f145d106s2, transmitting now," Bennu said as he pressed ENTER. "Xe41…" Smoke rose from the black metal box.

"Come on," Ahmed said, staring at the black room. "The circuits are going to melt."

"4f145d…" Bennu said.

Shepard leaned in next to Ahmed and asked, "What are those numbers?"

"The electron configuration of mercury," Ahmed said. "Think of it as an address for the electrons that surround the atom itself."

"Isn't that electricity going to throw off the charge?" Shepard asked.

"That's the purpose of the black box," Eshe said. She was standing behind him. "It cancels out any charge, radiation—anything that can possibly change the configuration of what's inside the black box."

Shepard stared at her over his shoulder and said, "You seem very prideful of this box here."

"Well, I created it, so…" Eshe said with attitude.

She walked away from Shepard, focusing back on the black room.

"106s2," Bennu said. "Got it!" He hit ENTER on his keyboard.

The rumbling of the metal boxes came to an abrupt stop. A small flame ignited at the back of the black room. Zaidi ran into the black room holding a fire extinguisher.

"It's the heating coils," Ahmed said. "Happens after every experiment. Do you want to see what's inside?"

Shepard scoffed. He shuffled his way through the congested monitoring room and stepped into the black room.

"Wait," Eshe said, holding a pair of oven mitts. "Take these."

Shepard took the gloves from Eshe and put them on as he approached the black box. He pressed down on the top latch of the box, which caused the four walls to pop open and reveal liquid mercury in the shape of an infinity symbol. Shepard squinted his eyes.

"Hmm…" Shepard said. "That's not possible."

"It is now, Mr. Black," Zaidi said, walking into the black room. "And I'm afraid North Korea owns this intellectual property."

"How far can you move objects?" Shepard asked.

"I told you," Zaidi said. "Anywhere on the planet."

"Can this thing move people, supplies, weapons?"

"No," Ahmed said shaking his head. "You see, the program works because it can identify the location of electrons in space. An element is no more than a group of clones that will react exactly the same. The computer captures this location, and if one electron is off, it doesn't work. A molecule composed of different elements? The computer would have to calculate probabilities in the trillions. It can never be done, at least not in our lifetimes."

"Then why do I care about all of this, Zaidi?" Shepard asked with a shrug.

"Listen to what I am saying, Mr. Black," Zaidi said, folding his arms. "I can move *any* element."

Shepard looked at the linoleum floor. A flash of insight came across his face.

"Uranium," Shepard said. "Plutonium."

"That is correct, Mr. Black," Zaidi said. "It doesn't take much. They plan to open dummy companies throughout the world. Starting with South Korea, they want to piecemeal the other parts and then, with this device, transmit enough plutonium to blow Seoul off the face of the earth."

Shepard looked down at the liquid mercury.

"We burn this place to the ground," Shepard said.

"That's more like it," Zaidi said.

"I need your data, though. All of it. That is the trade. You want asylum and free passage for your family, then that is what I need."

"Take it," Zaidi said raising his hands. "Americans can be evil, but you are not without sanity."

"Get your family together, doctor."

"You're looking at them," Zaidi said pointing his thumb back at the monitoring room.

"What?"

"This is my family," Zaidi said. "My children. I adopted them, took them off the streets of Egypt, and taught them science. They are my biggest achievement."

Shepard surveyed them, working throughout the lab. He looked through the computer-room window, watching Eshe readjust Ahmed's fingers for a proper Vulcan salute.

"They're just kids," Shepard said softly. "Lot of hormones in there, doc."

"Nine, Mr. Black," Zaidi said with pride.

Shepard gave a slight smile and nodded.

"OK. I'll get you all out."

"Out of the question," Bradshaw said. Bradshaw stood leaning against the elliptical wooden conference table in Ashcroft's office. Ashcroft was at his standing desk, looking over Shepard's report. He viewed the documents while periodically scratching his long Auburn-and-silver beard, raising his head to glance at Shepard, who was sitting on the other side of the conference table next to the door.

Santiago, dressed in a black suit and black tie, leaned back in his seat with his legs crossed and his hands resting in his lap. He looked over at Barbara, dressed in dark army fatigues, army boots, and a gray tank top. She kept her feet propped on the table as she disassembled her nine-millimeter and mumbled to herself.

"Barb?" Santiago asked. "You want to pay attention?"

She let out a loud snicker.

"Attention is a state of mind," Barbara said, adjusting her body in her chair.

Santiago looked at Ashcroft.

"Just continue," Ashcroft said, rubbing his forehead.

"Shepard," Santiago said. "I understand you want to help people. I do. But that's not 7721's purpose."

"I understand that," Shepard said. "But this is not like our typical sweeps. Wiping down a piece of intellectual property from some jihadist is one thing. We do this…"

"You don't have to explain to us the details of what happens, Black," Bradshaw said, shaking his head. "I know the drill. You guys go in, take all components of said property, including the creator. He disappears," Bradshaw said, making air quotations as he said "disappears" before continuing. "The property and creator are ripped from existence. World is a safer place. Well, kinda. Why should this be any different?"

"Because you are dealing with children!" Shepard shouted. "It's not just Zaidi who's the creator. They all are. The youngest is thirteen. These are extenuating circumstances that need to be discussed before we just…" Shepard closed his eyes and took a deep breath. "I am asking permission to handle this one differently."

"How so?" Santiago asked.

"That technology has to go," Shepard said. "We torch the facility. Zaidi and his kids are the intellectual property," Shepard said. "We extract all of them and burn the place down."

"And with no one being aware of their existence," Santiago said.

"No one will care," Shepard said, smiling. "It'll just be another random, accidental fire."

Santiago looked at Bradshaw and shrugged his shoulders.

"I'm never against salvaging human life when it can be helped," Santiago said.

Shepard looked at Santiago and nodded. They both waited for Bradshaw, who was slowly shaking his head.

"I don't know," Bradshaw said. "It's just…" He was interrupted by Barbara's high-pitched, ominous laugh. She slammed her assembled gun on the table and spun it. She then leaned over and stared at Shepard with a sardonic grin.

"This reminds me of a story," Barbara said with excitement. "An Aztec couple are farming in their fields when the king's soldiers approach the husband. His wife has just been given the honor of being the Friday-night sacrifice."

Barbara sat back in her chair, smiling. She watched as everyone in the room stared at her, frozen, with narrowed eyebrows and gaping mouths.

"OK," Santiago said. "Then what?"

"Oh," Barbara said, confused. "I thought it was clear that my story was finished. Well, it is. The moral is that in order to keep the sun god happy, you gotta be willing to gut a coupla kiddies."

Shepard closed his eyes and said, "Sir, is there a reason why her presence is required?"

"It's not murder, Shep," Barbara said, laughing. "It's a sacrifice."

Shepard locked eyes with Barbara.

"Bitch," Shepard said, pointing his finger. "Keep trying me."

"Call me a bitch again, and we'll see who gets fucked tonight, big boy," Barbara said chuckling.

"Yeah?" Shepard asked, raising his voice. "I always wondered how you kept your dick so well-tucked, Barb."

Barbara grabbed the thick wooden table. She broke off a piece and stood up.

"Here it is," Barbara said with a calm voice. Her grin widened. "Let's see if it can fit up your ass," she said, walking toward Shepard.

"Enough!" Ashcroft said.

Barbara froze. She dropped the wooden chunk onto the floor and sat back down. Grabbing her gun, she kicked her legs back up on the cracked tabletop and went back to disassembling her weapon, mumbling to herself as she took out the magazine. Ashcroft leaned forward at his standing desk.

"The answer is no," Ashcroft said. "We are not changing our M.O. just because you saw a bunch of kids and found that you have a heart. The only platitude we work in, Agent Black, is that the ends justify the means. There is no immediate gratification of what we do, my friend. We'll never see how many lives we've saved. Only the body count is in front of us, but keep this in mind: 'And darkness was on the faces of the deep when God said let there be light. And there was.' Genesis 1:1. Light comes out of darkness. Find some solace in that. If you can't, take up drinking. My preference is twenty-year-old scotch. Now get out."

Shepard sighed. He stared at his superiors calmly before darting his eyes at Barbara and walking out of Ashcroft's office. Barbara hoisted her feet back on the table and rested her hands on her stomach.

"This guy," she chuckled to herself.

"Barbara," Ashcroft said sternly. "That means you too."

Barbara stood up. She walked past Bradshaw, who was on the other side of the table, holding up her middle finger.

Bradshaw grimaced at her seductive stare and stood up from his seat.

"Alan, wait a minute," Ashcroft said. He looked up from the papers in front of him and smiled at Bradshaw. "Got a sec?"

Bradshaw nodded and sat back down. They waited for Barbara to close the door behind her. Bradshaw looked over at Santiago, who was swiveling his chair from side to side and holding a black pen. Ashcroft straightened his black military uniform and brushed a piece of lint from the single black star embroidered on the left breast.

"Alan," Ashcroft said with a smile. "Do you like pussy?"

Bradshaw's face jolted at the question.

"Excuse me, sir?" Bradshaw asked.

"Pussy, Alan," Ashcroft said again. "Vagina. Do you enjoy it?"

"Y-Yes sir," Bradshaw stammered.

"Well, that we have something in common," Ashcroft said. He stepped from behind his podium desk and sat down at the conference table. "'Cause I am a big fan. So many shapes and sizes. So accessible."

Bradshaw squinted his eyes and nodded slowly.

"Yes, sir. I-I guess."

"You know another thing?" Ashcroft asked. "You can get it any and everywhere. Day or night. It's like good Chinese food. You like Chinese?"

"Uh…I do," Bradshaw said.

"Of course you do!" Ashcroft said, chuckling. "Who doesn't like Chinese food?" Ashcroft glanced at Santiago, who slid a manila folder across the table to Bradshaw. "So, Alan, I ask you, if you have so many options for good Chinese food, why would you eat where you shit?"

Bradshaw opened the folder. He gasped for air as he sunk in his seat. Ashcroft's smile transformed into a rage-filled stare. He stood in front of his seat and placed his hands on the table. Santiago, hands clasped, looked at Bradshaw with a blank stare.

"I-I don't think…" Bradshaw stammered.

"You don't think what?" Ashcroft asked with a deep, deliberate tone.

Bradshaw took each picture from the folder and slid them onto the table. He looked straight ahead and said, "I think these pictures were taken…"

Ashcroft closed his eyes and said, "If you insult my intelligence, Bradshaw, I'll kill you myself. Of all the women you could have chosen to fuck, including your wife or your mistress, you chose a DAMN WEAPON?!"

"James, I think we're overreacting here," Bradshaw said, giving a nervous chuckle.

Ashcroft, stupefied, stared at Bradshaw. He looked at Santiago, who was also baffled. Ashcroft walked away from the table and turned his back, placing his hands on the podium.

Santiago leaned forward in his seat and asked, "Do you not grasp the gravity of what you've done?"

"Don't talk to me like a child, Santiago," Bradshaw said.

"If it appears that I am talking down to you, then you're not as obtuse as your actions make you seem," Santiago said.

"What did you just say to me?" Bradshaw asked.

"You created an affair with a genetically engineered super soldier who is emotionally and mentally unstable," Santiago said. He clasped his hands as if he were praying and continued. "Someone who will, if you so much as hold a door open for another women, make you swallow your own tongue and proceed to kill everyone in this building. You have to understand that, don't you?"

Bradshaw's left check twitched. He took a deep breath and sunk back in his seat.

"I didn't think about that at the time. No."

"*Stop talking*," Ashcroft whispered. He walked over to the conference table and sat down. He took a deep breath and said, "Santiago, can you kill her? If it comes to that?"

"Head on? No," Santiago said. "If Sean were still here, maybe, but between the two of us, she remains the strongest physically."

"Just sneak up on her and put a bullet in her head," Bradshaw murmured.

"Good idea," Ashcroft said with sarcasm. "You want to go give it a shot?" Bradshaw looked away.

"There is an option," Santiago said. "We make her angry."

"We what?" Ashcroft asked.

"You've seen Barbara when she loses it. She's like a bull headed in one direction. Complete tunnel vision. At that moment she'll be totally caught off guard. We take that opportunity to terminate her."

"Terminate?" Ashcroft asked, raising his eyebrow. "You don't have any affection for the person you grew up with?"

Santiago chuckled, "Am I supposed to have emotions for a fellow lab-rat general? Place her in charge of this next 7721 assignment. I'm sure she'll be ready to kill Shepard."

"And that will be the opening you need to end this?" Ashcroft asked.

"Given the right catalyst, timing, and environment, it's probable."

Ashcroft nodded.

"And Shepard?" Santiago asked.

"What about him?" Ashcroft asked.

"If he disobeys orders?"

Ashcroft took off his glasses. He leaned forward in his seat.

"If that's the case," Ashcroft said. "All of them. One fell swoop."

Eleanor

"Man," Charlie said, wiping the sweat from his neck, **"it's a sauna out here."**

"It is warm," Sayf said.

The two were sitting at a lime-green plastic table, several feet from a small, washed-out yellow food truck. The truck's tables spilled into the uneven asphalt road to accommodate Sayf and his Slokranian special forces. They each sat at different tables dressed in civilian clothing, trying their best to blend in. About a hundred yards from the makeshift restaurant came a dead end, at the end of which was a tall, multicolored, brick apartment complex. Many tenants were on their balconies. Some were washing clothes while others stood slumped over the railing, wiping the beading sweat from their foreheads.

Sayf took his plastic spoon and stirred the melting ice in his orange-colored Thai iced tea. He stared at the complex, which shimmered in the scorching hot sun. Sayf sipped on his tea, helplessly swatting at insects buzzing by his ear.

"Not bad, is it?" Charlie asked, watching the teenagers play soccer on the opposite side of the street.

"What?" Sayf asked.

"The pups over there playing the *joga bonito*. If they had a proper pitch, it could've been interesting, yeah?"

"Charlie," Morgan said, "no one cares about that fucking game right now." She was standing on a rooftop three buildings away, surveying the street through a pair of black binoculars, her right hand in the pocket of her tan kahkis. Two Slokranians were by the fire escape, standing guard. "Chief, I don't like this. We should have more men on the ground," she said, adjusting her black shades that dangled from her blue polo shirt.

"Morgan," Sayf said after sipping on his tea, "we're not trying to scare them, and I don't want an unnecessary shootout. All right?" Sayf brushed down the short sleeves of his light-blue dress shirt as he looked around. "This shanty is a front for organ trafficking. I'm pretty sure that even with all our manpower we still wouldn't be the biggest kid on the block."

"Size is irrelevant," Charlie said with a smile. "No need to be the biggest if you're already the meanest."

"I'll drink to that," Sayf said.

Moments later, a small old man approached the table. He was wearing an off-white linen suit and a straw hat. His gray bangs dangled behind his red-tinted glasses. He walked up to the table with his hands in the air. Charlie and Sayf glanced at each other.

"Here we go," Charlie whispered.

He took a seat at the lime-green table. The old man cracked half of smile, causing the skin around his right eye to wrinkle.

"Mr. Sayf," he said, smiling, "have you ever been to Bangkok?" Sayf shook his head. "It's a cesspool of degenerate drug dealers, prostitutes, and sodomites." He held up his index finger. "It's New York with a tan." A man from the food cart opened a blue cooler and grabbed a beer from the ice water. He ran over to the table, placed a napkin in front of the old man, and put the beer on top. "My friends call me Kiet."

"Alright then, Kiet," Sayf said, cracking a smile. "You know…"

"You may call me Mr. Pan."

Sayf snickered and said, "Alright. Mr. Pan, you know why we are here?"

"Yes, Mr. Sayf, I do," Kiet, said, taking a sip of his beer. "Normally, I wouldn't waste my time with the likes of you but…"

"Oi!" Charlie shouted. "What the fuck is your—" Sayf placed his hand on Charlie's shoulder.

"Take a breath, mate," Sayf said. "My apologies, Mr. Pan. You were saying?"

"People around here don't even say her name," Kiet said staring at Charlie. "It's almost sacrilegious."

"At least we are on the same page," Sayf said as he rubbed the top of his sweating head. "Tell us what we need to know, and we'll be on our way."

"It's not that easy," Kiet said.

"Why isn't it, then?" Charlie asked.

"It never is. Is it?" Kiet said, shaking his head.

"Mr. Pan," Sayf said. "I've come a long way to find a very dangerous person. Now I'm certain you did a background check on who I am and what it is that I do. Yeah?" Kiet nodded. "Now a sane man would realize that I am not one to be toyed with. So, shall we start over? Kiet, where's Barbara?"

Kiet stared at the ground. He scoffed and said, "You know he always brings me beer. I cut off his finger a few months back when he brought me the wrong drink. Ever since then he brings me beer. Funny thing is, today your *cha yen* looks very refreshing." Kiet stood up and dusted his linen pants. "Think I will join you and order one."

"It's your city," Sayf said.

"That's right, Mr. Sayf," Kiet said in a deep, monotonic voice. "My city." He turned around and walked toward the food cart.

"That...little...piece...of shite," Charlie said.

He looked over at Sayf, who was sitting back in his seat, scratching his face. They watched as Kiet strolled by each table, analyzing Sayf's Nazi commandos. Each wore regular clothing with cutoff sleeves, and their bare arms were covered in swastikas and Aryan tattoos. He turned around and gave Sayf a thumbs-up, walking backward toward the food truck.

"We're gonna do some torturing, right?" Charlie asked. "Pop the trunk? Observe how our primate buddies administer affliction?"

Sayf was silent. He looked around at the scene in front of him.

"He's too calm," he whispered to himself.

"Chief, are you listening?" Charlie asked.

"This..." Sayf sat up in his seat. "This is off. He's too calm."

"What you think is in store for us? Look around. The Third Reich is sitting all around us. I'm glad he knows. Makes him less liable to fuck with us. Maybe he hasn't realized that his tan little sandbox has gotten a lot bigger."

"Charlie..."

"Wha? It's true isn't it?" Charlie looked over at the teenagers playing soccer and shook his head. "I know you disapprove, chief, but I got to scratch this itch." He got up from his seat.

"Where the hell are you going?"

"That short little fullback over there." Charlie pointed in the direction of the teenagers. "His passing has been driving me crazy. Gonna show how's it's done."

"You must be joking," Sayf frowned.

"Boss, you can yell at me later. I'm pretty sure how this is about to go down." Charlie glanced back at the soccer game. "What if one of those kids over there is struggling to get out the ghetto? Me, the white savior, goes over there and teaches him the proper way to pass. He's inspired. Grows up to become the next

Ronaldo, Agbonlahor, or Pelé. He grows up to take Thailand to their first World Cup appearance. They make a movie where I'll be played by—"

"Here it comes."

"Jason Statham."

"You look nothin' like him."

"I look like him on the inside."

"Thought you didn't watch TV?"

"I don't, but the ex fancied him. Riled her up. Was a good shagging afterward."

"Yeah," Sayf said, chuckling. "Have you heard from Eleanor?"

"That tart?" Charlie scoffed. "The bank probably done her weeks ago and never got around to telling us."

The two of them looked at each other and laughed.

"Probably" Sayf said. "We did frame her for nearly four billion."

"I heard the bank offed the entire floor after we left. All nine jackals dead." Sayf cut his eyes at Charlie. "Sorry, chief. I know you don't like that description of us."

"Not surprised. What you gonna do?" Sayf asked as he stared at the food cart. "We all live by the sword. Bound to get shafted lingering in this lifestyle long enough. Right? Doesn't matter. We needed the loot to finance Ashcroft's plan."

Charlie nodded and jogged across the street, yelling at the children to pass him the ball.

Sayf chuckled to himself, shaking his head. He looked up at the sun, which sat at high noon in the cloudless sky.

"Chief," Morgan said in his earpiece. "what the fuck is he doin'?" Sayf shrugged his shoulders. "I can't really make a visual on this Kiet fella. There's some kind of reflection from the building at the end of the road."

Sayf looked up at the building. A young girl was standing on the balcony holding a mirror. Sayf's eyes widened.

"Hold on," Sayf said standing up. "That's because she's shining a light in your face."

"What's that, chief?" Morgan asked. Her voice sounded muffled. "I'm losing you."

Sayf looked over at Charlie circled by adolescents passing the soccer ball back and forth. Charlie looked back at Sayf, giving him a salute with two fingers.

"Get off the roof, Morgan," Sayf said in a stunned, steady voice.

"What's that, chief?" Morgan asked.

Two barefooted boys broke from the passing circle and dashed toward Charlie from behind.

"No," Sayf said.

A sudden wave of shock came over Charlie's face. He stumbled forward, grunting at the sharp pain he felt in the middle of his back before looking down at the machete blade protruding from his abdomen. He then looked up at Sayf, standing across the street, frozen, and smiled with irony. The two boys both put a foot on Charlie's back to pry out the machete. Charlie fell to his knees. He closed his eyes as one of the boys pulled his head back to slit his throat.

Sayf's nostrils flared at the sight before focusing back on the food cart. In that moment, Kiet and the cook were behind the food truck each holding AK-47s. Sayf's neo-Nazi commandos sitting next to the cart didn't even see the gunfire. Chairs and tables flipped over. Those who tried to run didn't make it two steps before a hail of bullets riddled their backs.

Sayf pulled out his nine-millimeter and fired a couple of shots before diving into a nearby alley. Bullets trailed behind him before bouncing off the corner of a red brick wall. He placed his back against the wall and grabbed a piece of broken glass, holding it up in front of him. In the reflection, Sayf could see the cook reloading while Kiet continued firing.

"What the fuck?" Morgan said, staring at the carnage. She picked up her rifle.

"Morgan!" Sayf shouted. "Get the fuck off the roof!"

Morgan brought the rifle scope up to her eyes to return fire. She placed her hand on the trigger and felt cold steel pressed against her head. The force of the bullet propelled her body off the rooftop, crashing onto the cracked concrete. The noise from the fall caught Sayf's attention. The sight of Morgan's broken body prone across the sidewalk enraged him. He cocked his 9-millimeter back and returned fire. The remaining Slokranian commandos found cover alongside the narrow side alleys. Kiet and his cook continued shooting until they ran inside the complex at the end of the street. As soon as Kiet disappeared through the doorway, his men came rushing out of the building, firing automatic weapons.

Sayf saw an armored Humvee pulling up to block the street. The rest of the Slokranian commandos hopped out of the vehicle and began firing back. They pushed down the street and regrouped with their comrades—twenty of them continued to fire on Kiet's men. The Slokranians marched down the street, forcing Kiet's team back into the building. At the front of the assault, a redheaded Slokrainian with an army-green swastika tattooed on his forehead held up his fist. The Slokranians stopped firing. They slowly marched down the bullet-riddled street until they stood in front of the silent, dilapidated building.

Moments later, the tenants of the building walked onto their balconies. Couples, the elderly, young children—each held an automatic weapon.

"Fuckin' hell," Sayf whispered.

They opened fire on the commandos. Kiet's men walked nonchalantly out of the building as the tenants extinguished Sayf's second wave. Kiet stepped out from the shadows of the building and walked over broken concrete and corpses. He wiped the dirt off his suit and raised his red-tinted glasses on the bridge of his nose.

"Do you understand what I mean by 'my city,' Mr. Sayf?!" Kiet shouted. "There is a Greek legend about a boy named Icarus who flies too high!" He walked over to one of the Nazi commandos, still squirming in a pool of blood. "Too close to the sun! His wings melt and he falls from the heavens!" He pulled out a handgun and shot the Slokranian twice in the head. "Do you hear me, jackal?! I'm not some warlord with delusions of grandeur!"

"We got clearance," a Slokranian voice spoke into Sayf's earpiece. "Should I watch for collateral?"

"There is no collateral," Sayf said.

"Do you hear me, Sayf?!" Kiet asked smugly. "I am a king!" There was a moment of silence followed by an ominous roar of laughter that echoed through the desolate street.

"You know what makes this so wrong?" Sayf shouted. "I just had a question."

Slowly, the echoing was being drowned out by a rumble that continued to crescendo. Kiet grimaced as he stared at the shaking ground.

A black Heuy helicopter blotted the sun like an eclipse, swooping down from the sky. Kiet and his men stood frozen in front of the armed chopper hovering over them.

"Your orders?" the voice spoke into Sayf's earpiece.

"Fire," Sayf replied.

Flashes of white flickered from the rotating Gatling gun. Kiet's men were ripped apart. The tenants on the balconies continued to fire at the chopper. Bullets rang off the black metal nose. The chopper redirected the gunners and opened fire on the balconies. One surge from left to right put down the complex's hostile welcome.

Smoke and steam bellowed from the Gatling guns slowing down before coming to a complete stop. The chopper floated backward several feet above the ground before finding a clear spot to land. When the blades came to a stop, six Slokranian soldiers including the pilot hopped out of the chopper. Sayf came from the alley and walked toward the pilot. He was a tall Slokranian with a blond Mohawk. He scratched his blond mustache, looking around at the carnage.

"This was trap?" he asked.

"You think?" Sayf said sarcastically. Sayf walked down to the end of the street. He looked at the bodies scattered across the rubble. Mostly elderly men, families, young women. "These aren't drug dealers," Sayf said, staring at the mangled remains of a pregnant woman. "These were tenants. We were slaughtered by the common folk." Sayf said, laughing hysterically. "The bloody townspeople." His eerie laugh lasted for at least thirty seconds until he was able to regain his composure.

"Sayf," one of the Slokranian soldiers said. "Kiet is not here."

"Of course not," Sayf said, staring up at the building. Bullets from the helicopter had pierced the concrete complex. Pieces of crumbling cement fell in the surrounding smoke. "Cockroaches can survive an atomic blast. That's what Kiet is: a fucking cockroach."

"You might want to see this," a soldier shouted in Slokranian from inside the building. Sayf looked at his pilot before stepping through the concrete entrance. Inside was a dark corridor that reeked of cat urine. The fluorescent lights flickered a dim green. Pastel-colored graffiti lined the walls of the corridor. He walked to the back room to find three of his soldiers standing over a balding middle-aged man. Blood dripped from his right leg onto the floor. He hugged a windowless steel door, scratching away at the metal with his bloody hands. Two Slokranians pried him from the door, dragged him to a wooden chair, and forced him to sit down.

The soldiers placed C-4 on the latch of the door and stood

back. One of the Slokranians pushed a mini detonator, which popped the door off its hinges and slammed it to the floor. Smoke covered the entire room. Sayf sniffed the air and winced at the wisp of rotten flesh.

"What is it?" A Slokranian asked.

"Death," Sayf said.

As the smoke cleared, a little girl with big light-brown eyes was staring at Sayf, her lifeless body dangling in the air. The smoke continued to clear, revealing bodies hanging from ropes. The middle-aged Thai man bellowed. He fell to the floor and began crawling toward the little girl. He held up his left hand as if he were about to caress her face. They pulled him from the ground and put him back in the seat. Sayf grabbed an old wooden stool and sat down across from him.

"Who are they?" Sayf asked in Thai.

The man's body convulsed. He slowly lifted his head as if an imaginary force was pressing it down. His red tear-filled eyes locked with Sayf's but stayed silent.

"Blackie's tongue is well-versed," one of the soldiers said in Russian. Still looking at the Thai man, Sayf pulled out his nine-millimeter. He placed it on his knee.

"Call me Blackie again and I'll rip out your vocal cords." Sayf said calmly. The soldier tightened his grip around his rifle and cleared his throat. "Now, my friend. Who were they?"

"M-My daughter," the man murmured.

"And the rest of them?" Sayf asked.

"They lived here. She took them away from us. Our mothers, sons, dau…" The man was overwhelmed by grief. Sayf looked at the room of dangling corpses. Then his eyes widened.

"Her?" Sayf asked.

"Kiet is nothing more than a two-bit hustler," he stammered. "It was the devil. S-She handed him the keys to the kingdom. That's why we fear him."

"The devil? What does this...*devil* look like?"

"The devil with brown hair. Who could..." His eyes started to roll back. His head drifted down. The blood hemorrhaging from his leg had formed a growing puddle that almost touched Sayf's shoes. "...crush bones into dust."

"Hey!" Sayf shouted. He grabbed the man by his tattered gray T-shirt. "Listen to me. I am not your enemy. The person who put your families in that box and turned you into a militia—that is your enemy."

"They took her," he whispered.

"Who took her?" Sayf asked.

"Men... bronzed skin...goats tattooed on necks..." His head fell limp and his entire body slid out of the seat into the pool of blood.

Saint Mary Le Bow

"This isn't a good idea," Rosa whispered to Jonah. They sat in the back of a black taxi crossing the Thames River. She was wearing a black business dress and a long black wig. She adjusted her thick, brown, square glasses and tugged Jonah's sleeve. "You don't understand. If I walk in there, they are going to kill me."

Jonah looked at her and saw the fear in her eyes. He straightened his navy-blue tie and flattened out the gray suspenders under the lapels of his dark-blue suit.

"How long has it been, Rosa?" Shepard asked. His deep voice startled her. Annoyed, she ran her fingers along the flesh-colored audio piece jammed in her left ear.

"Not long enough," she whispered.

"Keep in mind companies like this want to appear legit," Shepard said. "The heavy hitters they make disappear. Small-time embezzlers like yourself, they let the law handle it."

The driver slowed down and pulled off the road. Rosa planted her black six-inch stilettos on the concrete sidewalk and steadied herself out of the taxi. She looked up at the glass skyscraper, balling her hands into fists and rubbing cold sweat between her French-manicured fingers.

"Shepard, listen to me," Rosa said. "This is not what you think. You set up an appointment with a global finance officer."

"You mean a jackal," Graham said.

"Whatever you want to call it," Rosa said. "They pay governments a visit. Not the other way around. Besides, they don't deal with personal investments. It's going to come off as suspicious."

Jonah placed his hand on the small of her back.

"You always said money is money, right? It'll be fine," Jonah said.

The meager expression of hope on his youthful face put Rosa at ease. She cracked a smile, and the two walked through the revolving doors. Rosa followed behind Jonah, down the open glass atrium. Office workers wearing different shades of dark walked briskly across the gray granite floor.

"Listen," Shepard said, "you two are here to see a Marcus Sayf."

"W-who?" Rosa stammered.

"Marcus Sayf," Graham said. "Ever heard of him?"

"Name doesn't ring a bell," Rosa said.

"Good," Shepard said, "We don't want anyone to recognize you. Remember the cover. You made close to five hundred million dollars last year in the commodities market and are looking to invest in something sexier."

"Pork bellies are sexy. You ever had a piece of bacon?" Jonah said, approaching a dark circular desk in the middle of the atrium. An older gentleman with dark silver hair wearing a navy-blue suit and a red tie stood at the desk.

He gave a plain smile and asked "Hello, how can I help you?"

"Focus," Shepard said. "You're going to tell him…."

"Mr. Tompkins and Mrs. Potter here to see Marcus Sayf," Jonah said to him.

He looked at Jonah with a fading smile before staring down

at the computer screen lying flush on the tabletop behind the counter.

"Ah, yes," he said. He pointed at five elevators about twenty feet behind him. "Take the elevator on the far right. Go to the eleventh floor. When you get up there, you will see a young man at the front desk. He will take you to Mr. Sayf's office."

"Much obliged," Jonah said.

They walked to the elevator and stepped in.

"This is crazy," Rosa whispered.

"Calm down," Jonah said as he pushed the button. The doors closed, and the glass elevator began its ascent. Rosa looked down at the people in the atrium, who appeared smaller and smaller until they looked like ants scurrying between tunnels.

"Why did you guys ask me to do this?" Rosa asked.

"You know the building," Graham said.

"You remember when I first met you, Rosa?" Shepard asked, "That unkempt hair? The B.O.?"

"Fuck you," Rosa said.

"Seriously," Graham said. "You were like a mouse. I promise no one remembers you."

"Besides," Shepard said. "That dress I picked out with the wig? You bad, girl."

"Oh, fuck off!" Rosa whispered loudly.

They stepped off the elevator and walked onto the floor. It was an open room with black leather couches and dark-gray granite walls. A man with dirty-blond hair stood behind the desk wearing a red tie with a white dress shirt. His sleeves were rolled up to his elbows.

"I picked out this dress," Rosa whispered.

"Stop lying," Shepard said.

"The two of you—shut the fuck up," Jonah said through grinning, clenched teeth. They walked up to the desk. "Hi. We're here to see—"

"Yes," he said, sticking out his hand. "Mr. Tompkins, pleasure. My name is Mr. Stewart. This way, please."

Stewart came from behind the desk and pressed his hand against the wall to open a hidden door. He motioned for them to follow him.

"Forgive me, but Mr. Sayf is not here at the moment," Stewart said as they walked down the dimly lit gray corridor.

Rosa stared at the mahogany-framed black-and-white pictures on the wall. Each picture showed different financiers playing with children in different countries. They stopped in front of an oak door with the initials M. S. carved in gold plating. Across from Sayf's office was an empty glass room.

An emotionless Rosa stared at the room and mumbled to herself, "It's as if I don't…"

"In here, please," Stewart said, smiling.

He opened the door to Sayf's spacious office. It had dark flooring with autumnal-tinted reading lights turning on as the three walked in. Behind the glass desk was the London skyline. Dark clouds swirled in the slate sky.

"I have been placed in charge of Mr. Sayf's affairs while he is away." He walked over to a brown globe. "May I offer you a drink?" Jonah and Rosa gave a polite smile and shook their heads. "Fair enough. You don't mind if I indulge?"

"Please," Jonah said.

Stewart smiled and opened the globe. He took out a bottle of gin and a glass.

"Early, I know," he said filling his glass. "Please." He pointed to the leather seats in front of the glass desk. "So, why Mr. Sayf?" Stewart asked as he sat.

"Well, my partner and I saw an article in *Forbes* a few years back," Jonah said.

Rosa's eyes wandered around the room, staring at the photos of friends and dignitaries plastered throughout the office.

"Shit," Rosa whispered.

"Mrs. Potter?" Jonah asked. His voice snapped Rosa out of her trance.

"I'm sorry?" She asked.

"I was just saying to Mr. Stewart how a couple of Yanks like us got ahold of Marcus Sayf."

"Oh yeah," Rosa said, nodding. "The magazine. It had quite the impact on us."

"Yes," Mr. Stewart said. "Well, he is very good at what he does. However, I'm afraid he has moved on from the private sector and has focused his endeavors in a more philanthropic direction."

"What do you mean?" Jonah asked.

"I'm sorry," Stewart said, staring at Rosa. "You remind me of someone."

"Shit," Graham said.

"Don't panic," Shepard said. "He may have seen you in the cafeteria or somewhere in passing. Just laugh and tell him you get that a lot."

Rosa looked at Stewart for several seconds with a blank expression on her face, then busted into a high-pitched laugh. Jonah winced. His eyes darted back and forth between Rosa and Mr. Stewart. The laugh came to an abrupt stop with only a nervous and disjointed grin left on Rosa's face.

"I get that a lot," she said with a serious expression.

"Very well," Stewart said, raising an eyebrow. "Company portfolio with a net worth of close to a half-billion dollars is something that we take very seriously. That is why we are having this meeting. Although Mr. Sayf is occupied at the moment, I'm certain we can make other arrangements."

"Such as?" Jonah asked.

He glanced over at Rosa. Her head was completely turned, staring at the empty office across the hall.

"Do you want to know what happened?" Stewart asked.

"I'm sorry?" Rosa asked, whipping her head back around.

"There was a global finance officer who worked here. Quite plain-looking thing really. Always wore some dreadful pants suit that she probably grabbed from the bottom of a bin at some decrepit department store. Hair was always out of place, which for the life of me I could never understand, given that she had so many pencils up there." Stewart laughed before taking a sip of his gin. "Her appearance never mattered because the woman was a financial genius. I swear to you the woman dreamed in numbers."

"Sounds like a winner," Jonah said smiling. "I want her. Did she move to another office?"

"No, she didn't," Stewart said, looking at Rosa. "You see, she stole from us."

"You don't say…" Jonah said.

"You know something, Ms. Potter?" Stewart asked. "I couldn't put my finger on it, but I don't remember you. I remember the black dress." He leaned forward in his seat and turned around one of the photos propped on the table. It was a picture of Sayf, Morgan, and Charlie. There was a woman wearing the same black dress with long brown hair. Her arms were wrapped around Charlie's waist. "You see, Ms. Eleanor, that is part of what made you so remarkable. Your profound ability to make people forget you."

Jonah stared at the picture. He looked at Rosa, paralyzed in his seat.

Rosa gave a nervous smile. She chuckled and said, "OK. I think I'll have that drink now."

"Please do," Stewart said.

Rosa got up and walked toward the brown globe. At that moment a black cylinder can rolled to Jonah's foot. Jonah looked down and saw a flash of light. Jonah lost consciousness for the next several minutes. When he opened his eyes, Sayf's office was now blindingly bright. The ringing in his ears continued to echo in his head. He looked over at Stewart, who was being helped up by two men dressed in dark suits. Jonah could only make out slow-motion images of Stewart pointing at him. The men each grabbed one of Jonah's arms and placed a black bag over his head.

⤙

Rosa hurried down box-shaped spiral stairs. When she got to the fifth floor, she could hear shoes stomping against the cement floor echoing toward her. Loud, inaudible voices resonated through the stairwell. She climbed down another flight of steps and walked through a metal door with a large red *4* painted on it. She stepped into a large, empty hallway and sounded the fire alarm propped next to the fire exit. A crowd of people emerged from the glass offices and headed for the stairs. Rosa went with the tide of people heading for the exit. Her black attire was blended into the sea of dark-suited businesspeople. When she got to the ground floor, Rosa placed her back against the wall and peeked through the open door. Security guards dressed in white shirts and red ties were waiting at the atrium exits.

"Shit," she whispered.

After a few moments of panting, Rosa took a deep breath. She bent down and slipped through the fire exit. She waded against the masses who were rushing toward the atrium and headed for the cafeteria, her wig and breasts bouncing with each stride. She took off her high heels and hopped over the buffet line for the kitchen.

"OK, OK," she whispered to herself.

She opened the door to an empty back alley. The smell of garbage filled her nostrils. Next to the door was a brown metal dumpster. She pulled the flesh-colored audio piece from her ear. A clear, thick film remained on the rim of her inner ear. She looked at the sticky fluid that adhered to her index finger and thumb.

"Gross," she whispered.

She flung the earpiece into the metal dumpster and hurried

down the alley, looking over her shoulder every few seconds. When she reached the street, it was crowded with people staring at the skyscraper. Rosa looked at the nearby intersection and saw a red-and-blue cab slowing down for the red light. She scurried to the cab and opened the door, looking over her shoulder one last time before hopping in.

"Bit of a scene there isn't it?" the driver asked. "Where to?"

"Cleveland Street," Rosa said.

✍

Rosa stepped out of the cab and walked through the revolving door of a high-rise apartment complex. She tiptoed past a tan front desk. A tall doorman was sleeping, his cherry red-nose vibrating with each snore, his bulky frame propped up by a wooden countertop. Rosa slipped into the empty elevator and pushed the button for the sixth floor. She stood on the side with her back against the wall. When the door opened, she peeked down the hallway. The doors were painted gray with black trim. The walls had travertine wallpaper plastered on them, giving the illusion that they were made of gray limestone. Rosa stepped onto the hardwood floor and edged down the corridor. When she reached her door at the end of the hallway, she slowly turned the knob left, then right. It was still locked. She took out her house keys and opened the door.

She slowly peered in and sighed with relief at her empty flat. She could tell by the faint smell of pine that her cleaning service had recently come by. Her pile of books on economics and finance was stacked on her table. The double-glass-door entrance leading to her balcony was riddled with mathematic equations written in black marker. In the space across from the couch where most would have a TV were three shelves filled with books. Next to the bookshelf was a metal safe.

Rosa hurried over to the safe and pressed the combination

pad; it popped open. She grabbed a set of car keys and two thick stacks of hundred-dollar bills. After leaving the safe open and rushing for the door, she grabbed the silver knob and stared again at her empty flat. She shook her head and ran quietly into her bedroom. She pulled a pair of blue jeans and a gray T-shirt from her dark-brown drawer covered in Hello Kitty stickers. She put on her clothes, hurried back into the living area, and picked up the keys and cash. She walked to the door, turned around, stared at her empty flat, and shook her head again.

Rosa opened the door and stared down the empty hallway. She closed the door, went back into her apartment, and walked over to the stainless-steel fridge. She pulled out a carton of milk and opened the top, gagging at the rotten smell.

Rosa grabbed a bottle of orange juice and placed it on the tan counter across from the fridge. She opened the cabinet over the kitchen sink and pulled out a glass bowl and a box of cereal. She poured the cereal and orange juice into the bowl at the same time. Rosa stirred and crunched away at the orange juice–cereal concoction. She closed her eyes and gave a sigh of satisfaction, staring out at her balcony. Rain droplets tapped away at the glass door. Dark black clouds churned in the sky, thunder rumbling in the distance. She looked down at her cereal and glanced across the kitchen sink. She stopped crunching. She panned her eyes back across the countertop, hoping that the Glock, resting on a self-help book titled *You and Me: How to Lose Weight and Gain Happiness* was a figment of her imagination. She edged toward the gun and picked it up.

The toilet flushed. Rosa gasped at the guest bathroom across the flat next to the entrance. She held the gun by her side and approached the bathroom door. She held the gun up against the door as whoever was on the other side washed their hands. The silver knob turned and the door creaked open. It was a burly man wearing a black shirt with a cream-colored tie. He wore a pair of yellow-tinted glasses and had a thinning hair line. His sleeves were rolled up, exposing his thick, hairy forearms and sausage fingers. He stared down the barrel without flinching. The two stood in silence. Rosa looked at the man and cracked a slight grin. She pulled the trigger but it didn't budge. She tried again. The trigger refused to pull back. The calm, arrogant expression on Rosa's face was replaced by fear.

The man smiled. He gently put his right hand over her wrist and put the gun down by her side. He then carefully grabbed the weapon from her shivering hand.

"You see, darling," he said with a deep British accent, "the thing is a gun don't shoot if the safety is on." A tear fell from Rosa's trembling cheek as she looked down at the gun. He drew his hand back and drilled the bridge of her nose. She stumbled back, falling onto the floor. He pointed at her and shouted, "You fucking tart! You have any idea how long I've been waitin'?" He drew his leg back as if he were about to kick a soccer ball. The force of his kick made Rosa's body curl around his leg, and she slid a few feet back. "Fucking cunt," he murmured. "Oi! Wankers! Get your arses in here!"

There was a muzzled sound of several creaking doors opening in the hall. A young man with curly dirty-blond hair popped open the door to Rosa's apartment. He looked over and saw Rosa squirming on the floor, her nose dripping with blood, agonizing with each breath.

"Is that her?" the young man asked.

"What the fuck do you think, Tommy? Aren't you supposed to alert me to things? Where were ya?"

"Bob, I-I" Tommy stammered, "I didn't even hear her."

"Well, I guess I can't be too mad at ya. A real mouse, this one is." Rosa rolled onto her stomach and crawled for the door.

"Where are you going, mouse?" Bob asked, grabbing her hair. He dragged her over to an off-white love seat. Still with a grim grasp of her hair, he lifted her off the floor and placed her in the seat. "Let the blokes in the hallway know, and tell them no one is to be on this floor but us."

Tommy nodded and left the room.

"Wait," Rosa whispered.

"What's that, sweetheart?" Bob asked. He grabbed Rosa by the throat with his bloody right hand and started to squeeze, lifting her body from the seat. Rosa grabbed his hand and tried to loosen his grip. He stared at her red face, veins popping from her neck. "Four months I've been in this dump waiting for you," he said with clenched teeth. "Let me tell you how this works. You don't talk unless I tell ya, you don't pass out unless I tell ya, and you don't die unless I tell ya." He released his grip. She fell onto the couch. Before she could catch her breath, Bob yanked her by the shirt and slapped her. The sound echoed through the open flat. "But if you would like, feel free to experience pain anytime."

Tommy walked back through the door and closed it behind him.

Bob glanced over his shoulder and continued.

"When mice like you steal, normally the World Bank lets the authorities handle it. But when the number is to the tune of four-point-two billion dollars, it fucks with their minds. They want justice served with a side of savagery, ya see?" He grabbed her chin. Her brown hair draped over her eyes. Her mouth and nose covered in blood and sweat. "Now, do I look like the former or the latter?" Rosa panted fearfully. "Speak up, darling."

"T-The latter," Rosa murmured.

"I'm glad we at least have this portion of our discussion under wraps. Now, Ms. Eleanor, let's get down to it. Before you tell me where you hid that money, what are the whereabouts of Marcus Sayf and your shit boyfriend, Charlie Parker?"

❦

"How did we miss this?" Shepard asked. He marched down the empty cobblestone sidewalk with his hands stuffed in the pockets of his dark-gray trench coat. He walked with long, purposeful strides in the steady rain. "Look at this bullshit. Always rain with this country," he said, annoyed.

"Minor mistake," Graham said over Shepard's earpiece.

"This wasn't a minor mistake," Shepard said, shaking his head.

"Well…"

"Graham, she was fucking one of them and we missed it! That's minor?"

"We sent the kid, remember? He probably liked her from the beginning. Didn't vet her, I guess."

"Fucking millennials," Shepard said, shaking his head. "They'd cut off their arm for a piece of ass."

"Ten minutes till go time," Graham said.

"And the language," Shepard said.

"What do you mean?" Graham asked.

"The Brits. It's this obnoxious, pretentious, always speaking in prose. Shakespeare died like four hundred years ago, right? You can stop speaking in fucking riddles."

Shepard stepped through the revolving door. He glanced at the red-nosed doorkeeper sleeping behind his desk. The doorkeeper opened his eyes to the sound of Shepard's black dress shoes. He got up from his seat, wiped the drool from the side of his face, and stepped from behind the desk.

"Oi," the doorkeeper said.

"Fuck my life," Shepard whispered. He looked over his shoulder, studying the sturdy old man. "What's your next line? Fe fi fo fum?"

"What did you just say?" The doorkeeper asked. Shepard remained silent. "Listen, you have to call a tenant from my phone to go upstairs."

"I live here."

"No, you don't," the doorkeeper said, scrunching the left side of his cherry-tinted face. "I know every single tenant in this bloody complex, and you ain't one of 'em."

"Old man," Shepard said staring at the elevator stopping at ground level, "you need to fall back."

"Wha?" The doorkeeper said grabbing Shepard's shoulder. "I sug—"

The elevator door opened. The doorkeeper let out a strained wheeze. He looked down at Shepard's elbow in his chest. His knees buckled. Before he could fall, Shepard grabbed him by the head and rammed it into the elevator wall.

"Shut up!" Shepard shouted.

The doorkeeper laid unconscious with his back propped against the elevator wall. Shepard pulled out his nine-millimeter and pointed it at his head.

"Shep," Graham said. A couple came through the revolving door, laughing and wiping the water off their clothes. They looked up to see the open elevator with Shepard hovering over the motionless doorkeeper and froze as Shepard mouthed the words, *Walk away*. When the door had closed and they began to ascend, Shepard cocked his gun and pointed it at the doorkeeper's head.

"Shepard," Graham said with a stern voice.

"What?!"

"We're the good guys, remember?"

Shepard looked at his pistol and rolled his eyes.

"Can't good guys have bad days?" Shepard asked, putting the pistol back in its holster.

"Bad days? Sure. Bad decisions? No."

Shepard pulled out a cigarette and lighter from the lapel of his trench coat. He lit the cigarette and waited for the elevator to stop at the eleventh floor. When the door opened, three men were standing in the hallway. The one closest to Shepard squinted his beady eyes and said, "Wrong floor, mate."

Shepard didn't respond. He took long drags off his Rothmans, sauntering down the corridor as if no one was there. "You deaf, mate?" he asked. He walked toward Shepard with his broad shoulders hunched over. "What's yo—"

Shepard jammed his lit cigarette in the man's eye and pulled out his pistol. He grabbed him by his black wool sweater and shot him in the stomach. The other two men in the hallway drew their weapons and fired back. Shepard used the man as a shield and shot down the other two in the hallway. He then pushed away his human shield and kicked him in the chest. His lifeless body crashed through Rosa's thick wooden door. The scene startled Bob and Tommy. Before they could react, Shepard stepped into the flat and fired two shots, one for each head. Rosa jolted out of her seat.

"Thank God," Rosa whispered.

"I wouldn't thank him just yet," Shepard said calmly.

Rosa looked down at the pistol in his hand.

"Shep-Shepard, I…"

"Choose your next words carefully, Rosa," Shepard said. He looked down at the coffee table and saw a thick hardback called *Quantum Finance*. Shepard picked it up. "You were saying?" He turned the book over and studied the back cover.

"How did you find me?"

"Your earpiece."

"But I threw that away."

"The goo you felt on your ear has nanites that act as a tracker. Part of the Blackout."

"Shepard, this is a misund—"

Shepard grabbed the book by its spine and flung it like a frisbee towards Rosa's head. He assumed she'd catch it effortlessly with one hand. Instead, she slammed her eyes shut and turned her head as the textbook clipped her on her right cheekbone. Her knees wobbled, and she held on to the counter behind her to keep herself from falling. Shepard looked at Rosa confused. Her face turned bright red. She panted and stared at Shepard with ferocity.

"You were supposed to catch that," Shepard said.

"What the fuck, Shepard?" Rosa bellowed.

"Why didn't you…I mean, there's no point in continuing the act…."

"What act?" Rosa asked, waving her hands.

"This… What you're doing…"

Rosa wiped the blood from her nose and snickered.

"Shepard, sit down."

"You do realize…"

"Sit the fuck down, Shephard!"

Shepard looked around for a moment and sat down on the sofa in front of him, his pistol resting on his leg. Rosa paced back and forth.

"You don't want any ice?" Shepard asked.

"I don't know your world, Shepard! I'm not some Shaolin Power Ranger secret-agent ninja! Got it?! I'm not some big-tit crime fighter who wears fucking bifocals to keep appearances." She picked up her glasses from the floor. "You see these?" She asked jabbing at the lens. "They're so thick you can fry a fucking egg." She flung them in the air. "When I was twelve, I ran my bike into a big van, Shepard. It was bright red and it was parked. I'm blind, OK?"

"O-OK," Shepard said as if he were a child.

"You get it, Shepard?! The only costume and lasso I have is the one in the bedroom I used to wear for Charlie," she said, her voice cracking.

"I didn't need to hear that last part."

Rosa touched her bruised face and walked over to the sofa across from Shepard and sat down.

She took a deep breath and said, "Shepard, the only ability I have in this world is that I can add and subtract really fast."

"Well, how long have you been one of them?" Shepard asked timidly as he scratched the back of his neck.

"That's the thing, I'm not." She leaned forward in her seat, blood and sweat dripping from her face. "GFOs have been around for decades."

"Who?"

"Global financial officers, or jackals, as everyone calls them. Once upon a time, their job was to just give newborn republics a chance to grow. To help the Che's of the world become great leaders. In the end though, they realized even freedom fighters, once they took control, were no different and sometimes worse—than their predecessors." Rosa patted the blood from her face with the back of her hand. "Have you ever asked a guy with control of an entire army to pay a loan?"

"Point taken," Shepard sighed. "But I still don't understand. If part of the job title for being a global financial officer is," Shepard made a quotation gesture with his right hand, "finance with some light killing, why hire you on? Your coworkers must have been confused when they hired some American girl straight out of college with no ops training."

"You still don't get it, do you?" Rosa said, smiling. "Shepard, you can't call people coworkers when you're in charge."

Shepard's head tipped to the side. He closed his eyes and asked, "What?"

"Guess how much it is to kill a dictator. Six hundred and fifty million, on average."

"You're getting gypped. I know dudes back in Baltimore who'd take care of that for forty grand."

"It's not enough to just kill a man in power. There's too much global oversight. Big Brother is watching. If you're going to extinguish a flame, it has to look like the wind took it out. You can't be caught holding the bucket of water. Starting a radical government, paying off rioters, providing the weapons and supplies to make Molotov cocktails, every detail leading up to that GFO or whoever is pulling the trigger has a monetary value."

"So how did you become in charge?"

"Over the past several years, GFOs became more centered on the killing than finance. They started hiring ex-MI-6, -KGB, -CIA. Some of them don't bother to negotiate. They just execute."

"And I can imagine killing a client doesn't necessarily keep the lights on either."

"Better believe it," Rosa said, probing her swollen face. Shepard got up and walked over to the fridge. "The Global Finance Department was hemorrhaging money. The jackasses were killing off clients before the ink could dry on their contracts."

Shepard gave Rosa a kitchen towel packed with ice.

"That's why they hired you?" Shepard asked.

"My job was to make the Global Finance Department profitable again. Which meant less killing and better investments. This department does not exist. My title on paper was *foreign translator*."

"So where does Marcus Sayf fit into this equation?"

"He worked for me." Rosa scoffed and said, "The guy is British, African, or Jamaican. Sayf isn't his real name. It's Arabic for *sword*. Probably an alias he took a liking to when he was working for MI-6."

"So, he's some kind of fake-ass James Bond?"

"I guess you could say that, yeah. It's through him I met Charlie, my ex-boyfriend."

"What happened to the relationship?"

"I might be a wallflower but I'm no punching bag. He hit me and I told him to pack his shit." Shepard sat up in his seat and leaned forward, clasping his hands together. "After I broke up with Charlie, Sayf came to me with three assassination requests.

Three dictators in South America. After reviewing his proposals, of course I told him no. He told me these three countries were sitting on one of the biggest oil reserves on the planet. Apparently, some archeologist stumbled on it. He brought in scientists, representatives from OPEC. Of course, this needed to be confidential. I mean if the media or anyone caught wind of what we were trying to do..."

"They would rightfully try to stop you," Shepard said.

"Don't judge me," she said, pointing her dry, bloody finger. "You don't get to do that to me. The revenue stream would equal five times the investment. It just made sense."

"You signed it?" Shepard asked. Rosa nodded. "Did you ever go to South America?" Rosa shook her head. "There was no oil, was there?"

"Just fossils, no fuel," Rosa said, sighing.

"How much did he get away with?"

Rosa took a deep breath.

"Over four billion." Shepard squinted his eyes. "Yeah. He doctored the online banking information to make it look like he was using offshore bank accounts in my name. Marcus and Charlie disappeared and left me holding the check."

"Why come back?"

Rosa shrugged her shoulders.

"Rosa?"

Tears started to glaze over her eyes. She turned her head away to wipe the tears.

"For Jonah," she whispered. "I thought if anything happened, I would know the best plan of escape. But when it came down to it, I only cared about myself. I'm such a piece of shit."

"Fair enough. They caught Jonah."

"I know, Shepard!"

"That's your boyfriend, right? Or is he just your current flavor of the month?"

"Go to hell, Shepard," she said, raising her voice. "My intention was to grab his arm and run together. But the way he looked at me when he saw the pictures of me and Charlie I…I panicked."

Shepard leaned back in his seat and took a deep breath.

"OK," he said, squinting his eyes. "Step out on us again, and I'll continue where my man here left off. Grab your things. We better get going."

Rosa wiped the tears from her eyes and nodded.

"Should be fine," Rosa said. "I think they rented out the entire floor."

"Come to think of it," Shepard said, scratching his cheek. "I'm concerned about the unconscious doorman riding the elevator right now."

"Oh," Rosa said raising her eyebrows, "OK. Let me grab my bag. Shepard?"

"Yeah?"

"You think Jonah will forgive me?"

"I don't know, Rosa," Shepard said.

᪥

"A tough tart this one is."

Jonah heard this in between the crunching sounds of brass knuckles ramming into his ribs. His face was still covered with a black velvet bag, his hands bound behind him as blood and sweat dripped from his chin onto his bare chest.

"Tough fucking tart this one," the voice said again. Jonah could hear him take a few steps back. He smirked at the fact that his attacker was out of breath. "Right then," the voice panted. "Mate, I don't know who you are or how you got involved in all of this, but I need something." Jonah could hear the footsteps circling around him. "Do yourself a favor." He was standing behind Jonah. Jonah felt a sharp pain surge through his arm and then a pop from his shoulder. "Tell me what you know!" His shoulder was dislocated. Then through the pain, Jonah let out a thunderous laugh. The captor kicked the chair and shouted, "What the fuck is so funny?!"

"You're asking me what I know," Jonah said, catching his breath. "The thing is, I don't have the foggiest fucking clue as to what's going on."

"You know what?" the captor asked as he wiped sweat from his dirty-blond hair. "I'm inclined to believe you, mate. Too bad for you my inclinations are fleeting before I start cutting off appendages. So, I suggest you give me something."

"Let's trade information," Jonah said.

The captor looked at the other men in the room and chuckled.

"Trade information? You think you're in a situation to negotiate?"

"I'm not negotiating," Jonah said. "I used to run with a mob syndicate back in New York. I've been where you're standing. I know how this ends."

"Well, mate, if you cooperate maybe…"

"Fuck you," Jonah said. "I know how this ends. Answer my questions and I'll answer yours. When you're done with me, kill that bitch. She's the reason I'm in this situation to begin with."

He looked down at Jonah scratching his stubble. He grabbed a chair, sat down in front of Jonah, and removed the bag from his face.

"Mr. Stewart," Jonah said, grinning. "I thought it was you."

"All right then," Stewart said, taking out a cigarette. "We'll play it your way." He lit the cigarette, took a drag, then placed it in Jonah's mouth. Jonah puffed away as his captor held it. "You first. Talk."

"I met her in the States," Jonah said. "We killed off my syndicate and made away with some cash."

"Which syndicate?"

"The Mayada crime family."

"You killed the Mayada family?" Stewart laughed. "We're off to a bad start, mate. This doesn't work if you don't tell me the truth."

"The newspapers. They say it was a fire, right?"

"That's right."

"It was poison. Garden-variety poison. The fire was her idea." He stared at Jonah's unwavering eyes. He gave Jonah another puff.

"Go on."

"I need to stand," Jonah said.

"What?" Stewart frowned.

"My legs cramp if I sit too long and you know what? I'd rather die standing."

"Go fuck yourself, mate."

"I'll stand over there," Jonah said, nodding his head in the direction of the back-right corner. Stewart gave a sharp sigh. He shook his head and reluctantly pulled himself from his seat. He pulled out a knife and cut the ropes binding Jonah's legs. He grabbed Jonah by the neck and yanked him up from the chair. Jonah gave a slight nod, gesturing at the lit cigarette between Stewart's third and fourth digit. He shook his head and stuffed the cigarette in Jonah's mouth.

"Now, where were you?" he asked, irritated.

"Not much else to add," Jonah said as he blew smoke out of his nose. "I thought we were a thing. So, I followed her here. I thought I knew her, but I don't know her any more than you do." Jonah looked down at the cracked cement floor. "Why'd she come back?" he mumbled to himself.

"If I were in your shoes, mate, I'd be asking the same bloody question. She had to have known we were waiting for her. We didn't think she would be so stupid as to walk through the door. But just in case..."

"Why? I mean, what did she do?"

"She stole over four billion dollars! I say fuck the gallows—straight to the torture chamber with that one, yeah?"

"That bitch," Jonah murmured.

"Alright mate, unless there's anything else..." At that moment, the fluorescent lights in the ceiling started to flicker. "What was that?" The guards drew their handguns and left the room, closing the steel door behind them. "These your people?"

"I don't have any more people," Jonah said. "I told you I worked for the Mayada family. The only people I had was her."

"Tough br—"

"Come in!" a voice screamed over the walkie-talkie. Jonah's captor brought the set close to his ear.

"Problem up there, lads?" Stewart asked.

"We need help, backup, anything—fucking help us!"

"Rory," Stewart said. "Calm down, mate! What's going on up there?" Gun shots and screams crammed the airwaves. "Rory?"

"Help!" Rory screamed. Two close-range shots pounded against the captor's eardrum, followed by silence. He looked at Jonah's calm expression with concern. An explosion went off, causing the entire room to shake. Crumbled drywall fell from the ceiling as the lights continued to flicker. Jonah backpedaled until his back was pressing against the corner of the wall.

"So, you , have friends coming for you," Stewart said.

"I wouldn't call them friends," Jonah said.

"It was you and them who took down the Mayada crime syndicate."

"Well, I never said we did it alone."

"Stay back!" Stewart shouted at the metal door. "Stay back or this little shite is as good as dead!" Jonah took another puff of his cigarette.

"Listen, buddy," Jonah said, "We don't have a lot of time here."

"You mean you've been where I'm standing right?" Stewart asked with a nervous grin.

"You know how this is going to end? Fuck you."

"Man, you catch on quick."

"You by the door?!" Graham's muffled voice shouted.

"Nope!" Jonah shouted.

"How many in the room?!" Graham asked.

"Just one more question, Stew," Jonah said, staring at his captor standing a few feet away from the metal door.

"Go fuck yourself."

"You wouldn't happen to know a psychopath American by the name of Barbara, would you?"

"Wha?" Stewart replied, confused.

"Shit," Jonah whispered. He turned around and faced the wall. "Never mind."

Jonah covered his face and turned around. BOOM. The thick metal door popped off its steel hinges. The door glided through the air, crashing against Stewart's head. A red laser beam flashed past his eyes and was pointing at his chest. Jonah could see a shadow appear from the smoke.

"You get any information?" Graham asked.

Jonah didn't respond. He stared at Graham for a moment.

"Yeah, Graham, I'm fucking fine. Thanks for asking."

∽

Knock-knock. Rosa gasped. She stared at Shepard and tightened her fist on the kitchen countertop. Shepard placed his index finger on his lips, gesturing for her to be quiet. He picked up his nine-millimeter from the coffee table and walked stealthily toward the door. Graham and Jonah were standing in the broken doorway.

"Door's open," Shepard said, placing his gun back in its holster.

"I see that," Graham said, walking into Rosa's apartment. "Figured you'd be on edge, so I knocked."

Shepard nodded. Jonah walked in behind Graham and

locked eyes with Rosa. His eyes widened. He could feel his heart bursting from his chest. His breathing labored. Rosa stared back with her mouth open, desperately trying to speak, only to stutter before letting out a shallow sigh. Jonah pulled out his handgun and pointed it at Rosa. The draw was so quick, Shepard barely got out of the way before Jonah opened fire. The bullets rang through the entire apartment, smashing through the refrigerator, cabinets, and white tiles. Rosa didn't blink, only shuddered at the sound of the gunfire. Jonah emptied his entire clip into the kitchen. She stood frozen, staring straight ahead into Jonah's eyes. He looked at her as he holstered his gun. He closed his eyes and took a deep breath as the intense expression that had been on his face faded. He opened his eyes and looked at Rosa, emotionless and calm.

"Well, that's how I feel," Jonah said. He let his head fall limp to the side. "We better get moving," he said in a monotone.

Shepard walked toward Rosa and snapped his fingers. The loud pop jolted her back to consciousness.

"Gun shots, dead people—we need to leave."

She looked at Shepard, nodding with detached tears streaming down her face.

"Sh-Should I talk to him?" she asked meekly.

Shepard and Graham looked at each other. Shepard looked down at the floor and sighed before walking out of the room. Graham placed his hands in the pockets of his black slacks and smiled.

"Maybe you give him a little space," he whispered.

Assumptions

Pink and purple glittered confetti shimmered from the night-club rafters. The crowd, gyrating on the multicolored LED dance floor, cheered. Onlookers from the second-floor balcony pointed and gawked with amusement at the debauchery below. Scantily clad waitresses dressed in schoolgirl uniforms strutted through the club. A young Thai girl with long brown hair was sitting on the lap of an American patron. She had tied the bottom of her white oxford shirt into a knot. The loud, thumping base of tribal house music brought her bubblegum-glittered lips close to his cheek. The whiff of her knockoff Chanel perfume and gentle ear nibbles was all it took. She grabbed him by his dark gray T-shirt and led him out of the club. Kiet watched this and smiled from his VIP seat in the far-left corner of the club. From this point of view, he could see the balcony, the entrance, and the exit, which was to the left of his seat. He was surrounded by his men, who were slamming shots so hard their pistols bounced on the large metal round table. A restless woman sat in his lap. She rocked her hips to the rhythm of the music. Her long black hair had purple extensions that matched her skin-tight purple dress. She laid her body close to his, wrapping her arm around his head and gently scratching his clean-shaven face with her long purple fingernails. She leaned her head back to kiss his cheek. A young waitress crossed through the dance floor and approached the VIP table. She bowed apologetically and crawled to Kiet. She presented to him a cellphone as if it were an offering.

"What is this?" Kiet asked.

The young waitress was silent. Kiet pushed his private dancer off of him and grabbed the cellphone as she crawled back to the crowded dance floor and disappeared. Kiet and his men winced at the phone before it started to vibrate in his hand. He pressed the green button and held the phone to his ear.

"Nice club," Sayf said.

"Sayf?" Kiet frowned.

"The schoolgirl uniforms are a nice touch. If you're into that sort of thing."

"This is everyone's thing," Kiet said as he stood up. He snapped his fingers at his men, signaling them to pick up their weapons. "Fucking is fucking right?"

"Not everyone aspires to fuck a child."

"More than you think," Kiet said, looking around. "Where are you? Let me buy you a drink."

"I'm right across from you, mate." Kiet stood on his chair and saw Sayf sitting at a small table under the balcony on the other side of the dance floor. He held up his glass. "I see you. As you can see, I already have one. Little watered down, actually."

"You had a chance, Mr. Sayf. You had a chance to run and instead you choose to antagonize me."

"And fifteen dollars?" Sayf grimaced. "It might not be a lot to you but to the traveler on a budget? That's a lot of money."

"You know what? I'm not going to kill you. I have thirty men in this building. Seven on the dance floor, eight at the bar, seven sitting with me, and five above you." He got down from the chair. "I'm gonna take my time with you. Gonna send monthly pieces of you back to the World Bank!"

"That's not thirty. It's twenty-seven." Sayf took his last gulp and slammed it on the table top. "You assume that I'm a representative of the World Bank, when that can't be further from the truth. And finally…" Kiet looked up. A string of Slokranian soldiers lined the balcony, each holding an Uzi. "What makes you think I came here alone?"

Kiet's eyes widened as he stared at the firing squad above him.

"I thought they killed all of them."

"Ah!" Sayf said, pointing at Kiet. "Assuming is an extension of an inability to pay attention to detail. It's lazy, Kiet! And you're better than that, mate!"

"You won't kill all of these innocent people just to get to me," Kiet scoffed.

"Kiet, my friend," Sayf said, sighing, "You are overestimating my respect for human life."

The soldiers on the balcony raised their weapons and opened fire. Bystanders crouched and ran for cover while Kiet's men tried to fire back. Bottles on neon displays exploded, glass shrapnel showering the backs of bartenders lying flat on the floor. Sayf watched the carnage with his back against the wall. A curly haired bouncer dressed in a black suit and tie came rushing in, toting a Glock. Sayf, who was standing in the corner by the entrance, drew his nine-millimeter and pulled the trigger. The hollow-tip shell ripped through the back of the bouncer's head. Brain matter and skull pieces splattered all over a go-go dancer's face. She screamed and ran out of the club. Sayf placed his gun back by his side and continued to watch. The first hail of bullets, which were intended for Kiet, had ripped through his men and his private dancer instead. He kicked over the large circular metal table and took cover. He pried an automatic Glock from the lifeless hands of one of his men and darted for the exit behind the DJ table.

Sayf slid along the brick wall of the club with his nine-millimeter close to his chest. The remnants of Kiet's men pushed, shoved, and shot patrons as they tried to get to Sayf. The Slokranian soldiers on the balcony mowed them down before they could get halfway across the chaotic dance floor. Sayf skirted past the DJ table and was headed for the back exit. A bouncer stood at the exit, holding a young woman dressed in a black-and-white plaid Catholic school uniform as a shield. Sayf fired two shots into her chest and one into the bouncer's forehead. Sayf put his handgun down and ran outside. Before he could catch a whiff of the city air, shots rang past his ear. He dropped to the ground and crawled to a green-and-yellow taxi. Bullets ripped through the cab and into bystanders trying to escape the club. Sayf ran as the hail of bullets followed him from car to car. He crouched behind a small pink Datsun and looked up. It was a dark, narrow alleyway. Sayf crossed the street and placed his back against the wall of a brick building next to the alley, edging his way to the corner. Sayf quickly retracted his head when he saw flashes of white coming from the alley. Brick was pulverized where his head once was.

Sayf peeked around the corner again. It was quiet. He slid off the wall and cautiously crept down the alleyway. He looked to his left and saw old homeless men. They held onto cardboard boxes and covered themselves, too drunk and scared to run away. The alley smelled like a fusion of stale Indian and Chinese food. He passed a bullet-riddled motorcycle with a lifeless biker and an Uzi next to it. He smirked and whistled "Paint It Black" as he began strolling down the narrow alley. When he got near the end, he could hear whispering. The alley opened to a concrete clearing with a series of cement balconies. The residents had all run inside, staring through slits of their tattered curtains. Kiet was sitting at the dead end of the alley, holding a machete.

"Out of bullets, mate?" Sayf asked.

"Put the gun down," Kiet said. "Fight me like man."

"What?" Sayf scoffed. "What movie you think we're in, mate?"

Sayf raised his gun and shot Kiet four times, one bullet for each limb. Kiet fell to the ground, screaming. Sayf kicked the machete out of the way and leveled his pistol at Kiet's head. Kiet looked up at Sayf with blood oozing from his limbs, spewing profanities in his native tongue between each labored breath.

"You kill me, you will never find that woman."

"See, that's the thing, I already know where she is," Sayf said before firing two shots into Kiet's skull.

A Good Night's Sleep

A black Super Stallion helicopter flew through the clear midnight sky. Its blades rotated in near-silence, only emitting a faint high-pitched scream while cutting through the crisp spring air. Twelve soldiers sat strapped in their seats, loading their rifles. Their faces were covered with black camouflage and night-vision goggles.

"Sam," Mark whispered. Sam looked up from her rifle. "You think you can spare a cigarette?"

"I gave it up," she said, loading her rifle. "Hubby got me back on the patch."

"You've got to be fucking kidding me! When?"

"When we decided we want to have a baby."

"Fine time to pick getting pregnant."

"We haven't officially started," Sam said, shaking her head.

Mark sighed and said, "Hate to be the bearer of bad news, my friend, but there is a high likelihood that you guys may never start. You get him out of the country?"

"Yep," Sam said, removing the goggles. "He's staying with family in Canada."

"Good girl," Mark said.

He rested his head on the back of his seat and closed his eyes.

"Mark?"

"Yeah?"

"You were here when it was the three of them. Was that other Wolf as crazy as Barbara?"

"Who, Sean? No. He was actually the voice of reason."

"So why'd they kill him?"

"You'd have to ask Barbara that. Go ahead. Just before she snaps our backs in two for this dumb shit we're doing, make sure to ask her."

"You think this is a bad idea?" Sam asked, squinting.

Mark glanced at her from the corner of his eye, sighed, and said, "Not bad. Just dumb."

Shepard sat on the edge of the open helicopter. He stared down at the landscape of greens beneath him, his feet dangling from a quarter-mile up. He held onto the gunner and looked over his shoulder.

"Thinking of jumping?" Graham asked through his microphone.

"Naw," Shepard said, "Just admiring nature."

"You know if we run into some turbulence, you could bounce right off sitting like that."

"Thanks, Mom." Shepard turned around and smiled at Graham, who was holding up his middle finger. "Better save that aggression."

"I'm not worried about them," Graham said, holding onto to his colt MA1 assault rifle. "You know she's gonna kill us, right?"

"No, she won't."

"Yeah," Graham scoffed. "She will."

"Right is right. Fuck Ashcroft. And definitely fuck her. I'm not killing children."

"Obviously," Graham said, sighing, "You're not the only one. The *aye's* of 7721 had it."

"And you know what, Graham? Fuck you, too."

"Fuck me? Why?"

"Because you voted to kill 'em!" Shepard said. He glanced at a snarling Graham before looking back down at the forest beneath him. "Cowardly fuck."

"You know that wasn't from a place of fear. It was a calculation."

"Graham…"

"Shepard, listen to me. We do this, Barbara is going to kill all of us. Or have you figured out how to stop a Wolf?"

"No, I have not."

"Then like I said, this is a fucking suicide mission, and it doesn't need to be!"

"Graham, we're the good guys. Or least we're supposed to be. 7721 is not."

"Stop with the lecture."

Graham looked down at his sniper rifle resting under his boot. He unbuckled his seat, grabbed his Colt MA1 and his sniper rifle. He walked over to the open hatch door where Shepard was sitting and looked down.

"If you're so against this, why are you here?"

"Because in the end, as futile as all of this is," Graham said as he threw his weapons over his back, "I agree with you."

Shepard looked up at him, and the two bumped fists.

"Just keep that bitch in check," Shepard said.

Graham smiled and nodded. He put on his night-vision goggles before jettisoning himself from the helicopter. Shepard watched his body free fall through sky before a black parachute appeared.

"Shepard," the pilot said. "We're about five hundred yards

out from the drop point." Shepard pulled himself up and walked to his seat.

"Listen up," Shepard said, standing over his soldiers. "I'm asking you guys to do something that goes directly against Ashcroft's orders. The last time someone went against a Blackstar general's orders the repercussions were…severe."

"To hell with 'em, chief," one of the soldiers said.

Shepard smiled.

"Do the rest of you feel the same way?" Shepard asked.

"Yes, sir!" they all shouted.

"OK, then. Once on the ground, the south unit will jam communications and power. From that point on, we go dark. Any soldier you come across catches a bullet. Any receptionist working late gets a bullet. If you come across anyone that is not wearing a lab coat, they get a bullet. I aim to make this complex disappear tonight. Got it?"

"Yes, sir!" they shouted.

"Good." Shepard stomped his feet twice. "Ashes to ashes."

"Dust to dust!" they shouted.

In front of the research compound, a young Korean stood guard in front of a black electric fence. He held his pistol up in the air with his back against a gray brick pillar, pretending to shoot down airplanes as they passed over him. "Pow-pow," he whispered. The young guard took off his navy-blue cap and ran his fingers through his short brown hair, sighing. He reached into his back pocket and pulled out a magazine. Soon after he started to flip through the pages, a man appeared from a forest across from the compound.

He limped across the wide dirt road toward the gated building. His torn blue jeans dragged across the ground as he carried a tattered red-and-white polka-dot hiking bag. He stopped in the middle of the street and stared at the young Korean guard. The guard placed the magazine by his side and the two stared at each other for a moment.

"*Bonjour*," the man said, "um…*pouz*…um…*maider*?" The guard shook his head and shrugged his shoulders. "Why can't you speak English?" he whined. "It's bad. I know. So American, right?" He said, chuckling. "In another man's country, and you still expect them to speak English."

"What do you need?" the guard asked with a thick Korean accent.

"Oh, thank God," the man said, sighing with relief. "Listen, buddy, I need some help. I was camping on the other side of the hill and I fell down a ditch. I think it might be a sprain but I need to call a cab to get back to the hotel."

"Stop!" the young guard shouted. He grabbed the holster of his pistol. "You can't come in!"

"Whoa," the man said. "Easy. Look I just need to borrow a charger and I'll be out of your hair." The guard furrowed his brows. He sighed and grabbed his walkie-talkie from his jacket. The man stood in the middle of the road, leaning against his walking stick, listening to the Korean conversation. The guard nodded and placed the walkie-talkie back on his hip.

"OK," the guard said. "I have charger. Give me phone."

"Thank you so much," the man said.

He walked across the street to the guard and handed him his cellphone. It was a black square with no dial pad. A blue light flashed in its right-hand corner. The guard took out a circular pad and placed the device on the charger.

"Who make this phone?" the guard asked, studying it.

"I don't know," the man said. "It was free with my plan." The guard placed his back against the brick wall, staring at the black square device.

"I didn't get your name," the man said sticking out his hand.

"Shepard Black." The guard looked at Shepard's hand and continued studying the device. "OK, then," Shepard said, putting his hands in the pockets of his jeans.

"What a gorgeous fucking night to kill children," a voice said over Shepard's earpiece.

"Isn't this a gorgeous country?" Shepard asked the guard.

"The question is, who do I shoot?" the voice asked. "You or K-pop? Did I tell you the time I fucked a thirteen-year-old girl?" Shepard could hear the voice crunching on potato chips in his ear. "Yeah, it was back in Iraq. Fucked her with my hunting blade. She had this olive skin with gray eyes." Shepard was in the crosshairs of a sniper rifle. The black device in the guard's hand flashed green.

"This..." the guard said grimacing. "This is not..."

"So what's it gonna be, Shep? You or K-pop?"

Shepard remained silent.

"What this?" the guard asked.

"Let's leave it to the song of fate," the voice said, cracking another chip into her mouth. "Eeny..."

The guard dropped the black device and grabbed Shepard by his shirt.

"What is this?!" he shouted, pushing Shepard.

"Meeny..."

The guard continued yelling at Shepard as he reached for his pistol.

"Miny..."

As the guard was unholstering his weapon, Shephard heard the person on the other end of his walkie-talkie lock and load their rifle.

"Pop."

She pulled the trigger. It took less than a second for the hollow-tipped bullet to cut through the sky before going through the guard's head. Speckles of blood splattered onto Shepard's face.

The square device turned red. At that moment, the entire research facility went black.

"7721, this is Barbara. Everyone dies in that building. The cleaning lady, the front desk…" Barbara continued to give a list of random job titles through her earpiece.

Shepard laid the body on the ground, took off his camping backpack, and unrolled it. He pulled out a bolt cutter and started to clip off metal bars from the fence. Four shadowed figures crossed the road, their faces covered by night-vision goggles and dark-green camouflage.

"What the fuck, Shepard?" Mark asked as he loaded his rifle.

"Can't worry about her right now," Shepard said, popping off the gait hinges. "We stick to the plan."

"What about the non-hostiles?" Sam asked, staring at a man and a woman running out of the building.

"What about them?" Shepard asked.

"They're not armed, sir," Mark said.

Shepard sighed. He looked up at the hills behind him, knowing that Barbara was watching him through her scope. Shepard raised his rifle and shot them in the head.

"She's watching," Shepard whispered. He turned around and stared venomously at the hills behind him so that Barbara could see his face. "Seargent, this isn't the fucking Boy Scouts. Wolf said to kill everyone. Best you get in line." Shepard turned around and waved for them to follow him. "This is Shepard. South entrance breached. Status?"

"North unit," a voice said in Shepard's earpiece. "North entrance breached. Coming in through the back."

"East unit," another voice said. "East side flanked. No entrance, though. Planting inferno on the building generator. We are setting up to scale the wall to the third floor. Where's the package?"

"West unit," another voice said. "West side flanked. Inferno planted. Moving through side door now." Gunshots could be heard in the background. "Engaging now. Packages are on the ninth floor. Heading to the eighth now. Will have more intel in a minute."

"Listen," Shepard said. He walked across the broken glass door frame of the front entrance. "Set your infernos to fifteen minutes each. We're on that helicopter in thirteen."

"Yes, sir!" they all replied.

"Shep," Mark said, pointing at the stairwell entrance.

Shepard nodded. They walked toward the stairwell. Sam and Shepard stood alongside the door with their rifles close to their chests. Shepard glanced at Mark and nodded. They could hear footsteps stomping down the stairwell. Flashlights flickered under the wooden entrance. Mark kicked the door off its hinges and unloaded an entire clip. The guards tumbled down the steps to his feet. Sam walked past Mark and looked up at the square-shaped stairwell.

LED flashlights bounced in the darkness while guards shouted in Korean. Sam looked at Shepard and pointed up. Shepard nodded, and the five of them started to head up the steps. They moved quietly, popping around each corner and shooting down anyone traversing down the stairwell.

"This is east unit," a voice said through Shepard's earpiece. "We are on the eighth. Shepard, your location?"

"Just opening the fire exit to the ninth," Shepard whispered as he opened the door. He was blinded by bright fluorescent lights. Just before the flash, he saw the distorted figures of three guards raising their pistols. Shepard closed his eyes and ducked as bullets flew over his head. He raised his rifle and fired three shots. Shepard lifted his goggles onto his forehead and opened his eyes. The three guards laid motionless on the floor.

"How the hell did you do that?" Mark said, walking past Shepard.

"Tip drills," Shepard said standing up. "Keep a perimeter. East unit, you copy?"

"They must have generators on this floor," Sam said.

She squinted as she took off her goggles.

"East Unit," a voice said over the airwaves. "We're under the lab and we got the X-ray up and running."

"Report, East," Shepard whispered. "'Cause we're flying blind." They traveled down the corridor in a box formation with Shepard in the middle. Moments later Shepard and his unit were standing in front of Zaidi's lab.

"There're two rooms," East Unit reported. "Room one..."

"That's the black room," Shepard said.

"The packages are in there," East Unit said. "They're sitting down, legs crossed. Hands in their laps. Two hostiles are in there. They appear to be arguing."

"And the white room?" Sam asked.

"Nine guards," the voice said.

"What's the plan?" Mark asked.

"East Unit," Shepard said. "You got any quicksand?"

"Of course," the voice said. "But if we sink that white room, the two hostiles in there with Zaidi and his packages might get trigger-happy."

"We got em," Shepard said, walking over to the black-room door. "Nitro." Mark grabbed two cylindrical tubes with *liquid nitrogen* written on the top and placed it on the hinges of the door. "Get it ready. On my call, you crumble that floor."

"Roger," the voice said.

Shepard looked at the stopwatch on his wrist.

"Six minutes, thirty seconds, guys," Shepard said.

"This is exciting!" Barbara said over the earpiece.

"Listen," Shepard said. "If you don't have anything to add, shut the fuck up."

"I just want to let you know, Shepard," Barbara said chuckling. "You're gonna die in there!"

"Shepard," East Unit said. "Quicksand set and ready."

"What's gonna happen? What's gonna happen? Whats gonna happen," Barbara continued whispering in the background.

~

Zaidi and his family sat on the floor of the black room. They sat quietly in a circle as two pistol-toting guards hovered around them. Zaidi looked from the corner of his eye at the argument taking place among the guards in the white room. He looked around at his foster children. Black-tinted tears fell from Eshe's mascara-lined eyes. He crawled on all fours over to her and put his arm around her wiry shoulders.

"Soon over, my child," Zaidi said in Arabic.

Then, in the midst of the silence, Zaidi heard a faint sizzling sound. It was coming from the door. Frost foamed at the foot of the door and slowly ascended. The sizzling sound changed to ice cracking against itself. The two guards stared at the door as it started to crack. They looked over at the guards in the white room arguing, unaware of what was happening in the black room. The metal door, now a brittle sheet of ice, collapsed on itself. Smoke from the door blew into the room and the two guards turned their heads away. When they looked up, Shepard was standing at the doorway with his rifle pointed at them.

"Drop 'em," Shepard said.

The floor of the nine guards in the white room dissolved from under them. Shepard fired two rounds from his rifle into the temples of the guards in front of him. Eshe crawled away toward the window to the white room. Her trembling hands grabbed the windowpane and pulled herself up. Eshe shrieked at the horror below her. The nine guards were mowed down execution-style by a flurry of bullets. Their bodies shook and splattered the wall behind them bloody red. Zaidi ran to Eshe and covered her eyes.

"You made copies of the work?" Shepard asked. Zaidi nodded. "Let's move! We have less than three minutes to get to the roof. "

They marched down the corridor to the stairwell. Zaidi's children whimpered at the sight of bodies strewn across the wide stairwells. They climbed up to the twelfth floor and merged with the other three units. Shepard kicked open the door to the roof. Two guards were on the ground facedown, each of them with a hole in their backs the size of grapefruits. Shepard looked up from the bodies and stared in the direction of the adjacent hills. The other units, Zaidi, and his children stood on the rooftop huddled into a circle behind Shepard.

"How much time we got?" Mark asked, staring down at the compound.

"About sixty seconds," Shepard said.

"Fuck me sideways," Barbara said over the intercom. "You got them all up on the roof, safe and sound." She stared at Shepard's expressionless face from the scope of her sniper rifle. "I didn't know you were about that life, Shep. Since no one is gonna survive, this was your plan? To watch them burn from the chopper?"

"I'm not leaving them, Barbara," Shepard said, stoic.

"Now we're talking, Shep," Barbara said, switching off the safety. "I've been waiting for a reason. If 7721 is gone, I could get back to harvesting for the Blackout myself, so please...." Her trigger finger and voice trembled. "Give me one..." A smile came across Shepard's face. "What?" she asked.

"Check your nine," Shepard said.

"My nine or your nine?" Barbara asked.

"Mine," Shepard said.

Barbara turned her head to the right and looked down at a beam wandering next to her hip.

"Hey, Barb," Graham said over the airwaves.

"Graham?" Barbara said with a chuckle. "You couldn't shoot me if your gun was pointed down my throat. I'm gonna watch your team burn, and then I'm gonna take that gun you got there and make you eat it."

"You think it's a rifle I'm holding?" Graham asked. "Shepard ain't going nowhere. Put your sights on me." Barbara's eyes glanced to the right for moment before she looked down her scope in Graham's direction. He was kneeling deep in a patch of forest about a mile and half away. A rocket launcher was pointed in Barbara's direction. "Got your attention now?"

"Even if you fire that before I pull my trigger, I'll be long gone before it hits."

"Normally, I would agree with you, but this here missile's been Blackedout. Did you know we all give off different heat signatures? Well, this guy can differentiate if programed, and boy does he have a crush on you."

A silent wind blew over Barbara like a blanket. It was a black Boeing Chinook flying toward the facility. Barbara placed her sights back on Shepard's grin.

"You want to play tag, friend?" Graham asked. "Then pull the trigger."

As the chopper made its way to the rooftop, four fires erupted like volcanoes high into the dark-blue sky. The flames slowly headed for the main building, incinerating everything in their path. The chopper hovered only a few feet over the roof. The four units placed the children and Zaidi on board before hopping onto the helicopter. Rage flashed across Barbara's face.

"OK," she said, breathing heavily. She bowed her head and smiled. "OK," she whispered. Through her scope, Barbara could see Shepard giving her one last wink before he hopped onto the chopper. Soon afterward, the building crumbled into the glowing molten steel beneath it.

The helicopter landed near Graham.

"By the way," Graham said, firing the missile. Barbara's eyes tracked the missile cut hundreds of feet into the sky before falling straight down. It rammed into Barbara's metallic Humvee parked at the bottom of the hill. Metal shrapnel flew past her.

Unflinching, Barbara continued to stare at the chopper picking up Graham. "We didn't Blackout anything. Just a regular missile."

Barbara continued to chuckle at the end of each labored breath and watched the chopper disappear over the dark horizon. She lifted her sniper rifle over her head and snapped it in two across her knee.

"DAMMIT!" she screamed.

❧

It was morning. The black Boeing chopper had just landed on the roof of a gray five-story building in Copenhagen, which stood behind a tall gray tile wall guarded by armed soldiers at the front gate. Zaidi and his children hopped off the chopper. Eshe smiled at the view of the sun coming over the Baltic Sea.

"Once again, Ray," Graham said, "not a moment too soon, right?"

Ray gave a grin and nodded. He powered down his helicopter and jumped out of the cockpit.

"I know, I cut it close," Ray said, coming around the corner of the helicopter. He glanced at Shepard unloading supplies. "I had to wait until your bluff went through. If the Wolf didn't buy it, she would've just shot at the gas tank."

"I'm just giving you a hard time, old man," Graham said. "Listen, when we get to England, first round of pints on me."

"Sounds good. What sounds better is all of us cracking open those two bottles of scotch I got in my quarters."

"You flyboys," Graham said, slapping Ray on the shoulder. "See you downstairs. You coming, Shep?"

"I'll be there in a second," Shepard said. "Just hold the elevator for me."

Graham nodded and jogged to catch up with the rest of the team. Shepard looked at Ray and sighed.

"Time for the lecture," Shepard said.

"What in the hell are you doing?" Ray asked.

"Working on a good night's sleep," Shepard said.

Ray scoffed and said, "You think this is funny? When Upstead planted you here, it was to fry bigger fish. Remember? Not…"

"Not what?" Shepard asked. "Saving a bunch of foster kids and their dad?"

"No, Shepard! Going against Ashcroft and his fucking Wolves!"

Shepard sighed. He folded his arms and looked away.

"You violated a direct order," Ray said. "That places you in the crosshairs of Ashcroft and that psycho."

"Look, I can—"

"Don't tell me you can handle Barbara, son!" Ray took another step closer. "'Cause you never could," he said, pointing at Shepard's chest.

"Are we finished, Lieutenant Hayward?" Shepard asked.

Hayward shook his head and stepped aside. Shepard walked briskly toward the elevator and stepped on with Zaidi, his family, and the rest of 7721. Hayward and Shepard locked eyes before the door closed.

꠸

Two soldiers standing guard at the front gates leaned against the gray tile wall, thumbing through Facebook messages. In the distance, a faint hissing buzzed at their eardrums. The two soldiers looked at each other before looking up. A small crop plane, rapidly dropping altitude, was heading for the entrance. The guards opened fired before running out of the way. The plane slammed through the gates, lifting dirt and cement and sliding through the front parking lot before crashing through the glass front entrance. Within seconds, guards carrying submachine guns surrounded the plane.

"Get out with your hands up!" a soldier shouted. The plane

door was kicked open. Barbara stepped out, holding an assault rifle. "Ma'am?" the soldier said, grimacing. "Why would you—"

"Where are they?" Barbara asked calmly.

"Who, ma'am?" The soldiers lowered their weapons.

"7-7-2-FUCKING-1!!!"

"Th-They just got here. The elevator should be…" Barbara shoulder-bumped the soldier out of her way. She hopped down eight flights of steps until she was in the basement. Barbara kicked open the doors to a large underground hangar. One of the scientists wearing a black lab coat waved his hands.

"Hey," he said. "You're not sup—" Barbara shot him in the kneecaps, not missing a stride. She reloaded her rifle. Her eyes fixed on the elevator shaft climbing down toward the hangar. Barbara stopped and pointed her assault rifle at the elevator door.

"Open. Open. Open. Open you motherfuck…" her psychotic rage was subdued by the sounds of several rifles locking. She looked over her shoulder. Eight soldiers made a half-circle around her with Santiago in the middle.

"Santi?" she asked.

"Hey, Barb," Santiago said, sighing.

"The last time I heard you say hi like that was when we killed Sean." Barbara looked at the ropes hanging from the rafters of the underground hanger. "You were waiting for me. I guess me dropping my gun won't change the inevitable, will it?"

"Not this time, Barb."

"What kind of rounds you boys got? Hollow tips?"

"You know it."

Barbara looked at the elevator as it approached the hangar floor.

"Aww," Barbara said smiling. "This execution squad isn't just for me is it?"

"No," Santiago said.

When the elevator doors opened, Shepard saw Barbara

standing in front of Santiago and his men, all holding rifles, all pointed at the elevator. He looked into Barbara's big brown eyes, her madness piercing through her intense, sadistic grin. Shepard placed his body in front of the elevator, stretching his arms as far as he could. Just before the first shot sounded, he could see Barbara mouth two words:

"I win."

The first rounds went through Shepard, hitting Graham, who was standing behind him. Bullet holes and blood covered the metal walls. Barbara was pushed into the elevator by the firing squad. Santiago and his men unloaded their rifles on the elevator. When Santiago fired his last round, there was silence. Smoke rose over the motionless bodies piled in the elevator. Santiago sighed, shaking his head at the massacre in front of him.

"What do we do with the bodies?" A soldier asked.

"Take them out to the Baltic and drop 'em." Santiago cleared his throat and said, "I never had the stomach for this."

Upscale Depravity

A jet-black limousine with halogen lights cruised down a congested Cotai strip. Hot-pink, yellow, and blue fluorescent lights shimmering from skyscraper casino hotels reflected off of the limo's tinted windows. The limo turned into a gold coach gate in front of a red-and-black casino. At the opening gates stood two giant gold-painted laughing Buddhas wearing bright-red monk attire with red-and-black beads to match. Valets wearing red polo shirts with black slacks hustled between cars. The driver stepped out, marched toward the passenger door, opened it, and stood aside, bowing his head. Sayf stepped onto the red carpet leading toward a red wooden double door. He wiped down his black shirt and black jacket, then straightened his bright-red tie before walking through the giant double doors. A waitress dressed in a red-and-black traditional Chinese dress approached Sayf.

"Welcome, Mr. Sayf," she said smiling. "Mrs. Luthra is enjoying a ballet in the west wing. Would you like for me to take you there?"

Sayf's eyes glanced over the woman, her silk dress tightly hugging her petite, well-toned body.

"That won't be necessary, darling," Sayf said.

He took out a cigar, which the waitress cut for him before pulling out a pack of matches. She lit it, then bowed deeply as Sayf walked past her. He stepped into a large foyer decorated with red lamps that floated over gold-plated marble tiles. The casino itself was the size of a football stadium. Glaring sounds of jackpot machines and fast-paced hip-hop attacked Sayf's senses. He strolled across the room with his hands in his pocket, watching as the patrons slammed shots onto dark wooden blackjack tables. He walked past the high-rollers table and took an escalator to the second floor. People stood in a circle watching acrobats performing backflips off craps tables onto chairs held by their partners' feet as they did handstands. He approached a door to the backroom manned by two bodyguards.

"Good evening, Mr. Sayf," one of them said.

"Been a while, fellas," Sayf said.

"Shall I guide you to Mrs. Luthra?"

"That won't be necessary," Sayf said walking past the guards. He walked into the kitchen. The chef stood at the saucier station, trying a green concoction made by his sous chef.

"What the fuck is this?!" he screamed.

"Sorry, chef."

"You're fucking up!" The chef looked around at the organized chaos and shook his head. "All of you are fucking up!"

"Yes, chef!" The whole room shouted.

"That's no way to talk to your employees," Sayf said.

"Who the fuck are..." The chef turned around and his face turned pale. He quickly bowed his head and stepped out Sayf's way. "Forgive me, sir," the chef said with a wavering voice. "I did not know..."

Sayf remained silent and continued to walk through the

kitchen. The sound of banging pots and pans started to fade as Sayf continued down a creaking wooden stairwell. When he reached the bottom, he walked through a glass door. Nattily dressed men and women wearing masquerade masks sat over circular pits throughout a large, oval-shaped room. It was quiet. No music to lighten the ambience. Security dressed in black suits carrying automatic weapons patrolled the perimeter, their black loafers crunching against the black, sandy floor. From each of the pits echoed different sounds: Flesh pounding against flesh, bones breaking, men gasping for air as they were choked to death, women screaming in ecstasy.

Sayf walked over to one of the pits and looked down. It was an old man sitting with his legs crossed hooked up to a heart monitor. His eyes were sunken, his body frail and deconditioned. The chatty crowd sat in leather chairs while sipping on cognac. Sayf took a puff from his cigar and continued walking. He walked to the elevator, receiving respectful nods from the guards. The elevator flew by the casino and stopped on a floor with no number. The wall behind him opened to the sound of Vivaldi lightly playing in the background. He turned around and stepped onto a red velvet balcony. A woman with long black hair was sitting on a gold velvet couch. She wore a dark-blue lace dress with a matching choker that covered an old knife wound across her slender neck. Sayf took a puff on his cigar.

"Marcus, the cigar," she said calmly.

Sayf handed the cigar to the guard standing at the elevator. He placed his hands in his pockets and walked over to the couch. He took a seat and looked down. It was a young girl walking a tightrope. Sayf looked over at the woman sitting with her hands in her lap, watching the show. Her striking facial features were content. Her gray eyes sparkled with the flashing lights.

"All the data out there about smoking, and yet you continue this habit." Her voice was raspy, with a subtle foreign accent.

"Been a long time, Isabella," Sayf said.

"It has," she said, smiling. "How do you like it?"

"It's quite the spectacle. There was something I saw on the way here. An old man, frail, looked as if he were dying, racked with pain to the point of delirium. Did he cross you? Is he an example of some sort?"

"No," she said, sighing. "He is here of his own free will. That man has bone cancer and bets have been placed as to how long it will take for him to die." Sayf grimaced. "It's funny. People think the gambling, the drunks lined up at the bar, the women selling their bodies to feed themselves are the atrocities. They're self-indulgence, but not atrocities. The real abomination is in that room, when the rich and powerful make wages like deities. Who shall live or die? Can a woman have an orgasm while she is being raped? How many breaths can a dying man take?" Isabella cracked her knuckles and shook her head. "It's sickening."

"Then why do it?"

Isabella shrugged her shoulders and said, "If they're going to do it anyway, might as well make a buck watching them."

Sayf scoffed and said, "Well, you made quite a name for yourself."

"I can't say I take *all* the credit. After all, if it wasn't for my world-class financier...how is Mrs. Eleanor?"

"My guess is, dead by now," Sayf said scratching his cheek.

"Dead?"

"Embezzlement," he said, squinting. "A sordid, complex affair."

"Poor girl. I liked her." Sayf nodded. "Does that mean you'll be in charge of my finances?"

"You haven't heard?"

"What's that?"

"I'm no longer with the World Bank."

Isabella's warm smile faded away.

"No," Isabella said in a deep voice. "I hadn't heard."

"Don't worry, I still have your accounts and have been managing your funds like always."

"Why are you here then?"

"Because it is eleven fifty-five and at the stroke of midnight I have arranged for ninety percent of your funds to go to charity."

"Bullshit."

"Well," Sayf said, getting up from his seat. "It's about time for the threats, yeah? If I remember correctly it was the roof you liked to toss people off, right? Come on, lads."

He started toward the elevator when Isabella raised her hand in the air. She patted his seat. Sayf walked back and sat down.

"What do you want?"

"How long have you been the warden for Novem?"

Isabella's eyes widened. She gasped sharply as if the wind had been knocked out of her.

"How did you…"

"Isabella, I need Barbara."

"No," she whispered. "Marcus, listen carefully. Whatever it is that you want with that woman, leave it be."

"How did she end up there? Was she working for one of the cartels?"

Isabella sighed. "The triads first. She showed up at the Jade Dragons doorstep reciting the thirty-six oaths, laughing the entire time. They took her out to the back alley. A few hours later she came back dragging the bodies. They sent her on suicide missions. Dignitaries, rival syndicates, missions that not even the coldest of killers would ever consider taking. But she did, and she kept coming back."

"Sounds like a gangster's dream to me," Sayf said. "Why send her to Novem?"

"She'd leave for a few days, next morning you wake up to a bloodbath. Mutilated remains lying in the streets. Heads of dignitaries stuck on pikes in front of their estates. The attention was too much. I was told she got bored with the 'red tape,' as she put it, and left. Thought she could have more fun with the Russians."

"And?"

"Even the coldest killer has a flicker of morality. Especially when it comes to killing children."

"Hmph…." Sayf said, rubbing his hands together. "So how did you get her to Novem?"

"You know what?" Isabella said, rubbing her forehead. "Why don't you ask her yourself?" She looked over her shoulder and said, "Make sure Mr. Sayf gets the coordinates." She looked at Sayf and said, "You can have her, Marcus. The criminal underworld is better off." Sayf stood up and brushed off his suit. "My money?" Sayf took out his smart phone.

"Safe and sound in your accounts where they shall remain." Sayf placed his phone back in his pocket. "A fallen demon?" Sayf scoffed. "How is that possible?"

"We're all human, Marcus," Isabella said with a slight grin. "Evil is a business, not a pleasure. For your friend, it is the latter, not the former."

Conscience

Shepard screamed before jolting up from a rusted dark-green cot. Sweat poured down his face, burning his eyes. He gulped as much salty, cold air as he could and coughed. He wiped the sweat with his quivering left hand and looked at his bare chest. Four blood-soaked bandages were wrapped around his sternum. Shepard whipped his head in all directions, surveying his surroundings. It was a burgundy tent of modest size with cold sand and grass as the flooring. The wind from the outside howled against the shuddering tent and forced sand to swirl in through the cloth entrance. He winced trying to stand up, only to collapse on his own weight.

"Don't bother," a voice said.

Shepard's eyes followed the voice to the tent entrance. All that Shepard could make out was a blurred image leaning against a wooden pillar. Hazy clouds of smoke spewed from the figure's mouth with each exhale. A few blinks later, the image came into focus.

"You've been out for five days now," Graham said in between puffs. He stared at the tent ceiling, spaced out. A makeshift sling kept his right arm pressed against his bandaged chest.

Shepard pulled himself up from the cold ground and

prompted his weighted body on the side of the cot. He bent over and groaned at a burning pain radiating from his chest.

"How long?" Shepard asked.

"Five days."

"Where's the rest of us?"

"Two survivors," Graham said, exhaling smoke.

Shepard balled his fists and placed them over his face.

"We're somewhere in Denmark," Graham said. "Some secluded beach. They buried us, you know. Dumped us in a shallow grave by the ocean. Really shitty work. An Islamic caravan saw the bodies, felt it was their duty to give their fellow man a proper burial. I was in and out. You were barely breathing." Shepard pressed his fists against his forehead and let out a guttural growl. With each grunt, blood oozed from his fresh wounds.

"Where is she?" Shepard asked in a deep, ominous tone.

"I counted the bodies twice," said a stoic Graham. "She's gone."

"Zaidi? The kids?" Shepard asked with tears in his eyes.

Graham took another puff from his cigarette before glancing at Shepard and responding with a quick head shake.

Shepard gritted his teeth. He held tight to the edge of the cot and pushed himself up. His wounds stretched and dripped blood. His legs wobbled underneath his athletic stature. He planted his feet, tunneling his toes into the sand for more balance. Hunched over, Shepard held his chest with his arms and limped across the tent. He walked past Graham and lifted the cloth doorway. The flash of light from the noon sun forced his forearm over his eyes. Under the small shadow of his forearm, all he could see were hazy images of huts with figures moving in and out. Sounds of livestock and children playing filled his ears. A few feet in front of him were a group of mounds in a row. Shepard didn't need perfect vision to know that he was standing in front of a graveyard. He fell to his knees.

"I'm sorry," Shepard whispered. "I am so sorry."

Graham stood at the doorway to the hut, smoking a cigarette. He stood there listening to Shepard's sobbing, and stared at the gray ocean.

✍

"Graham! Graham!" Shepard shouted.

"Hmm?" Graham asked. Rosa and Jonah sat on Shepard's couch in his apartment complex, staring at him. "Sorry," Graham said, putting out his cigarette. "Mind wandered for a moment." Shepard looked over at Graham. He was leaning against the windowsill, staring at the city skyline.

"That trip sure was a bust," Jonah said with a sigh.

"Maybe not," Rosa said, scratching her bottom lip. "Sayf's spreadsheets were all over his desk. I think the bank printed them, trying to figure out what he was doing. It's pretty encrypted, but there were a set of numbers I saw over and over."

"A set of numbers?" Shepard asked.

"The pattern is usually linked to a client," Rosa said. She leaned forward in her seat and placed her elbows on her knees. "7721 ring a bell?" The four numbers immediately set Graham's heart racing. The two men looked at each other. Rosa studied their reaction and said, "I take that as a yes."

"How far do these documents go back?" Shepard asked.

"Years. Before I was hired."

Shepard placed his hands in his pockets, turned around and walked away from the living area. He sighed and said, "If that's true, Ashcroft..."

"Can't trust anyone these days," Jonah said, staring at Rosa. "Can you, fellas?"

"You know what Jonah," Rosa said, "I'm getting sick of..."

"Stop it," Shepard said.

The room became quiet. Shepard folded his arms. He rubbed his eyes before looking over at Graham.

"You're kidding," Graham said.

"What?" Jonah asked.

"This is bigger than revenge, Graham," Shepard said.

"Who cares?" Graham asked.

"Graham…"

"You think this is about revenge or retribution?" Graham asked. "We should have killed her years ago!"

"Graham," Shepard said. "You're gonna have to trust me."

"Yeah, I trust you, Shep," Graham said, raising his voice. "So did Mark…" He stood up from the windowpane. "Sam…"

"That's enough," Shepard said.

Jonah and Rosa looked at each other, confused.

"Matt!" Graham shouted as he walked toward Shepard. "You remember Matt, don't you Shep? You visited his wife yet? Tell her where her husband is? Where she can pay her respects? Get some closure? They can't even mourn for the man 'cause his body is in an unmarked grave in fucking Denmark!"

"You made your point," Shepard said.

"What about Zaidi?" Graham asked. "You knew what would happen if we disobeyed Ashcroft. Once again thinking you're bigger than all of this. Our job was simple! Harvesters for the Blackout! That's it!" Shepard glared at Graham with his arms folded. "I told you it was bad idea. I pleaded with you. And I still followed you into the shitstorm. That's on me. We walked those kids—"

"They would still be dead, Graham," Shepard said.

"That's how you reason this shit?" Graham asked, frowning. "That someone else would come along and do the job? You remember Ahmed, don't you?"

"Stop," Shepard said, walking away.

"Bennu?"

"Graham, seriously."

"Eshe?!…*Ray?!*"

The name knocked the wind out of Jonah. He inhaled sharply and asked, "What?"

"Graham, stop talking," Shepard said, glancing at Jonah.

"That's right, Jonah," Graham said, staring at Shepard. "Your father…"

"Dammit, Graham," Shepard said. "I promised him…"

"Your father was a member of our unit," Graham said. He looked over at Rosa and said, "7721." Rosa's eyes widened.

"That's the connection," she said. "He's pouring billions of dollars into your old unit, which is probably funding this Blackout thing we stole, which, by the way, you still haven't told us what it is."

Jonah dropped his shoulders and sunk his body into the sofa. He leaned forward in his seat and asked, "So…this wasn't some random act? All this time…"

"She was after your father," Graham said.

Jonah's eyes welled. He stared at the ground for a moment and whispered, "OK." He got up and walked out of the flat. Rosa stared at Jonah with sympathy. She looked at Graham and Shepard, who were locked in a venomous staring match.

"Maybe I should talk…"

"No!" they both said.

The Ninth Circle

INDIAN OCEAN, PRESENT DAY

Sayf sat at the bow of a jet-black Corvette staring down at the crystal-clear water. His feet dangled over the edge of the speedboat. His body bounced each time the waves crashed against the hull. His eyes ricocheted between the water, a cigarette in one hand, and a nicotine patch in the other.

"Shit," Sayf whispered as he slapped the patch on his forearm. He placed the cigarette in his mouth and stood up. On the pink horizon was a silhouette of an island shaped like a crater. The inland wind made his blue short-sleeved shirt rustle. The Corvette tore through the ocean and came to an abrupt halt, bobbing up and down between the island's crescent entrance. Sayf and the Slokranian soldiers boarded a long, inflatable motorboat and headed inland. The cove was encircled by red rocks more than a mile high. Stingrays coasted in figure eights around them, pulling up purple sand from the ocean bottom. Sayf squinted his eyes at a single figure onshore.

It was a thin man with gray hair. He sat on a plastic foldout chair, carving a distorted wooden cross. Behind him was a tropical forest. Palm trees lined the purple-sand beach. Wide-based Kauri trees with huge roots towered over the cove. A giant cave made the ceiling of the tropical skyline. Sayf and the Slokranians jumped off the boat and waded the warm ocean water to shore.

"It's manmade," the man said.

"Sorry?" Sayf asked.

"That," said the man, pointing his Swiss army knife behind him. "Nature may be beautiful, but it's not a decorator. Everything you see behind you was manmade." The man looked up, glanced at Sayf from head to toe, and continued carving. "You appear young to be such an accomplished mercenary."

"I beg your pardon?"

"What are you, thirty?"

"I'm older than I look."

"Well, you jackals…"

"I don't take kindly to that title."

"Oh, yeah," the man said chuckling. "What's that Isabella told me again? Global financial officer. Am I right?"

"That's right."

"Tell me, Mr. Financier," the man said, getting up from his wooden chair. "How many deals have you closed without the client looking down the barrel of a gun?" He looked into Sayf's eyes and smiled. "Isabella told me that you would have company." He glanced over Sayf's shoulder at the Slokranian commandos. "You carry interesting company."

"Extenuating circumstances," Sayf said.

"Right," the man said. "If you don't mind, gentlemen—your weapons. Leave them on your rafts." Sayf pulled out his nine-millimeter and handed it to the man.

"I would appreciate it if you would hold this for me Mr…?"

"Call me Brunu."

"Sicilian?"

"Close, Sardinian."

"No," the giant Slokranian said.

Brunu stepped past Sayf and approached him.

"Come again?" Brunu asked, moving his ear near the giant Slokranian's broad chest.

"I follow the orders of my prime minister. And on his orders, I'm forced to follow this…this person." Sayf placed his hands in his khaki pockets and snickered. "I may have to take orders from him, but you? Kooryva *mat!* Half-breed."

"Half-breed?" Brunu asked. "What does the first part mean?"

"You don't want to know, mate," Sayf said, rubbing his forehead.

"A sense of duty," Brunu said. "I respect that in a young boy."

"I'm no boy! My name is—"

"That's not important," Brunu said, waving his hands. "You are not important. What *is* important is that you understand." Brunu snapped his fingers. The sound echoed throughout the cove. A moment later, infrared dots crawled across each of the Slokranian soldier's chests and stopped at their foreheads. "This is not a request," Brunu said, walking away. As he passed Sayf, he handed him the small wooden cross and asked, "You Catholic?"

"No," Sayf said.

"You of all people need to become one."

"Are we concerned for my soul?"

"Someone should be," Brunu said, walking toward the tropical forest. "With the current life you're living, Saint Peter may need a little encouragement calling out your name."

⮾

They walked for miles into the rainforest before they passed the columns of fortified wooden towers seventy feet high. Each tower was connected by narrow wooden walkways. Guards wearing bulletproof vests and army fatigues watched from above carrying

M16s. They observed Sayf and his men navigate through ung-roomed vegetation. Brunu lead the way, hacking vines and banana leaves in his path. When they reached the end of the rainforest, they stood in front of a cave giving way to an inside clearing the length of four football stadiums. It was barricaded by armored vehicles. The guards watching the entrance saluted Brunu.

"Stay on the path," Brunu said, stepping onto a six-foot-wide black concrete walkway. "Keep behind me." The cement network twisted around the entire cave. Twenty-foot diamond-shaped metal towers were scattered across the flat compound. Sayf glanced up at one of the guards standing at ease. The guard glanced down in the direction of the convoy. His finger wrapped around the trigger of an army-fatigue-colored machine gun. Like any other prison, the yard was a segregated sight. Young black inmates sprinted across a makeshift dirt basketball court—shirts versus skins. The older inmates stood and watched from the side-line. Muslim inmates, just finished with prayer, stood under a tower with their prayer rugs rolled up and tucked under their arms. The white inmates stood around rotting wooden tables. Their haggard faces gave Sayf venomous stares as they passed by them on the designated walkway. Other inmates stormed out from dark-green burlap tents. They walked alongside Sayf and the Slokranians, shouting insults and profanities.

"What is this place?" a Slokranian asked.

"What do you think it is?" Brunu asked. "It's a prison."

"Drug dealers made a prison for other drug dealers?" the giant Slokranian asked.

"You see, some criminals in this world are more valuable alive then dead," Sayf said. "Their connections, resources, and knowl-edge may be irreplaceable. When certain high-ranking syndicate members commit an act that is not in the best interest of their organization, they are brought here, their family erased as pun-ishment and their assets frozen."

"Huh," a Slokranian said. "And the cartels finance this?"

"The cartels, triads, Russians," Brunu said. "This place cannot be found on any modern map and it never will be. They all pay to keep this place from existing."

They continued for another four hundred yards before stopping in front of a wide metal platform.

"This is where we leave... them," Brunu said, circling his index finger at the Slokranians.

"Won't be long, lads," Sayf said, stepping on the metal platform. Brunu looked at the watch tower closest to the platform and nodded.

Platform Hydraulics hissed and creaked before it started its descent into the earth. Brunu and Sayf stood at a distance from each other.

"So, who's smarter?" Brunu asked, staring at the black volcanic shaft. "Good or evil?"

"What's that?"

"Isabella said you were once with MI6."

Sayf scoffed and said, "And you fink that made me good?"

"Maybe not good, per se. But the ends always justified the means, right?"

"Which is exactly what a man says to justify doing evil shit. But that is not your question, is it?" Sayf paused for a moment. He looked up at the opening, which they had just descended through. It now looked like a tiny hole. He whistled half the first verse of painted black before stopping abruptly. "Evil, of course."

"Why?"

"Look around, only the mind of a criminal could devise a prison based on the classics."

"Classics?" Brunu asked with a raised eyebrow.

"*Novem* in Latin is *nine*. There are nine circular penitentiaries. From my understanding, the lower the circle the more violent the criminals become. Not to mention the elevator shaft is a volcano." Sayf chuckled and said, "I wouldn't be surprised if I saw fortune tellers with their heads put on backward."

"Your deduction skills have teeth, my friend," Brunu said.

The elevator shaft stopped. In front of the two men stood a giant metal door. When it opened, there was a large room. The floors and the walls were painted a blinding white.

"I agree; evil is smarter," Brunu said. "The weakness that evil has is that we are too ritualistic."

"Ritualistic?"

"A ritual is a preprogrammed set of steps. If you know where we've been, then you will always know where we're going."

They approached the end of the room and stood in front of a long double fiberglass window.

"Well, now that you have determined our predictability, where are we headed?"

Brunu pointed at the window. The ninth floor of Novem was a hundred yards long. Three floors of prison quarters ran along the outskirts of the ninth circle. Inmates sat with their legs dangling over the edge of the walkways looking down at the chaos. Some inmates smoked rolled tobacco sitting on wooden crates playing poker. Others lifted buckets filled with lava rocks in a makeshift weight-lifting area. Two fistfights were occurring simultaneously while a newly lifeless body was being dragged back to a prison cell. The prison guards walked through the bedlam with metal rods strapped to their hands, their thumbs hovering over a blue tip.

"What are the detonators for?" Sayf asked.

"This is the ninth circle. Here houses men so vile that the underworld deemed them a threat to humanity. If one so much as touches the metal of that lift, we are to sink the entire island."

Brunu touched his earpiece and said, "Call her." He looked at Sayf and said, "You know Satan was in that ninth circle bound in chains." He laughed and said, "Who'd have thought this whole time that the devil was a woman?"

The overhead intercom turned on. "Inmate 7455, come to the white room." Silence broke across the entire floor. The inmates stared at one another for a moment before they parted a path in the middle of the penitentiary. At the far end of the hall was a woman sitting with her back turned from the white room reading *The Adventures of Tom Sawyer*. She sighed and ran her calloused fingers through her dark, curly, neck-length hair. She stood up and turned around. The sleeves of her black jumpsuit were tied around her waist, and she wore a thin gray tank top underneath. Her well-defined arms were covered in old bullet and knife wounds. The yellow light from the overhead lamps put a shadow over her face and slender feminine frame. She approached the room walking on her toes, but her head swayed from one side to another as if she were drunk. The inmates looked away as she walked past them. Some kissed the feet of their crucifix or murmured Buddhist chants.

When light gave way, a youthful, untouched face emerged. Her big light-brown eyes sparkled behind a sadistic Cheshire-cat smirk. She stood at the entrance to the white room and tapped on the glass. The double glass door opened. A stench of prison air ripe with blood and urine wafted into the white room.

Brunu leaned in behind Sayf's shoulder and said, "I'll let you introduce yourself." The two stood on opposite sides of the white room locked in an intense stare.

"Huh," Barbara said.

"What is it?" Sayf asked.

"I don't smell a drop of fear on you."

"Should I be afraid?" Sayf asked. Barbara scoffed and pointed to Brunu, who was caressing the detonator button. "There's very little that this world has to offer me in the line of fear," he smiled.

Barbara chuckled.

"Oh, I think we could workshop that assumption."

She walked over to a white chair and long rectangular metal

table in the middle of the room and tucked her book under her arm.

"I see you're a fan of the classics," Sayf said, gesturing for them to sit down.

"*Tom Sawyer*. I've been told these old books are really good. Never really had the chance to read so I figured while I'm here I was gonna take time out for myself, you know?" Sayf didn't acknowledge the question. "You ever read this book?" Sayf shook his head. "It's so racist. These people are far from being woke." She said gesturing air quotations. "It's about—"

"Do you know why I'm here?"

Barbara leaned back in her seat.

"I mean…no," she said, scratching her nose. "I don't even know your name. For an Englishman you're very…" Barbara closed her eyes and took a deep breath. "Discourteous."

"You can call me Sayf."

"Ahh," Barbara said, smiling. "The kind you kill people with?"

"That's right."

"I like it." She said nodding. "And the cockney accent. It suits you. Now, Mr. Bond, you go back and tell the sicarios I'm still on vacation."

"Not with the cartels. Ashcroft sent me to find you."

Barbara squinted.

"Remember that assumption of yours?" she asked, standing up. Sayf leaned back into his seat and crossed his legs. She looked down at his relaxed demeanor and scoffed again. "I must say, this tough-guy act you're putting on is—"

"Maybe because it's not a put on," Sayf said, cracking a smile. "Santiago's dead." Barbara's eyes widened. She sunk back into her seat. Water glazed over her eyes. "You didn't know, did you?" Barbara turned away. She laughed as she wiped the tears from her eyes.

"It should've been me. First Sean, now…" she looked down

at the floor before muttering, "OK. OK." She looked up and said, "What do you want?"

"The real question, Barbara," Sayf said, leaning forward in his seat, "is what do *you* want?" She sprung up and slammed her hands against the table.

"I'm about to twist every bone in that beautiful body of yours! So, what the fuck do you care what I want?" she said in a guttural voice. He pulled out Brunu's wooden crucifix from his pocket.

"Because your wants are aligned with my needs at the moment," Sayf said, admiring the craftsmanship of his new crucifix.

Barbara chuckled and said, "OK, I'll bite. What do you think I need Mr. Sword?"

"Do I really need to say it?"

"You might want to."

"You're a wildfire who needs a forest and I have a forest that needs to be set ablaze." Barbara's glare lightened. Her flushed hands relaxed, leaving two fist imprints in the thick metal table. Sayf glanced over at her seat, and she sat down. "Yes, he sent me to hunt you down, but no, I don't work for the general. The general and myself have some big plans for this world. That involves some demolition. A skill that I know you are more than suited for."

"Demolition?" Barbara said. "You want to kill a lot of people?" Sayf nodded.

"Why didn't you just come out and say that?"

"I would have if you didn't go on about that bloody book." The two shared a light chuckled.

"So, I would work for you?"

"Wildfires work for no one. I'll just provide the kindling."

"OK, why not?" she said in a cheerful voice. "One thing, though." The cheerfulness faded. "Wildfires have no allies, friends, no partners. What happens when this wildfire comes for you?"

"When that day comes, we'll see who gets extinguished."

⤬

Barbara and Sayf stood with their backs against the glass window of the white room, staring at the metal double doors to the elevator shaft.

"What are we waiting for?" Barbara asked flickering her left thumb against the bullet proof glass.

"Brunu went to get some people that I'd like for you to meet."

"Why is it taking him so long?"

"Say again how long you've been here?"

"Two years. Why?"

"You've forgotten how long the lift takes to get down here." Barbara rested the back of her head against the glass. Sayf glanced at Barbara's thumb, tapping away at the glass. A growing crack appeared at the point where she was tapping. "Ashcroft has told me quite a bit about you. I actually met Santiago. Tell me about this *Sean*."

"Sean? What's there to tell? He was one of us. He was a couple shades lighter than yourself. He sold us out for pussy and we killed him. Next fucking question," she said, sighing.

"All right. Why are you still here?"

"Here?" Barbara looked around and leaned into Sayf's ear and whispered, "R and R." Sayf leaned back and looked at the content smile across her face.

"What?"

"What is there not to like about this place? In the middle of the ocean, tropical weather, three square meals?"

"It's a prison. You *do* know that, right?" Sayf asked, grimacing.

"Labels, Sayf. Just labels. Hell, New York is a concrete jungle with two-dollar hookers and Broadway shows," Barbara said with a chuckle.

"They all seem to fear you," Sayf said, examining the healed bullet scars running across her clavicle into her cleavage.

"You ever read Sun Tzu?" Sayf shook his head. "In *The Art of War*, the emperor instructed Sun to teach his concubines military formations. A few of the concubines thought it was a joke. Kept messing up. When the emperor asked what to do about this, Sun said, *Simple, collect their heads.* Reluctantly, the emperor did what was suggested and don't you know it? The rest of the cunts fell in line."

"Is that what you did? Collect heads?"

"I'm one of the few women down here, you know? The only one, really. The underworld has a very chauvinistic way of thinking. The first night I was in here, one of the bigger, greasier inmates came into my bunker. He ripped my clothes off and well…" She paused for a moment as a shade of blush came across her skin. "I kinda like role-playing," she murmured.

"What?" Sayf grimaced.

"It was a rape fantasy, you know? It's kinda nice." Sayf continued to stare at her with a blank expression. "Come on, you've had to have had a fantasy where you…" Sayf shook his head. "He seemed to enjoy it."

"Good for him."

"I came like a dump truck afterward," she said, chuckling.

"Afterward?"

"Oh," Barbara said with a look of shock. "That doesn't get me off. Never has."

"I don't understand."

"The next morning during breakfast, I grabbed him." She whispered, her hands trembling. "I broke his arms and legs with my bare hands and dragged him to the middle of the communal area. Right there," she whispered, pointing out the window. "And that's where I fucked him with one of his own bones. It was slow, painful, and very public." She leaned closer and looked Sayf in the eyes. "Like a dump truck," she said, smiling.

Sayf took a deep breath and put his eyes back on the elevator.

Moments later, the doors opened. Behind Brunu were the Slokranian commandos.

"What is this, Sayf?" one of them asked.

"Band of brothers!" Sayf said, smiling.

"We are not your brother. Why bring us down here?" another one said.

Sayf laughed and said, "You're absolutely right, mate. We're not friends. We don't even like each other. Which is exactly why I am going to enjoy this."

"What are you talking about, Sayf?" the giant Slokranian asked.

Barbara looked at Sayf, confused.

"You don't buy the car without at least taking it for a test drive, yeah?" Sayf asked. Barbara's eyes widened. "Have at it."

Barbara cracked her arms and neck, sauntering toward the Slokrainians. She walked on the balls of her feet and extended her long, slender, muscular arms. The scars along her back, deltoids, and triceps stretched as if they were smiling.

"What is this, Sayf?!" the Giant shouted.

"Waking the Dragon," Barbara sighed.

A young Slokranian stepped forward. He walked toward Barbara with his arms crossed and head cocked to the side.

"Is it really possible that such a small, well-toned woman could be such a danger?" he asked through his cavity-riddled smile. He examined Barbara from head to toe, and bit his lip with the rotting stubs of his top canines. Barbara looked at him and smiled. "You have pretty mouth," he said in Slokranian. He placed his hands on his hips. "Perhaps we could put those lips to better use?"

He and the other Slokranians laughed. In mid-laugh the young Slokrainian gasped and strained. Barbara's palm was planted in his chest, his sternum split in two. Laughter in that moment was cut down by terrifying silence. Shock and awe came across the Slokranian's faces as their comrade buckled to his knees by the single blow of a woman less than half his size. Sayf glanced at Brunu, who was unsurprised. The Slokranians looked at each other before nine of them rushed her. The giant Slokranian glared at Sayf before taking a seat at the metal table.

Barbara dug her fingers into the young Slokranian's rib cage and lifted the six-foot commando off of his knees. She threw the body into two soldiers, and both of them landed on the floor with the young Slokranian on top. They looked up at the bright halogen lights and saw Barbara's silhouette, her knee aiming for their heads. She crashed through their skulls and broke through the white tiled floor. She popped up and rushed the next two Slokranians closest to her. One of them threw a desperate haymaker. She ducked the wide hook and threw one of her own, this time landing on his chin. A snap was heard. The Slokranian fell forward on his stomach, but in his last moments realized that he was staring at the elevator behind him. Barbara grabbed another Slokranian by the arm and shoulder threw him. He screamed for his life before she caved his face in with one stomp. The giant Slokranian sat at the table leaning forward, studying Barbara's movements. Sayf looked in his direction and gave him a subtle two-finger salute.

Barbara was grabbed by the rest of the Slokranians and dragged to the floor. They each raised their steel-toed military boots and stomped on her. She took each blow while staring at Sayf.

"Fucking bitch," one of them shouted in Slokranian.

Barbara grabbed one foot each from two different soldiers and twisted them like a bottle top. She rolled onto her back, drew her legs to her chest, and kicked out. Her feet rammed through the kneecaps of the other two Slokrainians. They tried to crawl away, but she grabbed each of them by a leg and mounted them. One at a time, she held their heads back and punched their throats. Crimson was painted across the white-room canvas. Barbara's hands were covered in blood and sinew.

Barbara whipped her head around and locked eyes with the giant Slokranian. She walked toward him, stretching her shoulders before settling into an intimidating kickboxing stance. When she was within reach, the giant Slokranian raised his monstrous arms and brought them down on her back. Head-first her body crashed into the floor. He drew his fist back over his head and plowed into Barbara's face. He picked her up over his head, turned around, and threw her against the wall. Blood erupted from Barbara's mouth after a barrage of kicks. Just when she thought she had a moment to breathe, he grabbed her by the hair and banged her head into the wall. He stopped and let gravity pull her flimsy body to the floor. Blood tracked down the white wall. He stared down at Barbara, who struggled to stand. The giant Slokranian raised his fist and waited for her to look into his eyes. He shouted as his arm hurled through the air. Barbara smiled. She threw a punch of her own that met with the giant Slokranian's fist in midair.

Sayf blinked slowly and wiped his mouth at the unsightly scene in front of him. Barbara stood on one knee next to the giant Slokranian, her short brown hair and face caked with blood, her well-defined arm extended. It happened so fast, the giant could barely fathom that his once-massive arm was now just mangled flesh dangling on his shoulder. He let loose with a high-pitched squeal before falling on his knees. Drool came down from the side of his face as he keeled over and tried to grab what was left of his arm. Barbara stood up and looked over her shoulder at the last of Sayf's Slokrians.

"That's the stuff," Barbara said in a sultry voice. She turned around and kneeled down. She grabbed the giant Slokranian by the face and stared into his blue eyes. "That fear, that raw fucking fear. I gotta tell ya, big boy, you're making me wet." She grabbed his mouth and started to squeeze. He shrieked as he felt his jawbone slowly cracking. She stared into his fearful eyes and cherished each moment of agony. "We need to be alone." She grabbed him by the leg and started to drag him. She stared at Brunu and said, "Open the door."

Brunu looked at the guards and nodded. When the door opened, the inmates scattered to the corners of the prison unit. Barbara walked past Brunu and Sayf dragging the giant Slokranian, who was rendered nearly mute by his broken jaw. She walked into her cell on the far-right corner. The giant held onto the bars as long as he could before his body was sucked in. A few moments later, a blood curdling scream echoed throughout the ninth circle.

The Blackout

Around a dark wooden circular table, a group of senators sat talking. Senator McCray was quietly leaning back in his chair, deep in thought. The door to the small conference room creaked open. General Ashcroft crept in with his arms in his pocket. He slipped into a chair next to the door, unnoticed by everyone except McCray.

"OK, next line of business," One of the senators said. "There is an odd irregularity in this one government-funded program. It involves nuclear waste." The senator picked up a printed document and examined it over the rims of his glasses. "It has no name, uh…7721. Senator McCray, I believe this is your neck of the woods. Can you elaborate on what this is and why it's costing the tax payer tens of billions of dollars?"

WASHINGTON, D.C.: 2008

"I'm sick of this bipartisan bullshit!" McCray shouted, knocking his coffee cup off his desk as his staff watched him pace back and forth in his office. "We have the house and senate! And what does he want us to do? Cross the aisle. I hate that shit!"

"Well," one of the aids said, "maybe he just wants a more open dialogue about policy."

"Fuck dialogue!" McCray shouted. "All I want to hear is them choking on whatever legislation we cram down their throats."

Knock-knock. McCray's secretary, a gracefully aged black woman in her late sixties poked her head in and said, "Walter! The language."

"Not now, Paula," McCray said.

"Not nothing," Paula said, setting her thick glasses on the bridge of her nose. "Act like you have some sense. Senator Upstead for you on line one."

McCray scrunched his face.

"What the f…" Paula glared at him. McCray sighed and said, "Did you ask what he wants?"

"No," Paula said tersely before closing his door.

McCray walked over to his desk. He grabbed the phone, pressed line one, and sat down.

"Senator," McCray said flatly, "to what do I owe the honor of this phone call?"

"Senator McCray," Upstead said. His smooth, laid-back country accent frustrated McCray to his core. "It's a pleasure. Saw the little outburst you had there on the Senate floor."

"Did you?"

"I did. Quite a spectacle. It got over a million views on YouTube."

"Senator Upstead. How may I be of service?"

Upstead laughed and said, "Straightforward. I like it. We need to talk."

"So, talk."

"No. I'm in the office myself. Meet me downstairs—we're gonna go for a little ride."

"What is this about?" McCray asked, squinting.

The phone clicked.

❧

Forty minutes had passed since McCray stepped into Upstead's black limo. They sat across from each other, making uncomfortable glances before looking away. McCray looked down at his empty glass of ice water. He looked again at Upstead, now on his third bourbon. He held up his glass and turned it back and forth with his wrinkled fingers.

"How far…"

"Why aren't you married, senator?" Upstead asked.

"I'm sorry?"

"Humor me," Upstead said, sitting up in his seat. "We got about another thirty minutes. Figured it would be nice to chew the fat a bit." McCray stared down at his empty glass.

"My parents have asked me the same question." He looked at Upstead and said, "I don't know. I didn't get into this job to be some future Fortune 500 CEO. I really wanted to make a difference."

"Fifteen years in the senate, and that feeling has gone away?"

McCray scoffed and said, "You'd think reality would set in by now, right?" McCray shook his head. "Not even close. When you care that much about making a difference, it's hard to find someone who understands."

"You gay, Senator?"

"What?!" McCray asked, wrinkling his forehead. "No. Is that what this is about!?"

"Calm down, Senator. It was a simple question." McCray continued to glare at Upstead for a moment. His eyebrows relaxed before he sunk back into his seat and straightened his charcoal slacks. "You will find, Senator, that you and I are a lot alike."

McCray laughed and said, "We are nothing alike."

"Is that a fact?"

"Yes. That is."

"Let's hear it. Go on. Tell me what your ninth-grade history book says about old John Upstead."

"I wouldn't use those books, Senator," McCray said, smiling. "Those history books say Columbus found America and the Trail of Tears never happened. I've watched you on the floor for fifteen years. Fighting to reestablish Jim Crow, voting against civil rights legislation, condemning people for practicing the Islamic faith. Galvanizing your party and base to perpetuate this hatemonger bullshit. It's no different than burning books."

Upstead gazed at McCray with a blank stare for a moment before bursting in laughter.

"You think it's funny?" McCray asked, raising his voice.

"I'm sorry," Upstead said catching his breath. "Every time I hear some of the things people have supported me on, I can't help but laugh." Upstead continued to laugh. His wrinkled red cheeks became sore as a tear welled up in his left eye.

"What are you…"

The limo stopped. The driver walked to the rear passenger door and opened it. Upstead gestured for McCray to follow him. When McCray stepped out of the limo, he saw a string of rusted metal silos standing hundreds of feet tall.

"What time will you need me back, sir?" the driver asked.

"Give us an hour," Upstead said, staring at McCray's confused expression. The driver nodded, rolled up his window, and drove back down the dirt road. McCray looked at the limo drive away until its red brake lights were swallowed by wooded darkness.

"These here silos absorb sunlight. An entire facility requiring nothing more than God's light to operate."

"Facility?" McCray asked. A small metal door to the middle silo slid open. Upstead walked inside. Hesitant, McCray followed behind him. "Shit," he whispered to himself. McCray ducked his head under the short doorway. It was empty. McCray's and Upstead's black loafers echoed throughout the entire compound.

Hundreds of feet above them was a large fan blowing down warm air. On the other side of the silo was a man dressed in black fatigues holding an AK-47. He stood at ease next to an old coal miner's shaft.

"Guerez," Upstead said smiling. "How are things?"

"Wonderful, sir. Thank you for asking," Guerez said.

"Coming on or getting ready to go home?" Upstead asked.

"Coming on," Guerez said with reluctance.

"Well," said a smiling Upstead, "the morning will be here before you know it." *What the fuck is going on here?* McCray thought to himself.

"You get that family taken care of?" Upstead asked.

"I don't want to be a burden, sir…"

"Nonsense," Upstead said, shaking his head. "Talk to me."

"It's my brother, sir," Guerez said. "They won't give him a green card."

"How long has he been here?" Upstead asked.

"Over twenty years!"

"Listen, give me his full name and driver's license in the morning. I'll have him naturalized by the end of the week."

"Thank you so much, sir," Guerez said, sighing. Upstead smiled and stepped onto the mine shaft. McCray walked behind him with a half-opened mouth and wincing left eye. Guerez looked at McCray, smiled, and pushed a green button on the control panel. Rusted metal chains creaked against one another, giving the old shaft a jolt before descending into the earth. McCray stared at Upstead standing next to him with his hands behind his back.

"Why'd you do that?" McCray asked.

"Do what?"

"You don't believe in immigration."

"Says who?"

"Immigration is nothing more than adult childcare, a

shitshow. Taking care of shitty people from shitty countries. That's a direct quote from you on the Senate floor."

"Let me show you something, Senator." Upstead reached into his pocket and pulled out a dark-brown wallet. He opened it and took out a picture. McCray's eyes widened.

"Is that…"

"Dr. King," Upstead said, nodding. "I met him in 1964. People understood he was brilliant, but I don't know if anyone realized how funny the man was."

"In 1964, you were fighting to keep Jim Crow afloat. What were you doing—"

"I asked you what you know about me. And the truth is you don't know a damn thing about me." The shaft stopped. They were surround by moist limestone. McCray followed Upstead off the shaft toward two soldiers standing guard in front of a double-wide door. Upstead nodded at the two soldiers as they saluted and opened the door for the senators. It was a single corridor the length of a football field with long glass windows on each side.

"You don't know me, Senator McCray; you know my parents. Spare me the history lesson this time, because I lived it. Their parents were slave-owners and built an agricultural empire. Tobacco, cattle, cotton. My grandparents left my father with more wealth than what was good for him. He married my mother out of responsibility. Unfortunately, that is where the responsibility ended. His adulterous transgressions put my mother on the bottle."

They walked past an operating room with a little boy on the table. His chest was open. McCray stopped. The surgeon was inserting a black oval-shaped object into the child's chest.

"Is that—"

"An artificial heart," Upstead said, without breaking stride. "Genetically fitted to his immuno composition, it will run for a hundred years, and the antivirals it pumps will keep him free from any viral infection. Please keep walking, Senator." The long windows frosted over. McCray could no longer see anything but moving figures. "You see, Senator, I was raised by a little old black woman named Patty Mae Smith. That woman fed me. Clothed me. She had eight other kids who are my true brothers and sisters. They're my family. So, when it came time to be an adult and decide what to do with my life and fortune I asked myself, *What would my parents* not *do?*"

Upstead and McCray walked through a red door into a roomful of people wearing white coats hustling between computer screens. McCray and Upstead navigated though the busy room, passing two men in a heated conversation.

"Shepard, for the last time," Ashcroft said. Stabbing his finger into the air. "If you continue to piss her off…"

"Sir, she's a psycho," Shepard said. "Pissing her off is a side effect of reason." The two stopped their conversation as Upstead and McCray passed by.

"Senator," Ashcroft said, "He's the—" Upstead gave a subtle head shake and glanced at Shepard, who answered with a slight nod. Upstead and McCray made their way through the room and started up a flight of steps.

"Every man has a defining moment," Upstead said. "Mine was World War II. That German gave mankind a key to self-destruction."

"You mean Einstein?" McCray asked.

Upstead nodded.

"Can you imagine the shock and awe? The fear when those bombs hit Nagasaki and Hiroshima? I realized that mankind's greatest enemy wasn't racism or communism. It's mankind's intellect and heightened sense of destructive creativity."

They walked into a dark room. In the middle was a ninety-inch computer screen hovering in mid-air. Blue light shined down from the ceiling. McCray stood in front of the giant screen. He didn't know if he was losing his mind, but every few seconds, it was as if the black screen moved.

"What is this?" McCray asked.

"If you are referring to what's keeping that screen from crashing to the floor, it's an antigravity device. The Russians were going to use it in their new engines. Jet fighters with the ability to manipulate gravity. You could go up, down, and diagonal on a dime."

"I...I don't understand."

"Yes, you do," Upstead said, smiling. "But you're in a bit of shock so let me guide you. Mankind is a child, Senator McCray. A child holding a gun to its own head, ready to blow its brains out. We just haven't found the trigger. Once I was elected, I took my family's blood money and funded a government project for nuclear waste removal. Under this government project a group was formed to keep mankind from killing itself."

"What do you call this...group?"

"No name, just a number: 7721. It's a random nuclear-waste project on a random fiscal spreadsheet."

"You fund technological espionage that you deem unfit for humanity?"

"I see your brain is catching up."

McCray scoffed and said, "You mean deemed unfit for a foreign power."

"You see that?" Upstead asked pointing at the levitating black screen. "That's where all the information goes. Once we test the technology and confirm it functions, the research is stored in a coding system." McCray looked at the black shape-shifting screen. "What you see moving on the screen are words, numbers, equations. Hundreds of languages and dialects from the greatest minds of the century blurring away."

"So, this is all—"

"Data from dangerous intellectual property. We retrieve it and store it away onto a multi-coded server that is uncrackable. We call it the Blackout."

"All these years you were—"

"A man can do more good if he is perceived as evil," Upstead said, smiling.

"Why are you showing me this?"

Upstead looked down and placed his hands in pockets. He took a deep sigh and said, "Because you're gonna replace me."

"What?"

"It has to be you, Walter."

"Wait a minute," McCray said, holding his hands up. "I-I can't do this."

"You'll learn."

"I didn't even serve."

"Irrelevant."

"There's got to be someone more qualified."

"No one."

"H-hold on one—"

"Boy," Upstead said with clenched teeth. "Will you grow a spine?"

"Did you just call me *boy*?" McCray shouted.

"That was not intended as a racial slur. I'm describing a man who is acting too childish to see that history is calling his name!" His voice echoed through the empty room. The two stood quiet for a moment. "I'm dying. Pancreatic cancer. Doc says I got maybe a year." He walked over to McCray and placed his hands on McCray's shoulders. "Walter, listen to me. Politics these days feeds your narcissism. That's it. You want to truly make a difference? How's saving billions?"

∽

"Senator? Senator McCray?" McCray looked around at the table of senators staring at him.

"I'm sorry," McCray said. "I'm a bit tired." He looked over at Ashcroft sitting by the door with his legs crossed. "It has no purpose." McCray said staring at Ashcroft.

"I'm sorry, Senator?" another senator asked.

"It's a nuclear-waste budget that is outdated."

Ashcroft sat forward in his seat, his eyes glaring at McCray.

"I say we freeze the assets for now. Me and my team will re-crunch the numbers and get back to you."

"Sounds good," a senator said. "All in favor say aye."

"Aye," they all said. McCray did so while raising his hand and staring directly at Ashcroft.

"The *ayes* have it," the senator said. "We will reconvene in the next few months."

❧

"A moment, Senator?" McCray looked over his shoulder to see Ashcroft leaning against an eggshell-colored wall outside the conference room.

"General," McCray said keeping a brisk stride, "I'm late for another engagement, so if you—"

"Cut the bullshit!" Ashcroft whispered while walking behind him. "What was that?"

"What?"

"You know what!"

McCray stopped. He turned around and stared Ashcroft in the eyes.

"I would say that's damn good fiscal responsibility," McCray said, smiling.

Ashcroft clenched his teeth.

"If 7721 loses funding," Ashcroft said while rubbing his forehead, "we lose all current Blackout activity."

"I know what you thought," McCray said, putting his hands in his pocket. "Some dumb, incompetent member of the Black caucus. Keep him in the dark…"

"Senator," Ashcroft said, shaking his head, "what in God's name are you talking about?"

"Don't give me that shit!" McCray leaned in next to Ashcroft's ear and whispered, "I know." Ashcroft grimaced. "That World Bank guy has an interesting name. You know Sayf means *sword* in Arabic." Ashcroft made a sharp gasp before regaining his composure. He took a step back from McCray and sighed with his eyes slammed shut. "I'm a money man, James. They say if you want to get to the bottom of a conspiracy you follow the money. Not always the case. Sometimes a trail of emails on a government-issued computer can serve the same purpose." Ashcroft squinted his eyes, breathing his seething rage through his nostrils.

"Do you know who I am?" Aschroft asked with a calm voice.

"Threatening now, are we?"

"No," Aschroft said. He stared at McCray for a moment before walking away.

⋙

"Sir," Bradshaw said, holding his cellphone a good six inches from his ear.

He was standing on the corner of 7th and D a few feet from the Penn Quarter Station. Rain fell from the dark-red sky with intermittent flashes of lightning in the distance. Two guards dressed in dark suits stood next to Bradshaw, one of them holding a black umbrella over his head. Drops from the umbrella dripped onto his charcoal trench coat.

"How did he…" Bradshaw grimaced. "He did what?! That's illegal!" Bradshaw looked up and saw a black limo cruising down Pennsylvania Avenue. "We can get him on felony charges." The limo pulled up next to him. One of the guards opened the door. Bradshaw stepped into the limo and wiped the droplets of water off his arm.

"For fuck's sake, Alan," Aschroft said. He was sitting diagonally across from Bradshaw, holding a glass filled with Scotch. "Do you want to be tried for treason?" Ashcroft rubbed his forehead and continued. "If we turn him in, the contents of those emails will be exposed."

"Why did you correspond with Sayf from your government email?"

"I don't need for you of all people to point out my..." Ashcroft could feel his anger raising. He calmed himself and looked out the tinted windows as the limo turned onto 16th Street. Lightning flashed, revealing an even brighter view of the White House as they passed. "I don't know." The limo honked its way through New York Avenue and turned onto Massachusetts.

"Any word from Sayf?" Bradshaw asked.

"No."

"Is he still alive?"

"If he found Barbara, probably not."

The limo pulled up in front of a four-story brownstone. The windows were boarded up as if the place had been abandoned. Ashcroft and Bradshaw got out of the limo.

"Are we meeting someone at the safe house?" Bradshaw asked.

"No. We're staying here until we figure out how to fix this."

Ashcroft stopped at a tall gray oak tree rotting in the unkept front yard. He stared at a termite-infested branch. On top of the branch was a camera scanning Ashcroft's face. The metal front door unlocked itself and creaked open. Ashcroft and Bradshaw climbed four cracked brick steps and walked inside. The lighting was dim. All they could see was the shadow of a couch and, across from it, a plasma flat screen propped over a gas fireplace. Flashes from the lightning illuminated the small kitchen every few minutes. Bradshaw looked at the freight elevator down the hallway. The doors to the elevator were open with the silhouette of a person standing inside.

"Identify yourself!" Aschroft shouted, pulling out his pistol. Overhead dimming lights slowly brightened the floor.

"Evening, lads," Sayf said as he stood by the fireplace.

"Where the hell have you been?!" Aschroft shouted.

"Come again?" Sayf asked. "I believe keeping up my end of our agreement." He walked over to the kitchen and opened the creaking fridge. "So, this is where your 7721 operatives stay when they're under heavy manners, yeah? It's nice."

"Think this is a joke?" Bradshaw asked.

"No, I don't," Sayf said.

"Did you find her?" Bradshaw asked.

"I did," Sayf said. He shook his head and shut the fridge. "We had a chat and—" Ashcroft fired off two shots at the ceiling. Bradshaw covered his head from the falling drywall. Sayf didn't flinch. He stared at the stoic expression on Ashcroft's face. "Aren't you worried—"

"Soundproof," Ashcroft said. Sayf gave a subtle nod. "Let me bring you up to speed. 7721 lost its funding. The Blackout has lost its funding. We had a five-year plan that is dead in the water without money!"

"Well, I think I have the solution for that," Sayf said.

"Yeah?" Ashcroft asked. "What's that?"

"We kill him," Sayf said.

Ashcroft took a deep breath and shook his head.

"We can't just kill him," Ashcroft said. "We need him alive to tell the Senate board to reappropriate the funds."

"Money?" Sayf asked. He scoffed and said, "Money is far from the problem. We all need to disappear, which means we need to close the loop. That's the senator. The bigger problem is retrieving the Blackout."

"What?" Bradshaw asked. "I thought you got it back from Barbara."

"Barbara didn't have it," Sayf said.

"I don't understand," Ashcroft said.

"Not the sharpest officer in the bunk, are you, General?" a voice said.

Bradshaw and Ashcroft's heads swiveled in the direction of the freight elevator. The dark silhouette walked towards them, her face shadowed by the overhead lights. When her face emerged from the shadows, Ashcroft and Bradshaw turned pale, as if they were staring at a ghost.

"Barbara?" said Bradshaw.

Barbara raised her Glock and shot Bradshaw in the groin. He fell to the ground and gawked at his mangled genitals hemorrhaging across the wooden floor. Soon after, the pain set in. He grunted and squealed. Barbara kneeled down next to him and rubbed his graying brown hair. Her big brown eyes were bright and glossy.

"So, this is your plan?" Ashcroft asked, staring at Sayf. "A double-cross?"

"You know me to be smarter than that, right?" Sayf asked, laughing. "I'm a money man. A mercenary. Not a general. You're a man of strategy, not a hunter."

Sayf pointed at Barbra. She gave a slight nod to Ashcroft as she relished Bradshaw's agony. He grabbed her ankle with his bloody hands and curled into a fetal position.

"What are you trying to say?" Barbara asked with endearment.

"P-P-P-PLEASE DON'T!!" Bradshaw screamed.

"Hmmm," Barbara said. She leaned closer. "Shhh," she whispered before licking the rim of his ear. "I just want you to know you have never pleasured me more than right now."

Ashcroft looked down at the two of them. Beads of sweat condensed on his forehead.

"Oi!" Sayf said, snapping his fingers at Ashcroft. "Now, James, ignore what's going on in front of you. Obviously, there's an issue between the two of them, and to be quite frank I would rather not know the details." Ashcroft's eyes oscillated between Sayf and Barbara. "We need the Blackout. We can't move forward without it. Agreed?"

Ashcroft looked down at Bradshaw, lying in a pool of his own blood and sighed.

"If it wasn't Barbara, then who hit the embassy?" Ashcroft asked.

Barbara laughed.

"How did you get this job, dad?" Barbara asked. She pressed her knee into Bradshaw's wound. A flash of happiness came across her face from Bradshaw's squealing. "You high officials couldn't find bin Laden in Utah."

"I'm not your father," Ashcroft said. "Your point?"

"Shepard Black?" Barbara asked, looking up at Ashcroft.

"That's not possible," Ashcroft said. "He's dead."

"I don't think so," Barbara said. She looked down at the growing puddle of blood around her military boots. "He was moving on the helicopter before I hopped off."

"Shit," Ashcroft said sighing.

"Sounds like a plan, General?" Sayf asked. "You get your forces together, I gather the appropriate funds, and we let your Wolf do what she does best. Hunt."

Ashcroft wiped the sweat from his face.

Bradshaw looked up. He was fading in and out of consciousness, staring at a blurred image of Ashcroft and Barbara standing over him. Their voices sounding muzzled and distant.

"For God's sake, Barbara," Ashcroft said with disgust. "Put the man out of his misery."

"Yes sir," she said, sarcastically. Bradshaw trembled at the barrel of Barbara's pistol before two shots were fired.

Pandora

Knock-knock. Shepard opened the door to his flat. He glanced at Jonah's blank expression before walking away. Jonah walked into the spacious flat and closed the door behind him. Salsa music from the unit under them thumped against the hardwood floors.

"You don't have noise ordinances around here?" Jonah asked.

Shepard scoffed. He walked across his flat and sat down at his glass desk. A 42-inch flat-screen computer monitor was standing on the glass desktop. He clicked his wireless black mouse and started scrolling.

"What are you doing?" Jonah asked.

"Looking for escorts," Shepard said with sarcasm. He minimized the screen. "What do you want, Jonah?"

"The truth."

"What truth would you like to hear?"

"What?" Jonah asked grimacing.

"The truth is a shade of gray, kid. But that's not what you want."

"Shepard, I—"

"You're angry. Angry that your dad lied to you all these years. So, you want a truth that's undisputed. One that will make your dad a hero and justify the lies or one that'll make—"

"Fucking stop it! All right?!" Jonah's voice echoed throughout the long empty flat. "Stop it with the fucking riddles and tell me the truth."

Shepard looked away from Jonah, shaking his head.

"Fine," Shepard whispered. He stood from his seat and leaned against the glass desk. "He was one of us."

"7721?"

Shepard nodded.

"He was a pilot, of course." Shepard said. His face lightened. He gave a slight smile and said, "When I was a kid, your dad…" Shepard paused. He looked up at Jonah's cloudy gaze and said, "Jonah, what we do…it's bad. We steal intellectual property from the world. It's not just weapons of mass destruction. Cures for diseases, prototypes that would provide clean air and fresh water, vegetable seeds you can plant in a desert that could grow crops as far and long as the eye could see. The inventors, the aids, anyone who has anything to do with what is downloaded into the Black-out, is murdered. We've caused just as much evil as we've stopped. That's what your father was a part of."

Shepard walked over to the arsenal cage and unlocked the door. He took out a black M-16. It had a laser propped under the shaft and rows of red shark teeth drawn in on the sides. Shepard grabbed two magazines and walked out of the cage. "This was your old man's. You see this?" Shepard said, pointing at the shark teeth. "This was his number of kills. He had three more M-16s just like this in his cage." Jonah's breaths were labored. He could feel the tears form in his eyes. Shepard walked toward Jonah holding the rifle flat against his chest. "You might have known your dad to be this wholesome, positive pillar of the community, but he was also this." Jonah looked down at his father's M-16.

The salsa music's bass got louder. It shook the ground with each thump.

Jonah sighed and said, "This may have been a part of who he was. But he was still—"

Shepard stuffed the rifle in Jonah's right arm and kicked his chest. The force sent Jonah sliding across the hardwood floor before crashing through Shepard's apartment door. Jonah laid in the apartment hallway, rubbing his sternum. Two magazine clips came sliding across the floor and hit his leg. Jonah pulled himself to a kneeling position and stared at Shepard. Shepard nodded. Moments later the floor disintegrated from under him. Jonah gasped. He crawled to the opening of the apartment door and looked over the edge. It was twelve floors of nothing. Shepard and his flat were gone. The couch, arsenal cage, and computer had yet to crash at the bottom.

Jonah closed his eyes shut.

"Fuck," he murmured.

Jonah loaded his father's M-16 and tucked the other magazine in his jeans. Graham opened his door holding a nine-millimeter. He looked behind Jonah and saw the floorless flat.

"Shepard?" Graham mouthed.

Jonah shook his head. Rosa walked out of her room, startled at the sight behind Jonah.

"Oh, my God," she said.

"Shhh," Graham said. He gestured for her to go back in her room.

The elevator lights to the twelfth floor turned on, and the elevator doors opened. Four metal cylindrical tanks were flung from the elevator. They spun in the air and landed in the atrium and down the hallway. Graham and Jonah nodded at each other before taking one last deep breath and closing their eyes. Within a minute, purple smoke filled the entire floor. Jonah got down on his belly, pointing his rifle in the direction of the elevator.

Sounds, Jonah thought to himself.

7721 stepped out of the elevator. They wore black gas masks and armored vests.

Different sounds.

Graham kept his back against the wall and snuck to the right side of the atrium, hiding under the smoke.

Different sounds.

Graham felt his way along the atrium wall and took a knee, raising his pistol. He opened fire. The bullets grazed past the armed men.

The bad...the worse...

Jonah pulled himself up to one knee, holding the rifle as if he were looking through the sights.

"Over there!" one of them screamed. They opened fire. Jonah's ears twitched at the sound of five SMG machine guns firing.

...and the fucked up! Jonah shouted in his mind before pulling the trigger.

M16 bullets rang through the atrium. A chest shot for each gunman. Jonah and Graham waited for a moment before getting up and making their way down the atrium. They took the gas masks from the soldiers and slipped it on their faces. Jonah ran into Rosa's apartment.

"Rosa!" Jonah shouted, his voice muzzled by the mask. He ran into her room. Rosa, unconscious, was on the floor by her bed. Jonah picked her up over his shoulders and walked out to the atrium. "How did they find us?"

"Doesn't matter," Graham said, looking around the smoke-filled atrium. "Up is the only option." They hurried back into Rosa's apartment and opened the window to a metal fire escape. They climbed four flights of creaky, rusted metal steps to the roof. Jonah could feel Rosa squirming on his shoulder. He propped her on her feet.

"Hey!" Jonah shouted, slapping her cheek. Rosa took one

deep breath of the crisp midnight air. She grabbed Jonah's shoulders and gasped as if she were having a nightmare.

"Wh-Where are we?" she asked, coughing.

"I'll explain later," Graham said, grabbing her arm. The three of them sprinted across the long cement rooftop. Graham could hear 7721 swarm behind them. Bullets rang against the cement. The edge of the rooftop was coming fast.

"We're running out of room!" Rosa shouted.

"No, we're not," Graham said. "There's more room on the next building."

"Wait! What?!" Rosa shouted.

Jonah and Graham each grabbed Rosa by an armpit and picked up speed. She screamed as the three of them leaped five feet over a three-story crevasse, landing on their feet. Graham grabbed Rosa by the arm as her knees buckled.

"C'mon!" shouted Graham.

They ran across the rooftop, which had an old pigeon coop near the edge. Graham looked over. Beneath them was a quiet street with cars parked on the sidewalk. Graham rushed into the coop. Gray-and-white collared pigeons flapped and gawked. Graham pulled out a bag. He dragged it back to the edge of the roof.

"These are bungee cords," Graham said.

"What?" Rosa said.

"Blackout technology," Graham said as he took out three harnesses. He handed one to Jonah. "The harness is a computer, the cords have nanites. When you're five feet from the ground, they slow the rope." He placed the harness on Rosa and tightened the shoulder straps. "As soon as your feet touch the floor, the harness will release. When we get to the—"

"Hubby!" a voice echoed in the distance.

The voice knocked the wind out of Jonah. A wave of goosebumps rippled across his back. He stood up, glaring in the direction of the greeting.

"It's her," Jonah said.

His eyes stared at the short-haired feminine figure on the other side of the rooftop walking toward him. She wore dark-gray fatigues with a matching tank top. Next to scar tissue of an old bullet wound on her chest were two dog tags that read SANTIAGO and SEAN GREEN. Her black army boots ground against the rooftop cement, as her wild, curly, dark-brown hair blew in the wind.

"Carol," Jonah said raising his SMG and walking toward her as if he were in a trance.

"Jonah," Rosa said. "We have to go." Jonah didn't respond. He continued to walk toward her. "Jonah! What are you doing!?" Jonah was about to remove his harness when he felt a sharp pain on the back of his neck. He fell to his knees. His eyes rolled into the back of his head before falling to the ground. Graham picked him up and dragged him to the edge of the rooftop.

"Listen," Graham said, digging in his pockets. "When you get to the ground, take one of those cars and run."

"Wait," Rosa said. "I can't—"

"Listen to me! We are out of time! You get to the bottom, take a car, and run!"

"Graham, I don't know how to hot-wire a—" Graham handed her a rectangular shaped object the size of a credit card.

"Put this against any car made after 2007. It will unlock and start it. Got it?"

"Wait! I don't…" Graham picked up Jonah and pushed him off the edge. Next, he grabbed Rosa by the shoulders and placed her on the edge. "I can't do this!"

Graham's adrenaline subsided as he gazed at Rosa's tearful face.

"Rosa," he said wiping her tears away. "If you're always afraid, you'll never fly."

He pushed her off the roof's edge.

Graham took the other two harnesses and kicked them off the roof. He holstered his nine-millimeter and waited. 7721 hopped across the roof holding SMG rifles with red scopes, making a line spanning the entire rooftop. Barbara broke the line and stood in front of her unit. The clouds parted, giving way to a moonlit sky that shined on the quiet rooftop. Graham and Barbara stood for a moment staring at each other, breathing the cold air.

"Graham," Barbara said, pulling back her short brown hair.

"Been a while," Graham said.

"Where's my husband?"

Graham laughed and said, "Gone."

"You saved him from me?"

"No," Graham said, shaking his head. "I saved him from himself. He thinks he can kill you." Barbara laughed. "Where's Shep?"

"I think we dropped him off a while ago." Barbara chuckled. "I'm sorry. Too soon? I know the two of you were bosom buddies."

"I never really liked Shepard. We only got along so well because we hated you more."

Barbara smiled. She raised her hand and gestured for the other soldiers to lower their weapons.

"Is there something you want to get off your chest, amigo?" Barbara asked, walking toward Graham. "Why don't you and me have a little chat," she whispered.

Graham cracked his neck. He ran toward Barbara and jumped in the air. His left fist grazed her left cheek. Graham landed square on his feet, throwing a hook to Barbara's ribs. Rage had taken over. There was no rhyme or reason to his attacks, just a flurry of thoughtless aggression. With each punch landed, Barbara laughed. She could feel the fatigue overcoming his anger. His breathing became more labored. Barbara dropped her hands to her sides. She studied Graham's worn-out stance and shook her head.

"Feel better?" she asked.

All Graham saw was a blur and in a second Barbara's elbow shattered his cheek bone. The blow whipped his head back before it was slung forward by a blow to his chest. Graham felt as though he was having a heart attack. He collapsed to the floor and rolled on his back. She knelt down beside him.

"It's just a broken sternum," Barbara said. "Crippling, but won't kill you. I had a cracked sternum after they shot us up in that elevator. On cold nights like this it still smarts like a fucker." She sighed. "Anyhoo, what's done is done." She reached into Graham's pockets and pulled out the oval-shaped thumb drive. She held the Blackout in the air. The light from the full moon bounced off the black thumb drive, causing her big brown eyes to sparkle. "Who'd a thunk Pandora would come in such a tiny package?"

Successor

It was a four-by-four metal box no bigger than a small bathroom. Graham sat slumped on a metal chair. He stared at a small matching metal table in front of him, examining the distorted reflection staring back at him, that of a beaten prison inmate wearing a tan jumpsuit with a swollen cheek bone. He twisted his wrists and ankles in the metal shackles that were chained to the ground. A yellow overhead light shined on his clean-shaven head with the number 2001 tattooed into the side of his scalp. Graham looked up as the thick metal doors to his cell creaked open. Ashcroft, wearing his black trenchcoat, stood with his hands in pockets. He pulled a pack of cigarettes from the breast pocket of his black coat and walked into the room. Ashcroft sat down, straightened his burgundy-and-gold-striped tie, and the two stared at each other.

"You know," Ashcroft said, breaking the silence. "My replacement was always going to be you." Graham gave a subtle scoff. "No, it's true. You think Bradshaw wanted this job? Fuck no. I certainly wasn't going to give it to Black. He thinks he has a heart of gold. But you?" Aschroft chuckled. "Adaptable. You do what's necessary. That's why I thought someday you were going to wear these stars." Ashcroft sighed. Graham lowered his head and continued staring at his reflection. Ashcroft leaned over and extended his arm, a cigarette between his thumb and index finger. Graham took it. He placed it in his mouth and leaned forward while Ashcroft lit it with a lighter.

"Appreciate you," Graham said grinning.

"Of course," Ashcroft said. He took out a metal flask and slid it across the metal table.

"This that black label you keep in your limo?" Graham asked opening the flask. Ashcroft nodded.

"Guard," Ashcroft said. "Remove the chains from this soldier." The guard walked into the room, uncuffed Graham, and walked out.

"How're you gonna do it?" Graham asked.

"How would you do it?"

"You're asking me how I would kill me?" Graham asked, squinting his eyes. Ashcroft smiled and nodded. "I don't know, Ashcroft," Graham said furrowing his brows. "I'm not suicidal."

"Well," Ashcroft said picking up the flask, "Maybe it would be easier—"

"How'd you find us?"

Ashcroft opened the flask and took a swig.

"I didn't."

"Barbara."

Ashcroft chuckled and said, "You gotta hand it to her. She's a tracker. That building you were staying in was an old federal building. You should've known we would've figured that out."

"No, you wouldn't."

"You're right," Ashcroft said. "Hiding in plain sight, huh?"

"You could say that."

"You gonna tell me where the others are?"

Graham let out a single chuckle before picking up the flask and taking another gulp. He slammed the flask in front of Ashcroft, shaking his head.

"Here's what's going to happen," Ashcroft said, clearing his throat. "You and your accomplices will be tried and convicted for the unspeakable act of terror you inflicted on this nation."

"Terror?"

Ashcroft took out his phone and slid it across the table, where it came to rest in front of Graham. It was the apartment complex. It was news footage from a helicopter view of the entire block encased in a fireball that touched the sky. The sight knocked the breath out of Graham. He turned the phone over and slammed it against the table.

"We're gonna try you in Oklahoma, put you in front of a firing squad. A soldier's death. It's the least I could do."

"People lived there. Children."

"That's right," Ashcroft said, standing up. "Families, babies… you're a monster, Graham." Graham panted. He looked up from the metal table and glared at Ashcroft. "A man who does something like this has an agenda that makes human life grossly expendable in comparison." The two locked eyes for a moment before Graham slammed his fist on the tabletop. "You know what? You don't have to tell me where they are. We'll find 'em." As Ashcroft walked out of the holding cell, he yelled, "I wasn't lying. I always thought it was gonna be you."

Rat Race

"Number 304! Two large dump burgers! No mayonnaise," the cashier shouted from behind the register. Rosa stood up and approached the counter. She rummaged around the pockets of her tattered gray jeans and took out a wad of cash. She tucked away her sweaty brown hair and pulled down a dark-blue hood over part of her face. She handed the cashier the wad of money, grabbed her change, and took the bag.

"Have a good evening," the cashier said.

Rosa nodded and walked out of the busy restaurant. She clutched the greasy white bag in her right hand, keeping her head down as she walked with a crowd down worn gray steps toward a subway station. She pulled out a card and waved it over a scanner, allowing her to pass through the gates. She walked with the crowd to a second lower level of the subway. From the crowded platform, she looked over at the empty subway tunnel. An old man sat on the floor with his back against a light-gray cracked-tile pillar. He held up a sign that read: I BEG SO I CAN DO DRUGS. I BUY DRUGS TO BE HAPPY. DON'T YOU

WANT ME TO BE HAPPPY? Next to the beggar was a teenager sitting on a bench surrounded by white buckets playing drum cadences. Rosa bumped her way across the crowded subway platform toward the back wall near the tunnel. Echoes from the oncoming train hummed across the platform. She looked up from the ground and saw a little black girl staring at her. Her pigtails showcased her pink glittered barrettes as the train flew. Her hood rustled against Rosa's face. Rosa looked at the child and cracked a smile. The child waved and smiled back, her front teeth missing. The little girl tugged on her mother and pointed in the direction where Rosa was standing, only to find an empty wall and a passing train.

Rosa walked for about a half-mile down the dark subway tunnel, looking over her shoulder every few steps. She stopped in front of a pile of plywood next to a large opening where subway tracks intersected. Rosa lifted the plywood. She crawled into an uncovered manhole and scaled down a twenty-foot drop using a rock-climbing rope before landing in the middle of a small rectangular space. LED lights illuminated the small room. Worn posters of old boy bands were taped to the solid cement walls. Jonah was sitting on a rusted black futon with no cushion. Rosa pulled out a burger and threw it at him before walking over to a green-and-white lawn chair on the other side of the room.

"What the hell is this?" Jonah frowned.

"Food," Rosa said.

"You call this fried pink puff shit *food*?" Jonah asked. Rosa ignored the question as she ravaged her burger. Jonah looked down at his meal shaking his head. The two ate in silence. The sounds of subway trains hurling over them rattled the entire space. "I'm surprised a debutante like yourself would know a place like this even exists."

"A debutante?" Rosa asked. "You grew up in the Midwest, taking hayrides and running through cornfields."

"What's that supposed to mean?"

"You don't know anything about me, do you?"

"I know you're a liar."

"Welcome to the human race."

"Fuck you."

"No, fuck you!" Rosa said, holding up her middle finger. The room was silent again.

"So, are you going to tell me how you knew about this place or not?" Jonah asked waving his hands.

"Look at the 112 poster."

Jonah contorted his torso to look at the poster behind him.

"What am I supposed to be..." Just under the group's feet was a signature that read, *To Rosa: Keep it real.*

"That was an awesome night," Rosa said smiling. "The last time I had a good set of foster parents."

"You were in the system?"

"It's not so bad when you come across good people," Rosa said, folding one of her legs in her lap. "But good people? Genuine people in this world?" Rosa clutched her knee. "Man, they're hard to come by. One couple wanted me to pull cons with them. This one guy took me in just so his wife could scissor me while he watched, but it wasn't until one couple almost human-trafficked me before I said fuck this. I ran. Ran until I came across some people down here. They set me up in this little spot. Checked on me. When I was old enough, I got a job, got my GED, and moved forward."

"I didn't know. Why didn't I know this about you?"

"I don't know." Rosa brought her knees up to her chest, cradling herself.

"There were a lot of things that you kept from us. Why?"

"Transparency. Remember?" Rosa asked while wiping the crumbs from her face.

"You don't think you should have been transparent before we got on a fucking plane to England?"

"What does it matter?" Rosa uncradled herself and placed her feet on the dusty ground. "Shepard is dead. God knows if Graham is still alive, and we're still on the run. I don't know what the next move here is, Jonah! Do you?" Jonah put his head down. "Do you?!" He raised his head, locked eyes with her, and shook his head.

"No," he whispered.

"Then transparency means fuck-all right now, don't it?"

Jonah shook his head wincing with his right eye.

"How long were you in England?" Jonah asked.

"What?"

"You just went Guy Ritchie on me."

Rosa bowed her head. She bit into her sandwich and chuckled between each bite.

"Shut up," she said.

Jonah looked at her and smiled as they sat and ate in silence. Mid-chew, Jonah raised his head, a bolus of hamburger still in his mouth. His eyes widened.

"Rosa?"

"What?"

"How did you pay for this?"

"I used cash, Jonah," she said, taking a deep sigh. Jonah parted his lips and breathed, nodding his head while chewing. The two shared another moment of silence before Rosa gasped and whispered, "Shit."

"What?"

"I used my MetroCard to get down here."

"Shit," Jonah jumped up from the futon and grabbed Rosa by the arm. "We gotta go."

"Wait, Jonah." He pulled her over to the rope leading to the tunnels. "Hold on. Maybe they haven't—"

"You know they have! Now go!"

Rosa grabbed the rope and started to climb. She was no more

than three feet off the ground when the makeshift plywood hatch to their bunker flew off. A train passed by the hole. A gust of natural wind hit Rosa's face before a gas-filled canister grazed her cheek. Light-blue smoke spewed from its sides. Rosa tried her best to focus on the opening that was becoming more and more distorted. She released her grip from the rope and fell onto her side. Jonah pulled out his pistol and hovered over her holding his breath. The entire bunker was filled with a light-blue mist. It became so thick that Jonah couldn't see his hands in front of him.

"Come on!" Jonah shouted. He felt a light tap on the shoulder. As he tried to whip his gun around he was blindsided by a right hook. Jonah was unconscious before his knees touched the ground.

Truth in Deception

WASHINGTON, D.C., PRESENT DAY

"You have an appointment with the chief of staff at eight a.m. sharp, a brunch with the D.C. Women's Rotary Society—"

"Rotary what?" McCray asked staring, at his black tablet. "Cancel that."

He sat at a small round table with dark-red linen across from his aide, using his index finger to scroll through the touch screen. Waiters wearing black ties and tan sport coats navigated through the crowded, upscale Georgetown restaurant. The setting sun shined a dim autumn light through the ceiling windows onto patrons sitting at their tables.

"Sir, you've canceled five of your appearances, and elections are in the next few months. If we don't make your base happy—"

"Fuck my base. Those days are done."

"Sir?"

"Nothing, Ben. Don't worry about it."

"Are we ready to order?" The waiter asked. The waiter glanced at the security guard standing five feet from them.

"Sir?" Ben asked.

"Another coffee," McCray said staring at his tablet. Ben sneezed. To the senator's disgust, green snot and phlegm flashed from Ben's nose and mouth. "The hell is wrong with you?" McCray asked, grimacing.

"My apologies, sir."

"You guys make chicken and dumpling soup here, right?" The waiter nodded. "He'll have that and a glass of whatever juice you got back there." McCray turned his head and waved for his security detail. His guard walked across the crowded restaurant to McCray. "He's gonna finish his food and then you take him home."

"Yes, sir," the guard said. Ben wiped his nose and sniffed.

"Sir I—"

"Shut up," McCray said, going back to his tablet. "You're gonna eat your food, go home, and get some rest." He looked up from his tablet. "And Ben, if you fucking make me sick…"

"It's Benji, sir."

"What?"

"People call me Benji."

"What?" McCray asked scrunching his face. "I'm not calling you…what are you? A fucking puppy? You're trying to get into politics, right?"

"Yes, sir."

"I'm gonna give you some great advice, then you're gonna leave me alone, eat your food, and go the fuck home, OK?" Ben sniffed and nodded. "Image is how people perceive you. It's the cornerstone to politics, because if people perceive you as a leader, they will make you a leader. That's it. That's the big secret to politics and the kicker here is that you don't have to be a good person. It doesn't matter if you save kittens in your spare time or smoke crack—if people perceive you as a leader, they're gonna vote for you. Now do you think when people hear the name Benji, they're thinking, *This is a guy I want to have the nuclear codes?*" Ben cleared his throat and shook his head. "Right, now the name Benjamin? Senator Benajmin James

Thomas? West Point graduate? That guy sounds like Captain fucking America." Ben looked down at the table and nodded. "Now, the next time someone calls you Benji, do yourself a favor and smack the shit out of 'em." McCray went back to his screen.

"Sir, if you don't mind me asking, what are you looking at?"

"Someone who can answer my questions," McCray said. His finger stopped. He pressed the touch screen, where a mugshot and video of a man in chains being led to his cell appeared.

"Federal prison unnamed?" McCray whispered. "Just came in." He maximized the video screen. It was Graham in chains, being processed. McCray paused the video and enlarged Graham's image. He could see healed bullet wounds on Graham's chest and a tattoo on his clavicle with four numbers.

"7721," McCray said. He closed his laptop as the waiter brought Ben's meal to the table. McCray stood up. "When I come back, I want to see you eating."

"Yes sir," Ben said.

McCray walked through the dining floor and past the kitchen. He stepped into the bathroom and started to wash his hands.

"Long time, Senator," a voice said. McCray looked into the mirror and saw a figure standing several feet behind him.

"I'm sorry?"

"We don't have much time. They're coming for you."

"What?"

"Please don't make this difficult."

"Who are you?"

"I'll explain that on the way."

"Way? Where?" McCray took two steps. "Guar—"

He felt a sharp pain in his neck before passing out. The man caught the senator before he hit the ground and threw him over his shoulder.

᪐

McCray grunted and opened his eyes, which caused him to squint at the light that was shining in his face. Disoriented, McCray rubbed the back of his neck and blinked hard several times. He rubbed his eyes and looked around. He was sitting in a wooden chair in front of a long hardwood conference table surrounded by old law books with dusty, tattered spines, sitting on worn shelves. McCray continued to blink, trying to adjust to the bright room. He could barely see two figures standing up. Jonah stood with his back leaning against one of the bookshelves. Rosa was pacing toward McCray with her arms folded.

"What is this?" McCray asked, catching his breath.

"You're awake," Rosa said.

"Who are you?" McCray asked. "I had a security detail. They're probably tearing the city apart looking for me."

"You don't need to threaten us, Senator," Jonah said. "We arrived the same way you did."

"Knocked out?" McCray asked. The two nodded.

"Where do you think we are?" Rosa asked.

"If I were to guess," McCray said as he stood up, "this looks like the basement of the congressional library."

The doorknob behind McCray started to rattle. Keys jingled until the door opened.

"You three are lucky I move faster than them," Shepard said as he entered. "They were right on my heels."

Rosa closed her eyes and gave a sigh of relief.

"Dammit!" Jonah shouted. "Why?"

"Why what?" Shepard asked.

"Why did you put us out?" Rosa asked.

"Told you they were on my heels," Shepard said. "Literally. I could move you two faster if you weren't trying help. No offense."

"What?" Jonah asked.

McCray, squinting, walked toward Shepard.

"I know you," McCray said. Shepard nodded. "7721, you were with Ashcroft that day I came with Upstead."

"Wait!" Jonah said. "That was a twenty-foot climb. What the fuck do you mean it was easier carrying us?"

"I needed you unconscious for us to get out Jonah," Shepard said. "The place was crawling with 7721 after Little Miss Financier used her subway pass to get back into the tunnels."

"How did you get us out?" Rosa asked.

"The trains," Shepard sighed. "We got on one as it passed by your panic room."

Jonah and Rosa looked at each other with tilted heads and a glossy gaze.

"If you don't want to tell me the truth, Shep, just fucking say it," Jonah said, shaking his head. "I am sick of your bullshit lies!"

"That is the truth," Shepard said.

"How do you expect us to believe that, Shepard?" Rosa asked. "How? Those trains go up to fifty miles an hour."

Jonah paced back and forth, rubbing his face.

"Which means the force would rip off your fucking arm!" Jonah said.

McCray gasped. He looked at Shepard and said in a calm voice, "You're a Wolf."

Shepard glanced at the senator. The room was silent. Jonah and Rosa stared at Shepard's quiet affirmation.

"Graham?" Jonah asked.

Shepard shook his head.

"So, Ashcroft was lying when he said there were only three of you?" McCray asked.

"Nope," Shepard said sighing. "That's probably the only truth to ever come out of that man's mouth."

"I don't understand," McCray said. "There was Santiago, the psycho, and a guy named—"

"Sean Green," Shepard said. "Let's talk about him."

The Wolf

"**Ya!** Get in there!" he said to his cattle. Riding on the back of his brown-and-white spotted horse, the herdsman rode in the opposite direction of his sluggish steers. It was a small group of twenty. He looped back, his horse now galloping behind the herd of cows.

"Get in here so I can watch this game!" he shouted, straightening out his Redskins baseball cap. He howled at the herd as they moaned and pranced their way into a circular dirt clearing surrounded by a tan wooden fence. The last one, a young black steer, looked up at the ranch hand.

"Hurry up!" he shouted.

The little steer scurried into the crowd of cattle. The herdsman closed the fence. He hopped off his horse, patting down his faded red T-shirt and jeans. He wiped the dirt from his brown-skinned forearms. "Beer, football, shower. In that order," he murmured to himself.

He looked out onto the endless dirt pastures. It was dusk. Pink sunlight flashed just above the distant mountain range as the sun set. He directed his horse into a small gray-and-white stable before making his way toward the worn, unpainted front porch of his small ranch-style home. The herdsman climbed up four creaking steps and took off his boots before opening the ripped screen door.

"Trish?" he asked. He could hear Joe Jackson playing on the Bluetooth speaker in the kitchen. "Baby?"

"Oh good," Trish said, walking into their small, empty living room. A teal leather loveseat was propped against the tan vinyl wall. Across from the loveseat were two narrow doorways: one leading to a bedroom with only enough room for a single bed, the other leading to the kitchen. Sean could smell dinner in the oven. Trish wore a generic white apron with a pair of jogging pants and a white T-shirt underneath. "Come in the kitchen for a moment."

She motioned for him to follow her, scratching the light-brown scalp beneath her crinkled black hair. He followed her into the slit of space that was the kitchen. An old school-desk from the fifties covered with white linen made the dining-room table. A few feet from the makeshift dining table, Trish pointed at an analog TV with a thick, wooden frame. Black-and-white popcorn static was on the screen.

"Sean, we're going to miss the game."

"Joe Jackson again?" Sean asked. The fifty-inch television was too big for the small kitchen. Sean had to slide between the TV and the oven to get behind it. They placed the TV in the middle of the kitchen, facing the living room, so that they could watch it from the cracked leather loveseat. "You've got to be the only Joe Jackson fan in the world."

"You don't have five Grammy nominations and nineteen albums with just one fan."

"Shit," he said.

"You're never gonna fix it."

"Tinfoil."

"Sean?"

Sean brought his head from behind the television set and stared at Trish.

"Have a little faith. Tinfoil, please?" He asked with a smile. Trish rolled her light-brown eyes and walked over to the counter. She was only able to open the drawer halfway, knocking into the wooden frame of the TV. She yanked the box of tinfoil from the drawer and threw it at Sean's feet.

"Dumb question: Is stealing cable still a no-go?"

"You want—"

"I know. I get it. Baby, it's just that we must have missed eight games this season, three of them have been on regular TV and…"

Her slight frown lightened as a clear analog picture came on the screen.

"There we go," Sean said with a smile. He stood up and gave Trish a kiss on her forehead. "What's for dinner?"

"Salmon," she said with a devious smirk.

"Aww, honey," Sean said with a bitter smile. "Really?"

"Sean, how many times have we had steer?"

"I mean…"

"Sean, how many times?"

Sean shook and bowed his head.

"Right, if we're going live off the grid, as you say, I need you healthy."

"I am healthy."

"Not now. Forty years from now."

"Forty?" Sean asked turning his head to the side. "Is that all you're giving me?

"Fifty?" Sean grabbed her by the waist. "Ok, sixty!" He rubbed his nose against her neck. "OK!" Trish said, laughing. "How about a hundred years!"

"See now you're just making up num—" In the midst of

Trish's giggling, a faint red light flashed across the windowpane. Sean's head swiveled in the direction.

"You OK?" Sean was quiet. His green and blue eyes locked on the red beam shining in the distance. "Sean?" The red flash flickered a few times before fading. Trish looked at him for a moment and then asked, "Honey?"

"It's nothing. Thought I…"

Trish grabbed Sean's face with her hands.

"Baby, they're gone. Hey, look at me. Just me and you. OK?"

"Yeah," he said, sighing. "OK."

⤎

"So, what do you think?" Trish asked.

The two were sitting on the old sofa, hunched over bamboo dinner trays that rested in their laps. A clear analog picture showing the last quarter of *Sunday Night Football* beamed from the TV in the kitchen.

"What do I think of what?" Sean asked.

There was silence. Sean looked up at Trish, who was giving him a blank stare.

"What do you think I'm asking about, Sean?"

"I don't know, but if you want me to guess some more, I can."

Trish cut her eyes at him, shaking her head.

"You can be such an asshole sometimes."

"What are you talking about?" he asked, putting another chunk of fish in his mouth.

"Forget it."

"What?" Sean said, laughing. "I don't know what you're asking me about."

The two continued. Trish mumbling profanities under her breath with Sean repeating, "Should I guess some mo'? Should I guess some mo'? Should I guess some mo'?"

"The salmon Sean! The fucking salmon, do you like it?"

"Oh," Sean said furrowing his brows. "I mean…it's straight."

Trish glared at Sean.

"OK," she whispered. She got up and grabbed their plates. She stepped into the kitchen and slid her body across the bulky TV to the farmhouse sink behind it. Trish dropped the dishes into the sink loudly enough to startle him. He watched as she turned on the water and opened the freezer to their half-sized fridge. She grabbed a small tub of pistachio ice cream, picked up one silver spoon, and sat back down on the couch. She continued to watch the game, feet tucked under her legs, chipping away at the rock-hard ice cream.

"You just mad 'cause your team's losing," Sean mumbled to himself. "Told you: To be a Browns fan is to be a fan of shit."

"I'm sorry, what did you say?"

"Oh, I was just wondering if you were going to share some of that?" he asked with a childish tone.

"No."

"Thought so. Just checking."

⁕

Sean looked over at the clock. It was one a.m. A white space heater in the corner of the small living room illuminated the entire flat in bright orange. The TV showed a distorted, multi-colored end-of-broadcast-day signal. By now Trish had crawled into his arms and fallen asleep. Sean took Trish's head and neck and laid it down on the couch. He turned off the TV and walked outside to the porch. A full silver moon in the clear black sky shined across the countryside. Sean closed his eyes and took a deep breath of the crisp Midwest air. He placed a hand on one of the wooden porch columns, his index finger tapping. There was no music in his head, no song he heard earlier in the morning that was on repeat, but the tapping continued. Then he realized that the tapping was getting louder and faster. The tapping he felt

compelled to do was the rhythm of rotary blades from a helicopter approaching fast. Sean ran into the house.

"Trish! Trish! Wake up, love!"

"Sean?" she asked, confused. "What's going…" He picked
her up and took her into the bedroom. He kicked over their
single bed to reveal a trapdoor with a latch. "Sean?" He unhooked
the latch and opened the door. "Sean, are you going to talk to
me?" He could hear the fear in her voice. He grabbed her by the
arms and gave her a tender kiss on the lips.

"Listen to me," he said. "Whatever happens, you do *not* come
out of that box."

"What?! Sean what are—"

"Love, listen to me! We don't have a lot of time here. That's a
panic box. I put it there when I first built this place. It locks you
in. There is food and water. The combination is your birthday,
'cause you don't remember our anniversary," he said, laughing.
Sean picked Trish up and placed her in the panic box.

"Sean," Trish said, sobbing.

"Love you, too."

He smiled and closed the metal casing. The box locked. He
walked over to his dresser and opened a long bottom drawer. A
black Stinger rocket launcher was encased in gray foam. Next to
its shaft was a pair of black shades and a set of dark-gray rubber
gloves. Sean grabbed the loaded launcher, glasses, and gloves.
He walked outside and stood in front of his patio. He looked
down at the ground and took a deep breath before pointing the
launcher at the giant crystal-colored moon hovering above him.
Sean fired the single rocket into the sky, then put on the glasses
and gloves and stepped onto his porch. The dark glasses clicked
a few seconds before four video screens appeared in front of him.
Each video screen was from the missile's point of view as it flew
through the sky. A ticker in the right-hand corner of Sean's virtual screen read 20,000 feet. He held his right fist in front of

him. When the ticker read 30,000 feet, he opened his hands. The rocket split into four separate missiles, dropping back down from the clouds. Sean focused his attention on the first screen. It raced under the silver clouds, passing by the dark blur of an oncoming chopper.

"Black Hawk," Sean said waving his hand.

The missile whipped around. In seconds the first screen went black. Sean could see the explosion over the mountain range.

"Closer than I thought," he murmured.

He looked at the fourth screen, which showed three choppers moving in formation. Each chopper released two Hellfire missiles. Sean opened his right hand and held it upward at an angle. He used his other hand to open a command drop box, pressing the flare command. His fourth missile increased altitude and dropped flares in front of the Hellfire missiles. They each exploded. Sean then pointed his hand downward, causing the missile to crash into the tail rotor of the lead helicopter. It spun in the air before running into the other two helicopters and exploding in the distance.

"Stupid, you got all this space—why would you fly so close to one another?" he said, shaking his head. Sean looked at his second screen, which had just gone dark. A fireball in the sky soon followed.

"Shit," he said. "Got that one." A red light from the distance flashed across Sean's eyes. He ran into the house and leaped behind the kitchen countertop just before a hail of bullets ripped through the wooden ranch house. As the bullets flew past him, Sean closed his eyes and listened. He could hear the faint sound of assault rifles reloading and engines humming.

"Fifteen Humvees. Coming from the front."

The convoy continued to fire at the ranch house, collapsing the front wall, cattle caught in the crossfire as they stampeded through the wooden fence.

"Cease fire!" a soldier shouted.

They jumped out of their armored Humvees and made a half-circle perimeter around the house. The heat from the bullets set parts of the wooden house on fire. The cattle screamed and limped in terror toward the distant mountain ranges. The house creaked as if it were about to collapse, as the mini-platoon sat and waited in silence for any sign of movement. The lead soldier motioned for the rest of the platoon to move toward the house. Sean kneeled down in the corner of the kitchen. His eyes were closed, his right ear held up in the air. He held up his clenched right fist over his head, trembling with tension. As soon as the lead soldier took one more step, Sean grunted and dropped his fist down in front of him like a hammer. His third missile slammed into the middle of the platoon. Bodies were thrown from the explosion. The remaining survivors from the air strike scattered like roaches. In the midst of the chaos, Sean walked out onto his bullet-riddled porch with a M16. One bullet for each man. Headshots. Within minutes he wiped out what was left of the platoon. He looked down and saw the soldier in command crawl toward him. Sean walked down to the last step of his crumbling porch. The soldier's face was burnt from the blast. He looked up at Sean, blood dripping onto the dirt. Sean looked down at him with a stoic expression. They stared at each other and shared a brief moment of silence.

"Sir," the soldier said.

"Ryan."

The soldier's eyes widened. He bit his bottom lip and mustered the little life he had left to raise his firearm. Sean pulled out his pistol and shot twice. He looked at Ryan's smoldering body and took a deep breath. He climbed back up his creaking porch steps. He took two steps into the doorway before the force of an explosion threw him off his own porch and into the open field. Sean was disoriented.

Struggling to shake off the concussion, he was only able to make out two blurred images rushing toward him. He raised his rifle, but one of the blurred images kicked the M16 from out of his hands. The other flanked him and shocked him with a taser. Sean's knees buckled under eight thousand volts. Shadows came from every direction. They pinned him against the ground, placed titanium shackles on his arms and wrists, then pulled him up to a kneeling position. Sean stared into the distance, forcefully blinking his eyes into focus. Three dark figures were walking toward him. The one in the middle was wearing a long black trench coat that flowed like a cape. The remaining soldiers saluted and took several steps back from Sean. He looked up at the dark figures now standing over him. All he could see were the silhouettes of their faces, but he knew who they were.

"Santi?" Sean asked.

"Yeah, buddy?" Santiago asked.

"Can I bum one?"

"Sure," Santiago said.

Santiago pulled out a cigarette from the front pocket of his dark-green fatigues. He knelt down and lit it, using a small fire that burned on Ryan's corpse. He put it in Sean's mouth. Sean took two puffs and nodded.

"How are you doing, son?" Ashcroft asked. Sean looked away. "You were tough to find. We looked everywhere—and I mean *everywhere*. The whole time I thought you were on some tropical island somewhere, but you were here the entire time. Right in our back yard. Selling cattle, no less." Sean looked over at Barbara, who was licking her teeth. "Well Barbara, I owe you a Coke." She cracked a smile. "Barbara said you were in the States all along." Ashcroft knelt down and the two locked eyes. "So, what to do with you, Sean?"

"I have a few thoughts," Sean said.

"Let you go?" Ashcroft asked. "Let you continue to sell filets and ribeyes? Continue this American dream?"

"Something like that," Sean said. Barbara looked over at the burning house. She hopped up the charred porch steps and disappeared in the flames.

"What the hell is she doing?" Santiago asked.

"Sean, listen to me," Ashcroft said. "I need you back."

"Why?" Sean Asked.

"Why?" Ashcroft grimaced. "You know why, Sean! You're the leader of the pack."

"Let one of these two lead," Sean said.

"Santiago is calculating. To a fault. And Barbara?"

The three of them looked at the burning house.

"Damn, it's hot!" Barbara shouted from inside.

"Do I need to explain?" Ashcroft asked. "Son, 7721 ops got intel on very dangerous intellectual properties held by very unstable people." Sean sighed. "Look, you do these three assignments for me, I'll cut you loose."

"If you were going to cut me loose, why try to kill me?" Sean asked.

"Sean," Santiago said, "brute force was the only way that you would listen to reason."

"Yeah, and I killed Ryan in the process," Sean said.

"Fuck Ryan," Santiago said. "He was an asshole. Your words, not mine."

Sean looked at Ashcroft and said, "Three more. Three more and I'm done." Ashcroft nodded. "And get me a new fucking ra—"

Barbara emerged from the burning house, pulling Trish by the collar of her T-shirt. She hopped down the last porch step and threw Trish in front of her.

"Trish!" Sean shouted.

Trish looked around, confused by carnage strewn all over her front yard. She looked at Sean and ran toward him. Barbara looked at Sean and smiled. She pulled out her Glock and fired.

The hollow tip bullet put a hole through Trish's chest. Trish's body whipped forward and fell to the ground. Sean stopped breathing. He crawled over to Trish and rolled her over onto her back using his shoulders. He sat down next to her, using his legs to place her head in his lap.

"D-Don't leave me. OK?" Trish said, straining for air between each word. Tears streamed down Sean's face. He smiled and shook his head.

"What the hell are you doing?!" Aschroft shouted.

"Did you see that?" Barbara said, laughing.

"Dammit, Barbara." Santaigo said calmly.

"What is wrong with you?" Ashcroft asked. "We were talking! He was—"

"Who gives a shit!?" Barbara said. "You were gonna kill him anyway when he got what you wanted!"

"He didn't know you that, you fucking…" Ashcroft looked at Sean sitting on the ground watching the love of his life dying. "He's no good to me like this."

"Orders, sir?" Santiago asked.

"We're leaving!" Ashcroft shouted. "Ground forces stay. Wait until she dies, then shoot him."

"Yes, sir!" a soldier shouted.

Barbara walked over to Ashcroft and said, "If anyone should be killing Sean…"

"Shut up!" Ashcroft said. "Get on the damn chopper."

Barbara gave a loud, straining sigh. She followed Ashcroft and Santiago behind the ranch house. Minutes later, dust and wind blew as the chopper hovered. Sean bent over to rub his cheek against Trish's forehead. The remaining ground forces surrounded Sean. Four of the soldiers raised their rifles and pointed them at him.

"Wait," a soldier shouted, "the general said—" The four soldiers pointed their rifles at the other soldiers and opened fire.

One of the four walked over to Sean and pulled him away from Trish.

"No!" he shouted. "Don't touch her!"

Sean drew his head back and rammed his forehead into the soldier's nose. The soldier fell back on the ground. He looked up in terror as Sean's knee was about to cave his head in. The other three soldiers fired tranquilizers into Sean's neck and shoulder. Sean fell over and was nearly unconscious in seconds. He could still hear distorted voices.

"Is she still alive?"

"Barely. I got a pulse. Gonna start bagging her in a minute."

"ETA on that chopper?"

"Five minutes."

"OK, you got that IV in?"

"Yeah."

Sean opened his eyes. The blinding fluorescent light was unbearable. He tried to use his hands to shield his eyes, only to realize they were bound to a gurney by two thick titanium shackles. Sean scanned the empty bright room through his blurred vision. In the left corner of the room, he could see the image of a man sitting in a folding chair with his legs crossed. The image slowly came into focus. He was old, with a full head of white hair and a matching white mustache and was using his index finger to operate his smartphone. The old man looked up when he realized Sean was awake and blinking in his direction.

"How are you feeling?" he asked with a thick Southern accent.

"W-Where am I?" Sean asked.

"For starters, not dead. But you were well on your way." Sean took a deep breath. The events of the evening came flooding to his mind. Every muscle in his body flexed as he tried to break his restraints. "Now, Sean."

"Where is she?!"

"Sean."

"Where is she?! Trish!! Trish!!"

The soldiers who saved his life came into the room. One of them pointed his Glock at Sean. The old man gestured for him to lower his weapon.

"It's OK," the old man said. "We're OK." Sean continued to shout until he was out of breath. "Now listen," the old man said as he edged closer to the gurney. "Those chains were made for your kind."

"Your kind?" one of the soldiers asked.

"Sam. Please," the old man said. He looked at Sean and continued. "That's Sam, by the way. Her and Mark were on the ground. You broke Mark's nose. That old fart behind them is Hayward. He's the pilot that got your lady to safety."

"What? She's alive?" Sean asked. The old man nodded. "Who are you?"

"I see you don't watch the news," the old man said. "Or read the tabloids."

"One and the same," Hayward said.

The old man chuckled.

"Senator Upstead," he said. "The money man behind 7721."

"I don't understand," Sean said. "Ashcroft…"

"Reports to me," Upstead said. "Now I'm gonna unhook these chains and take you to your girl. I'm confident your civility will prevail?" Sean nodded.

After Upstead opened the shackles, Sean sat up and hopped off the gurney. He followed Upstead out of the room and into a gray hall. Upstead opened a sliding door with his security card, and the two walked in. The room was dark with electric-blue lights shining around the perimeter. In the middle was Trish, lying in a horizontal metal cylinder filled with fluid. She was connected to a respirator that hissed air with every breath given to her. Her vitals appeared as a hologram over the cylinder. Sean could only see her face through a small square window. He placed his hand on the cylinder.

"What the fuck is this?" Sean whispered.

"She was seriously injured," Upstead said. "Her lungs were torn to shreds. She damn near bled to death. Thankfully, we had Blackout tech for that, so…"

"Wait, what?"

"Blackout tech. In this case, artificial lungs." Sean's eye widened. "It's organic. Cloned from her own stem cells we had in the lab. That fluid she's floating in is talking to her immune system. Telling it not to attack her new lung."

"This is…"

"I know," Upstead said, smiling. "It's amazing."

"Forbidden. The whole point of the Blackout mainframe is to do just that—*black out* intellectual property."

"That's true," Upstead said, chuckling. "But you of all people know we've implemented some of the Blackout tech into administering 7721 assignments for quite some time now. And given we just saved your lady, I would think—"

"I'm aware, but Ashcroft's religious views made it forbidden for us to use this type of tech. He didn't even want the data stored into the Blackout. He just wanted us to eradicate the property."

"Ashcroft has been outsourcing maintenance of the encryption code for years. One of those Scandanavian countries. The program sits at a hard drive in the American embassy in said Scandanavian country while it's being updated. For that split-second, the data is opened to be reviewed and extracted. Pandora's box is wide open."

"Why would he do that?" Sean asked.

"Because Ashcroft plans to steal the Blackout."

Sean took a deep breath and took a step back from Trish.

"Before I left, he doubled the mission load. When we first

started, he'd allow us to give political asylum to nonmilitary creators. Lately, it's been just kill orders. Whole families."

"Sean, if Ashcroft gets the Blackout, my guess is five, maybe ten years? He could build an army of technological prowess unlike anything we have ever seen. You know what's in that Blackout. Technological advances that make it seem like we're living in the Stone Age. With the proper financing, the free world would not be able to stop him."

Sean closed his eyes and asked, "What do you want me to do?"

"I need you back in the fold."

Sean scoffed and asked, "You mean 7721? Not possible."

"As you, of course not." Sean grimaced. He took his eyes from Trish to stare at Upstead. "My people came across a piece of Blackout tech about a year ago. They've worked diligently and are confident it's safe for human use."

"What?" he asked with a blank expression.

"It's an antibody that attacks melanin. Kinda like that ah... veetaligo condition or whatever it's called. We gonna make you a shade or two lighter. More presentable if you wanted to join an Alabama country club someday." Upstead laughed. Sean still had a blank expression on his face. "The procedure, they say, may be painful. Once we finish it, plastic surgery will—"

"Whoa!" Sean said, pursing his lips and drawing his eyes together. "Plastic what?"

"Of course. We gotta get rid of those African features that for the life of me, I don't understand why you folks try to get rid of! God made you per—" Sean shook and tilted his head to the side. "What I mean is, the nose got to go. We gonna raise them cheekbones. By the time those boys are done, you'll be a completely different person." Upstead paused and stared into Sean's green and blue eyes. "We can keep the eyes, though. They suit you."

Sean turned around and stared down at Trish. He placed his hands on the capsule.

"You gonna wipe her memory?" Sean asked.

"Why would I do that, son? That's your retirement. You finish this and you go back to her. We'll keep her safe." Sean sighed. He looked into Upstead's hopeful baby-blue eyes and nodded. "When you get in, you watch that damn Blackout with your life. Do what you gotta do. Destroy it. Steal it. From this moment on, you are the shepherd of the Blackout."

∽

Everyone in the old basement conference room stared at Shepard, gaping. Every time Jonah tried to say something, the weight of what he had just heard would leave him speechless.

McCray stared at the floor and said, "Not only do you want me to believe that you're the third Wolf—which is bullshit, because by all accounts Sean was black—you also want us to believe they whitefaced you?"

"Senator," Jonah said walking toward Shepard, "You haven't seen Blackout tech before, have you?" McCray was silenced. "I have."

"Einstein said knowledge is nothing without imagination," Shepard said. "Senator, imagine a generation of Baby Boomers, desensitized geniuses creating weapons from the darkest depths of their minds. Man's psyche is so twisted that even good will be put to a fucked-up use."

Jonah stood in front of Shepard and studied his facial features.

"Did it hurt?" Jonah asked.

"Like someone dropped me in gasoline and lit a match."

"What's the next move?" Rosa asked.

"They have the Blackout," Shepard said. "Barbara's back with Ashcroft. She's gonna eventually kill him and then she's gonna set the world on fire. There's only one option I can think of, and it's a shit option." Shepard stood straight. He folded his arms and said, "Anyone who wants to leave for self-preservation, now would be a good time."

Shepard, Jonah, and McCray stared at each other and nodded in agreement. They turned around to the sound of flint sparking a light. Rosa was lighting a cigarette, her hands shaking. She took a drag and stared at the three men.

"Fuck it," she said.

⟡

Graham sat on the edge of his five-foot metal bed, staring at his thick metal prison cell door. He leaned forward, resting his elbows on his knees and clasping his cracked, calloused hands. Fresh blood was caked on his knuckles. Two guards stood at his door, each holding a shield and wearing riot gear. An old inmate, mopping blood from the metal floor, slid by the two guards. He squeezed reddish water from the mop into a yellow bucket. The old man looked up at Graham through the prison bars and flashed a smile. Gums and one gold tooth. Graham gave a slight chuckle before he buried his face in his hands and sighed. Distant footsteps echoed through his prison cell. The footsteps built to a crescendo until the sound came to a stop in front of his cell. The door opened. Senator McCray stood in front of him, adjusting his red tie and glasses. Graham squinted his eyes and studied the senator.

"Do you know who I am?" McCray asked. Graham nodded. "Ashcroft told me about you. Him and Bradshaw handpicked you. What were you before—"

"CIA. Field ops."

"Right," McCray said, nodding. "Ashcroft used to tell me what made you so dangerous was that you were a strategist on the field. That you had the ability to strategize as you improvised."

"Why are you here?"

"I think you know why."

"Help you fight Ashcroft? Save the world?"

"Something like that."

Graham laughed and said, "Senator, I don't think you've noticed, but I'm incarcerated. Twenty federal counts, one of them high treason. They're gonna keep me in a box for the rest of my natural life, which isn't long because I'm seeing a firing squad in a week. Not even a member of the security council can change that."

"I'm not a member of the security council," McCray said.

"Since when? I just saw your face on—"

"I'm the new Upstead." Graham tilted his head. "But that doesn't matter anymore. Ashcroft tried to kill me the other night."

"How do you know?"

"Because Shepard saved my life."

Graham scoffed and said, "Shepard's dead." McCray shook his head. Graham's eyes slowly widened. "That's not possible. They crumbled the floor from under him. He must've fallen a hundred feet."

"That's the other thing we need to talk about. I'll tell you on the way."

"On the way where?"

"Have you been listening? We're going after Ashcroft."

"Couple of problems with your plan. One, Ashcroft has loyal soldiers in 7721. Hundreds. Two, Barbara is with him. Three, I'm still in prison."

The door creaked open. Graham rose from his seat. The guards and the old inmate were gone. McCray rolled his sleeves and placed his hands in his pocket.

"Problem number three solved. Follow me outside and I'll show you the solution to problems one and two." McCray strolled out of the prison cell and down the hollow steel corridor. Graham followed behind, slowly and timidly. They walked past guards and inmates as if they were ghosts. At each checkpoint they walked past, a guard would open the gate and stand aside. "The old man wasn't stupid. He knew Ashcroft was gonna lose his fucking mind." They walked outside the prison along a cement walkway with tall chain-link fences on each side. Inmates on one side were playing basketball and lifting weights. When they got to the front entrance, a guard gave Graham a clear plastic bag with his belongings. "You can change on the way." A tall metal door with barbed wire on top stood between Graham and freedom. The double doors slowly creaked open. Outside, soldiers stood at attention. "Navy seals, Uncle Sammy's incorruptible. There are only twenty-five hundred in the world. Upstead got his hands on a little over a thousand. This was the reset button if 7721 ever decided to go rogue."

"This is your plan?" Graham asked, laughing. "Where do you think Ashcroft's soldiers come from? 7721's census, last time I checked, was about three thousand. We gonna just knock on the silos and have a gun fight?"

"Shepard has a plan. And take a close look at what they're wearing. I have no intention of having a shootout with anyone. Neither did Upstead." Graham looked at the large unit and shook his head. He paused for a moment before a flash of insight came across his face.

"Huh," Graham said nodding. "That…might work."

The Complex

"Where is this place?" Sayf asked.

An oval hardwood table on Ashcroft's personal 747 separated Ashcroft and Sayf. A band of twelve Spartan Airbuses flew around the plane in a wedge-shaped pattern. The planes were in their descent, cruising over red mountain ranges and an endless blue Atlantic Ocean in the distant horizon.

"Central America," Ashcroft said, "San Pedro, to be exact." He was sitting in a dark leather chair with his hands in his lap; he wore a dark-gray button-down short-sleeve shirt, khakis, and brown army boots that matched the brown leather holster resting on his chest. "The National Cricket Association had decided to have an international tournament. They thought San Pedro would be the perfect spot. They were wrong. It was a disaster. The country went bankrupt building the place. The stadium itself is finished from the outside, but when you step in there are no seats. No money, no stadium. No stadium, no money. Just a ghost town."

Sayf undid the first three buttons of his dark-green army fatigues and looked outside the cabin window.

"We will be landing in San Pedro in approximately twenty minutes," the captain said.

"You sure he's dead?" Ashcroft asked.

"It was a pretty long drop," Barbara said with her black army boots propped on the tabletop. She wore a dark-gray tank top tucked into her black fatigues, and her curly dark brown hair covered her face.

"Now that that's over we can move on to production," Sayf said. "I looked through the numbers for a few of the weapons you want to put in mass production. I think we need a hedge fund while we get our business off the ground."

"Business?" Ashcroft asked.

"The tools, raw materials, labor, research? Where do you think that money comes from? We need to have a steady source of income to—"

"Who said anything about a business?" Ashcroft asked.

"Why don't you stop being Mr. Fucking Clandestine and tell me what's on your mind?" Sayf asked, annoyed.

"You thought this was a business venture?" Ashcroft asked. "We have the most highly trained soldiers in the world with the most powerful weapons in mankind's history, and you think I plan on chop-shopping that power just to have a lot of crisp green dollar bills? That's the problem with you economists. George Washington and Ben Franklin have become your golden calf."

"Again, Mr. Clandestine, what's your plan?" Sayf asked.

"You open your hedge fund," Ashcroft said. "And we build. We build until we have enough to look the world dead in the face and say, 'Bend to our will or die.'"

A smile came across Barbara's face.

"Not everyone's gonna bend," Barbara said.

"My gift to you," Ashcroft said.

Barbara got up. She walked to the bathroom as the plane descended, clapping her hands.

When she stepped into the bathroom, Sayf looked at Ashcroft and asked, "You know she's going to kill us, right?"

Ashcroft chuckled and nodded.

"Well aware," Ashcroft said. "And she knows I'm aware. Barbara won't do anything as long we allow her to maintain her habit." Sayf sat back in his seat, his eyes narrow, his body tense. "You're not getting skittish on me?"

"You understand my job is to analyze risks based on history. Alexander the Great. Napoleon Bonaparte. Hitler. All tried to take over the world and failed."

"And failed gloriously," Ashcroft said, smiling.

The convoy was approaching a two-lane runway. A red flash flew by Ashcroft's cabin window with smoke trailing behind. It made a high-pitched scream before crashing into an Airbus behind them. The force of the explosion whipped Ashcroft and Sayf in their seats. The entire airplane shook as it crashed onto the runway, snapping the landing gear in half. Sparks flew from the bottom. When the plane came to a screeching halt, Barbara kicked open the door. She stuck out her head and surveyed the deserted airfield. Four of the twelve Airbuses were strewn across the runway in flames. Soldiers from the remaining planes flooded the runway armed with M16s. Barbara jumped from the airplane door, dropping twelve feet before landing in a kneeling position. As she stood up, a soldier tossed her an assault rifle.

"How many?" Barbara asked.

"We don't know, ma'am," he said.

"Do we know where the missile came from?"

"No, ma'am."

Barbara grabbed him by the neck and lifted him a foot off the ground.

"Find out," she whispered.

The soldier nodded his head.

"Enemies?" Sayf asked Ashcroft.

"Me?" Aschroft asked. "No." They climbed down a rope from the airplane door onto the black cement runway. "All of my enemies are…" Ashcroft gasped. Through the Central American heat, Ashcroft saw a distorted image of Shepard holding a Stinger rocket launcher. The two locked eyes before Shepard put on his shades. "I'm gonna kill him."

Shepard launched another missile into the air.

"Incoming!" Ashcroft shouted. He inserted a communication earpiece as he and Sayf ran for cover. "Barbara, get as many men as you can, load up the Humvees. Shepard is still alive!"

Shepard looked at the virtual screen in front of him. He raised his arms and opened both of his hands. The missile rose and split into five separate missiles. Shepard brought his hands down to his waist and let out a sharp exhale. Ashcroft stopped and looked at the sky. A high-pitched sound rang through the runway before a hail of missiles came crashing down. Sayf and Ashcroft hid under the hull of one of the aircrafts. The ground shook. Bodies were tossed into the air. Shepard looked at the runway engulfed in flames and waited. The wind had picked up, feeding the fires. Shepard took off the gloves to the Stinger and dropped them on the asphalt.

Shepard folded his arms and stared at the demolished runway. He could hear the rumbling of engines starting behind the wall of fire in front of him. A series of Humvees roared through the blaze. Shepard hopped in an old doorless military jeep and mashed the gas, steering the vehicle off the runway and onto a dirt road. Shepard glanced in the rearview mirror. He could see soldiers climbing onto heavy machine guns propped on top of the SUVs. Bullets rang past him, bouncing off the metal interior of the jeep.

"How many I got?" Shepard asked through his earpiece.

"A lot," Jonah said.

"Did we get 'em?"

"No, they're leading the pack," Jonah said.

"Who has the Blackout?"

"How should I know?"

"Forget it," Shepard said. "You and Rosa in position?"

"Yeah."

"Jonah, don't make a move until we got all of them on the bridge."

"Copy."

Shepard took a sharp turn onto a cracked concrete road, obscured by dark-green banana leaves and short palm trees. He glanced again in his rearview mirror at the convoy that was closing in on him.

"Can't keep your house in order?" Sayf asked Ashcroft.

They chased Shepard through the rainforest, the old jeep rattling along a cracked makeshift road. As soon as Shepard broke free from the jungle, the broken road gave way to fresh asphalt. Shepard looked in front of him and floored the gas. An empty mile-long concrete bridge stood fifty feet above calm ocean water. Shepard crossed onto the bridge. At the end of it, he could see a massive concrete stadium surrounded by an empty brick city.

"You see 'em?" Shepard asked.

"Yeah," Jonah said. "Coming in fast."

The soldier driving the Humvee leading the convoy looked in his rearview mirror. White flashes hailed down from the sky, hammering against the armor-plated Humvees behind him. A white flash hit the gas tank, causing a Humvee in the back to explode. The force of the explosion bounced against the other two Humvees. They twirled off the bridge before crashing into the teal ocean water. The explosions also shook Ashcroft's Humvee. He looked at Barbara. She and Sayf climbed onto the roof of the Humvee. On the left side of the bridge, she saw a Black Hawk chopper mowing down the back of the Humvee convoy. Rosa was manning the gunner. The recoil shook her entire body. Her eyes were wide and focused. Bullet shells fell from the chopper into the ocean.

Sayf crawled over to the driver and banged on the door.

He looked at the driver and said, "Rocket launcher!"

"They're requesting the launcher, sir!" the driver said to Ashcroft.

Ashcroft bent down and grabbed a black launcher. He handed it through the window to Barbara. She grabbed the rocket launcher and aimed it at the chopper. The remainder of the convoy opened fire. Rosa screamed and covered her face with her arms as bullets bounced off the chopper hull.

"We speed up to the front of the bridge and shoot overhead!" Jonah shouted.

He increased speed and altitude. As the chopper approached the front of the convoy, Barbara's eyes widened.

"Come on, come on, come on, come on," she whispered. She placed the launcher on her shoulder and leaned her head in against the sight, her finger poised on the trigger. The tint of the helicopter's windshield gave way to a flash of sunlight and the faint image of Jonah in the cockpit. Barbara gasped.

"What are you..." she whispered, lowering the rocket launcher.

"What in bloody hell are you doing?!" Sayf shouted.

He stripped the launcher from Barbara's shaking hands and pointed it at the passing chopper. At the moment he pulled the trigger, Barbara slammed the back of her fist into Sayf's stomach. He was thrown off the Humvee and plummeted into the ocean. The missile was thrown off trajectory and hit the tail rudder, spinning the helicopter out of control.

"Hang on!" Jonah shouted.

Rosa was too frozen with fear to scream. She wrapped her arms around the Gatling gun and closed her eyes.

Shepard crossed the bridge into the city. He watched the Black Hawk spin over him before falling out of sight near the stadium.

Strapped in the cockpit, Jonah covered his face from the flying glass and rotor shrapnel. The helicopter slowed down and came to a stop just a few feet in front of the stadium. Rosa unstrapped her seatbelt and climbed out of the wreckage. She crawled along the side and looked down. Jonah was struggling to unbuckle his belt. Rosa yanked at the strap. Moments later, Shepard pulled up to the crash site. He hopped onto the helicopter and reached into the cockpit. Jonah was still fumbling with the metal buckle.

"I think it's bent," Jonah said.

"Move your hand," Shepard said.

Shepard grabbed the buckle and bent it with his hands until it snapped.

"Shit," Jonah whispered to himself.

After pulling Jonah out of the helicopter, Shepard walked over to the jeep and unzipped a green duffle bag, grabbing four round black discs. He pushed the middle of each of them, and a red light started to flash.

"What's that?" Rosa asked.

"Blackout tech," Shepard said.

"What does it do?"

"You remember when the floor crumbled?" Shepard asked, sliding the discs across the concrete in front of the jeep.

"This isn't a floor."

"No," Jonah said, grabbing an AK-47 from the duffle bag. "There's a sewage system under us. What you think Shep? Fifteen-foot drop?"

"Let's hope so," Shepard said, grabbing another rifle from the duffle bag. "When they build these makeshift stadiums, they do shoddy work." Shepard stood up and reached behind him. He pulled out a forty-five-caliber pistol and handed it Rosa. "You know how to use this?" Rosa shook her head. "I turned off the safety. Don't point it at us, OK? Point it at them. Caress the trigger. Don't pull. Pulling is inaccurate."

Nervously, Rosa nodded, and the three of them ran into the stadium.

"You think McCray got Graham?" Jonah asked.

"Doubt it," Shepard said.

∽

The convoy sped past the bridge into the deserted brick city. They followed the smoke trail of the Black Hawk, cutting through side roads and alleyways. Barbara stood on top of the Humvee in a trance. As the convoy turned onto a main road, she could see the crashed Black Hawk and Shepard's rusted jeep. She walked to the front of the Humvee and kneeled down, squinting. It was faint, but she could see them: tiny black circles flashing red. Her eyes widened. She dropped down onto her stomach and smashed open the driver-side window. She grabbed the wheel and spun the Humvee. The military-grade SUV crashed into an oncoming Humvee. The grills of each SUV became tangled, and the two vehicles spun into the window of a department store. Barbara rolled off the top of the SUV and looked inside. The driver was dead. Ashcroft kicked open the door. He crawled out and coughed after he inhaled smoke and dust from the wreckage.

"What the hell was that?!" Ashcroft shouted. Barbara looked around at the soldiers pulling themselves from the wreckage and started to count. "What the hell are you doing?"

"There's five of us," Barbara said. "Call for backup."

Ashcroft stopped coughing.

"I beg your pardon?" Ashcroft asked, brushing the dust from his khakis.

"Backup. Call it."

"What part of disappearing don't you understand?"

She grabbed Ashcroft by his shirt and dragged him outside. One hundred feet down, the road was a gaping hole.

"We're it," Barbara said. "The rest of them are in there." She said pointing at the hole. "Besides, Sayf's dead."

"He's what?"

"Flew off when the bullets started flying," Barbara said, laughing.

"What the fuck is so funny?"

"It's like that book. You know the one you made me read." Barbara scratched her head. "Dammit," she whispered. "Literally on the tip of my tongue." She snapped her fingers. "That's it! The Bible! There was this line."

"A verse, Barbara?" Ashcroft asked.

"Yeah, a line. It says the stone the builder rejects will become the cornerstone." She stared into Ashcroft's eyes, pointing at each bullet wound on her chest. "Karma is a fucking beast, ain't it," she said with a sardonic grin. "Call for backup. because I want him alive. I'm gonna…" Barbara ran out of breath as if the wind was knocked out of her. "I'm gonna kill him with these here bare hands."

"Sir," a soldier said.

"Call it," Ashcroft said, staring at Barbara.

"What?" the soldier asked, confused. "But sir—"

"Call it!" Ashcroft shouted.

Barbara glanced over at the end of the street. Shepard was walking toward them, an M-16 by his side.

"Nice job, Shep!" Barbara said with a smile. The other three soldiers raised their weapons. Ashcroft glared at Shepard. Both sides walked down the street with slow, deliberate steps. "How 'bout that Blackout tech?" Barbara laughed.

"Shut up, Barbara," Ashcroft said.

"You hitched yourself to a winner there, Ashcroft," Shepard said.

Ashcroft looked over at Barbara's sadistic expression.

"A necessary evil," Ashcroft said.

Ashcroft's men slowly closed in on Shepard.

"Drop the rifle!" one of them shouted.

"This?" Shepard asked. He held up his rifle by the shaft.

"Drop it now!" the soldier shouted.

Shepard smiled and dropped the rifle on the cracked concrete street.

"So how long you think it'll be before she acts out her fantasy?" Shepard asked. Barbara grimaced. "You haven't forgotten, have you? Bane? That was your favorite story. Bane breaking Batman's back. I swear you must have read that a hundred times."

"How do you know that?" Ashcroft asked, squinting.

"Hey, Barb, you remember when we were teenagers?" Shepard asked as he walked toward them.

"Stop!" one of the soldiers shouted.

Shepard put his hands behind his back and continued.

"Teenagers learn how to deal with those raging hormones in different ways. We were a little different. We had just a touch more testosterone than most. Right, old man?"

Ashcroft, confused, stared at Shepard.

"Santiago was a bookworm," Shepard said. "Remember? Sun Tzu? Machiavelli?" Shepard looked down and put his hands into the pockets of his fatigues. "He must have read *The Five Rings* a hundred times."

"Get on the ground, Black!" the soldier shouted.

"Barb, you did something odd. You reverted to comics. The villains, man. I don't know how many times I would hear that bullshit about DC being better than Marvel. Batman." Shepard laughed. "Fucking Batman. You would say, 'Fuck the bat, it's all about the villains.' You remember when you were twelve and you snapped that golden retriever's back? Right on your knee. Just like Bane."

"I'm not going to tell you again!"

"Then you turned sweet sixteen," Shepard said. "Shit. Not a

damn thing sweet about it. Our concrete bones settled in and you were off to the races. What was it? Twenty guards? Ten tutors?"

The soldiers took their last step, finding themselves within range of Shepard's leg. Shepard kicked the rifle shaft of the soldier on the far right. The other two tried to adjust their rifles to aim for Shepard's chest. Shepard pulled a pistol from his hip and shot them each in the head. Shepard slipped behind the third soldier and grabbed his neck. Ashcroft winced at the snap. Shepard stood facing Barbara and Ashcroft with the soldier's twisted head in the palm of his right hand, his neck broken across Shepard's right shoulder.

Shepard sighed and said, "Me? I think I did the most reasonable thing a sixteen-year-old kid would do. Fell in love. You took that from me."

Barbara's face was expressionless. She tilted her head.

"S-Sean?" Ashcroft asked, squinting his eyes.

Shepard smiled. He let the propped soldier slide from his shoulder. As the lifeless body was falling toward the ground, Barbara grabbed Ashcroft by the back of his shirt. Shepard kicked the rifle on the ground next to him into the air. He caught it and opened fire. Bullets flew past Barbara just before she found cover behind a building. She threw Ashcroft against the wall. Shepard continued suppressive fire, edging his way toward them. Barbara and Ashcroft stayed crouched on the ground. Gray brick fragments crumbled over them.

In the midst of gunfire, Barbara's ear twitched at the sound of a pin unlatching. She looked down and a grenade was in front of them. Barbara grabbed Ashcroft by the shirt and took two steps before the blast went off. The force threw Ashcroft and Barbara through a windowpane. Barbara's ears were ringing, and her eyes were blinded by flashes of white. She shook her head and looked over at Ashcroft, who laid on the floor, unconscious. She pulled herself up on the windowpane. Her vision came into focus and she found herself standing in what was an abandoned convenience store. Barbara staggered toward a molded wooden door. As she was about to open it, Shepard's boot crashed through it and into her chest. The force of the kick threw her into the air. Her body put a hole in the rotted dark-gray drywall behind her.

"Why are you keeping that piece of shit alive?" Shepard asked.

Barbara got up, snickering.

"Man, I missed you," she said, holding her chest. "I haven't felt a kick like that in years." She dusted off her tank top and wiped the blood from her mouth. "It was you who killed Santi. Wasn't it?" Shepard didn't respond. "Did he say anything?"

"Happy to see you," Shepard said.

Barbara snapped her fingers.

"That's Santi," she said, nodding with approval. "He understood that this is who we are. How we show our affection." Barbara walked backward. She pressed her back against the wall and said, "I love you, man. You? Me? Santi? We're family. Although…" She put her hands behind her back. "I always wanted to know what it'd be like to…you know. You and me. I'm pretty sure I could feel it in my back. Long and hard…"

Barbara broke through the drywall. She catapulted across the room. A metallic blur rang across Shepard's face. Barbara twirled the metal pole and speared Shepard in the abdomen. She raised her arms in the air and swung the metal pipe as if she were taking a golf swing. The blow slammed into Shepard's jaw and lifted him off the ground. He went through the window frame of the convenience store, onto the cracked pavement. Barbara stepped across the broken glass and onto the street. Shepard tried to get up. He was on his knees when he felt Barbara's pipe hitting his ribs.

"Of course I remember," Barbara said. "Bane changed my fucking life! You know why I love bad guys, Sean? Because they are who they are! They have the guts to tell the world this is who I am! People are always trying to be good when the fact of the matter is ninety-nine-point-nine of us aren't!" She lifted the pole in the air over Shepard's head. "Me smashing that head of yours like a pumpkin is who I am. This is me loving you!"

"Funny fucking way of showing it," Shepard murmured.

"Before you go, one question. There was—"

Shots rang. Barbara could feel four bullets burning in her chest. She dropped the metal pipe on the ground next to Shepard, and her face lit up with happiness.

"Honey," she said, panting. "I was just talking about you." Jonah was on the other side of the street, holding a nine-millimeter. Barbara looked down at her chest. "Hollow tips," she said, laughing. Barbara staggered toward Jonah.

A bloodstained grin came across Barbara's face as she pulled out a knife and marched toward him. Jonah fired another shot before the gun jammed. She grabbed Jonah and stabbed him in his flank. Jonah fell to his knees and Barbara stared down at him with endearment. The love in her eyes subsided to an expression of madness.

"Till death do us part, right?" Barbara asked in a deep, distorted voice.

"After you…" Jonah whispered.

Jonah dropped down to the ground. Barbara felt the wind of Shepard's swing before the pipe landed and lodged in her neck. She fell to her knees, her body shaking as she smiled and stared at Jonah. Then her smile faded, leaving a blank stare. Shepard looked down at Barbara's kneeling corpse and let go of the metal pipe. He reached over and helped Jonah.

"Can you stand?" Shepard asked.

"I think so," Jonah said. With Shepard's help, Jonah pulled himself from the ground, looked around and said, "My wife was a bitch, but through it all…" He looked at a grimacing Shepard. The two chuckled for a moment before Jonah felt a sharp sting from his side. "Damn, that hurts!"

"You'll be fine," Shepard said, looking around. "Where's Rosa?"

"Oh, that cow!" Jonah said. "So, we're at the stadium and I tell her to stay here. She says OK."

"And…"

"I mean, you would think she would say, 'I'm coming along,' or come out of nowhere with some—"

"What is wrong with you?"

"She could have done something."

"Jonah, the woman ran into a red van when she was a child. How the hell was she manning that gunner?"

"Oh," Jonah said, looking up at the sky. "That was me. I was controlling it from the cockpit. She just needed something to keep her occupied." Shepard laughed, which made Jonah chuckle and writhe in pain. Their amusement was stopped by the sound of a gun being loaded a few feet from their backs. The two limped around.

"Rough day, Sean?" Ashcroft asked.

"Still with us?" Shepard asked, shaking his head.

"Gonna be more than just us in a minute, son," Ashcroft said, looking at the sky.

"How?" Shepard asked. "Your faction is dead."

"What?" Ashcroft asked. "This isn't my faction son, it's yours. You see, my men discovered a shadow faction in 7721 led by you and Barbara. Santi found out and that's why you killed him. We tracked you to here only to find you and Barbara in a heated argument. I held you off valiantly until backup arrived."

"Can he do that?" Jonah asked.

"Have you heard from McCray?" Shepard asked Jonah. Jonah didn't respond. "That's why he can do it. Dead men don't talk."

Shepard could hear helicopters in the distance.

"You know what made Washington a good general?" Ashcroft asked. "His retreats. Man could organize a retreat with the best of them. I'm taking one from our forefathers' playbook. I'm retuning back to 7721. I'm going to order them to kill you and burn your remains, and when I find the banker, we're going to have a chat about finance."

The helicopters were flying over them. Shepard glared at Ashcroft's smug expression. Ropes fell from the sky. In seconds, twenty soldiers dressed in black were on the ground. They stood behind Ashcroft, rifles locked and loaded. Humvees swarmed the empty streets. Snipers placed themselves on rooftops. Jonah and Shepard were surrounded.

Ashcroft smiled and said, "7721! Shoot these traitors." The platoon was silent. Only the sound of helicopters could be heard. Ashcroft scowled and turned around. "Are you lot fucking deaf?! I said shoot them!"

"They're not deaf," a voice said in the distance. He made his way to the front. Ashcroft's eyes widened. "7721 is under new management," Graham said. He stood in front of the platoon, staring at Ashcroft, who studied Graham's attire: black dress shoes and slacks, gray oxford dress shirt with a black tie, sleeves rolled up. A small acrylic black star insignia was pinned over his left chest. Graham looked over his shoulder and said, "At ease, fellas." The platoon followed his orders.

"I…I don't understand," Ashcroft said.

"These are the latest members of 7721. Replacements for you and your traitors. We intercepted your S.O.S. You and your unit were killed in a gunfight with Barbara. McCray reissued orders to find new recruits as well as a new Blackstar general." Ashcroft looked around and chuckled.

He looked at Graham and said, "Told ya. It was always going to be you."

"State funeral, a couple of statues," Graham said. "Your daughters will get your flag."

"Not even a fucking gold watch?" Ashcroft snickered. Graham walked over to Ashcroft. He reached into his pants pocket and pulled out two cigarettes. The two of them stood for a moment looking around at the sea of soldiers dressed in black fatigues surrounding them. Ashcroft took a last hard puff and said, "Well then…"

Graham took another puff and stuck the cigarette in his mouth. He took five paces away from Ashcroft and pulled out his pistol. Graham inhaled. The end of his cigarette glowed orange. He raised his pistol and emptied half his clip in Ashcroft's chest. He put his gun down, took the cigarette from his mouth and blew smoke. Graham holstered his weapon and walked over to Jonah and Ashcroft.

"What a shitshow," Graham said.

"The shittiest," Shepard said.

Graham looked over at Jonah, who was bent over and clutching his side.

"Get this man some medical attention!" Graham said.

Soldiers moved in and carried Jonah away.

"Rosa?" Graham asked.

"Hiding in the stadium," Shepard said, chuckling. Graham scoffed. "McCray didn't want to be here for this changing of the guard?"

"He said he's a man of the pen, not the sword," Graham said.

Shepard laughed.

"Bitch ass,"

"Here," Graham said, handing Shepard a Manila folder. "Your papers. You got a red eye for upstate New York. You live on a ranch. It's got like, I don't know. Couple hundred acres? Shit-ton of cattle. Couple million in the bank. You might want to hire some help. I think there's a barista somewhere near there who loves the outdoors."

He looked at Graham and patted the back of his neck.

"Aren't you the love doctor," Shepard said.

"Fuck off."

The Turtles

"Another drink," Sayf said to the waitress. She had on a black-and-white German *biergarten* dress. The checkered red corset pushed her breasts against the round wooden table as she cleared the empty glasses. "Oi," he said to her. "Aren't you cold?"

"Not that cold," she said smiling. Sayf sat back in his metal seat. It was a half-empty bar on an empty street. Sayf stared out at the snow drifting through the air and blanketing the ground. False light shined through an oval multicolored stained-glass window. A flickering overhead light dimmed over each table and swayed to the soft sound of techno music. The waitress came back and placed his drink on the table.

"Cheers," he said, smiling. Sayf leaned back in his seat and was about to take a sip. He stopped as the shot glass touched his lips. A young lady walked in, wearing a dark-blue mink trench coat with a long white scarf wrapped around her neck. She sashayed through the half-empty bar, her black suede boots pounding against the wooden floor.

She stood in front of Sayf and asked, "This seat taken?"

"Fuckin 'ell," he said, laughing. "Please."

Rosa nodded and sat down across from him. She stared at him with a half-grin.

"Miss," Sayf shouted to his waitress. "Bring another for the young lady here."

The waitress came to the table and smiled at Rosa.

"Sorry," the waitress said. "English poor. Drink?"

"I'll have what he's having," Rosa said in Slokrainian. The young waitress gasped and smiled. She came back with a shot. "Thanks," Rosa said, not taking her eyes off of Sayf's smug expression. He sat with his arms folded and eyes raised, sneering.

"How'd you find me?" Sayf asked.

"You thought if you're going to lay low, do it in plain sight." Sayf shrugged his shoulders.

"I'm certain you didn't come all this way for a drink." Rosa pushed her shot to the side and placed her hands palm down on the table. "So, it's not the how, but the *why* you're looking for. Am I right?" Rosa cracked a smile. "The why is simple. Money. Blue yen, pink euro, the green dollar. Money luv. Simple as that."

"This whole time, you and Charlie played me?"

"Wait…" Sayf said smiling. "You didn't fink…" He laughed. "Rosa…" Sayf said, shaking his head. "Of course you were being played. I mean, you're a pretty girl and all and don't get me wrong, Charlie enjoyed the shagging, but that was about it. The money, darling, was going to get him five of you. You understand? Five better versions of you, at that." Sayf tossed back his shot and slammed it on the table. "Now, before I go, how many Slokranian soldiers did you happen to bring?"

"I didn't."

"Well…" Sayf said, placing his hands under the table. "That was foolish. You fink you're some femme fatale because you've been hanging out with a couple of spooks?" Rosa was silent. "Before I send you off, is there anyfing else you have to say to me?"

"Draw."

Sayf smiled. As he pulled his gun from the table, two bullets popped through the stained-glass window. Blood splattered across Rosa's face. Sayf dropped his arms to his side, his gun falling onto the floor. He looked down at the wounds in his chest. The entire bar cleared as Rosa leaned back in her seat. The last patron left, the music had stopped, and the only remaining sound was Sayf's labored breathing. He looked up at Rosa and smiled. Blood dripped from the side of his mouth.

"Liar," Sayf said.

"I never said I came alone." Rosa picked up her shot glass, and Sayf watched as she turned it upside down and poured the clear liquor across the table. "My condolences." Rosa got up and walked out of the bar. She looked up at the cloudy red sky in front her. The snow was intensifying. She pulled out her cellphone as she walked down the street.

"You get him?" Graham said on the other line.

"Yeah," Rosa said sighing. "We got him."

"Jonah?" Graham asked.

"In the hotel room across from the bar. Should be meeting up with him in a few hours."

Rosa glanced at Slokrainian police cars driving past her.

"Listen, I'm up to my ears in training and we got some reliable intel about some fucking physicist trying to manipulate tectonic plates."

"Always the fucking physicist," Rosa said smiling.

"Always the fucking physicist. It's a lab in Istanbul. You turtle doves in?"

Rosa paused for a moment and smiled.

"Yeah, I think so."

The Dark Sacred Night/
The Bright Blessed Day

PRESENT DAY

Shepard sat at the coffee shop pretending to read the newspaper. His eyes wavered between his third cup of cold coffee and Trish filling beans in the espresso machine.

"Can I get you anything else?" the waitress asked. The question startled Shepard.

"Oh, no thanks," Shepard said.

The waitress nodded and walked away. He looked down at his phone buzzing. It was a text from Graham. HEY ASSHOLE! THIS IS DAY NUMBER 3! IF YOU DON'T ASK HER OUT I'M GOING TO HAVE YOU ASSASSINATED! Shepard turned off his phone and shook his head.

"Can't assassinate a nobody," he mumbled to himself.

"Excuse me?" a voice said.

Shepard put down the phone to find Trish standing in front of him.

"Y-Yeah?" Shepard asked. He could hear the nervousness in his voice.

"You want me to get you a fresh one?"

"Yeesssss," he said. Trish smiled and walked behind the counter. Shepard looked down at the newspaper, whispering to himself, "Just tell her. Just tell her."

"Here you go," Trish said, placing the hot cup next to Shepard's newspaper. He looked up at her and was frozen.

"Thanks," he said. Trish smiled and turned to walk away.

"Wait," Shepard said. She stopped and turned around. "You know, Joe Jackson is a legend."

"What?"

"Joe Jackson. I've been in here before, and when you're managing, you play nothing but Joe Jackson. I mean, 'Steppin' Out' is awesome, but 'I'm the Man' is a—"

"Stop," she said sitting down. "You did *not* just say 'I'm the Man' is his best."

"Hands down."

"Are you kidding?" Trish said scratching her head. "*Night and Day*? That album is fire!"

"I mean commercial fire, but there is no substance..."

"OK. Whatever." She laughed. "I can't believe I met another true Joe Jackson fan." She stuck her hand out. "Trish." Shepard looked down at her hand. He took a deep breath and blinked to dry the tears welling in his eyes. He looked at her and smiled.

"Shepard."

CPSIA information can be obtained
at www.ICGtesting.com
Printed in the USA
BVHW041049050623
665397BV00004B/37